CONSTANTINE

CONSTANTINE™

A Novelization by
JOHN SHIRLEY

Screenplay by
KEVIN BRODBIN and FRANK CAPPELLO

Story by
KEVIN BRODBIN

Based on characters from the
DC Comics/Vertigo *Hellblazer* graphic novels

POCKET STAR BOOKS
New York   London   Toronto   Sydney

An *Original* Publication of POCKET BOOKS

 A Pocket Star Book published by
POCKET BOOKS, a division of Simon & Schuster, Inc.
1230 Avenue of the Americas, New York, NY 10020

This book is a work of fiction. Names, characters, places and incidents are products of the author's imagination or are used fictitiously. Any resemblance to actual events or locales or persons, living or dead, is entirely coincidental.

ISBN: 0-7434-9755-4

First Pocket Books paperback edition January 2005

10 9 8 7 6 5 4 3

POCKET STAR BOOKS and colophon are registered trademarks of Simon & Schuster, Inc.

Manufactured in the United States of America

For information regarding special discounts for bulk purchases, please contact Simon & Schuster Special Sales at 1-800-456-6798 or business@simonandschuster.com.

*This is dedicated to all the writers and artists
who made the* Hellblazer *comics so very cool. . . .*

Acknowledgments

Thanks to Micky Shirley, Paula Guran, Charles Kochman, Steve Korté, Ed Schlesinger, and the writers and producers of *Constantine*.

"Exactly when the world is not expecting it,
exactly when we're sure of ourselves—
that's exactly when the Old Gods Return
and sweep our cities . . .
BACK INTO HELL!"

—Blue Oyster Cult, "The Old Gods Return,"
from *Curse of the Hidden Mirror*

ONE

The Sonoran Desert, Mexico

The devil rose up, and spun, and seemed to hiss at Francisco before settling back into dust. It was just a dust devil, a swirl of desert wind, but to Francisco, the desert's uninhabited places had always seemed invisibly peopled—and dust devils were a hint of that secret life.

He muttered an unfelt prayer to the Holy Mother and turned back to the dump, not so very far from Chihuahua, where more than a dozen human *basureros* crept about under the overcast afternoon sky. They were scavengers—like Francisco himself—the poorest of the poor, hunched over among the moraines of trash, picking at it the way field workers plucked at strawberries in the harvest up north. But here they searched for saleable clothing—especially shoes—pieces of copper, batteries that could be sold to the unwary as if they were new, appliances that could be repaired or might seem to be intact, even bits of edible food.

Families. Children digging through trash alongside rats and crows and sometimes turkey vultures. The *ninos* sometimes getting sick from the things they rooted about in: poisons from old computers, dumped chemicals. Syringes. Tainted food. It was dangerous work, but you never knew . . .

Once, Francisco had found some money in an old purse, enough for a whole evening's *chido caballo*, the best heroin he'd ever had. Remembering the purse, he bent over, poked gingerly at a Styrofoam cooler. Last month, opening one of those, a swarm of wasps had come up and stung him so much he was sick for a week. Still . . .

The cooler was empty but for a few dead flies.

Francisco sighed. He'd found nothing that day but a pair of mildewed tennis shoes he doubted he could sell. The dump was pretty much picked through.

He shivered, thinking about heroin. He was too poor to sustain much of a habit—the withdrawal was over long ago. But all he thought about was getting more. The relief of dope; the end of pain, until the dose wore off.

There had to be a way to get out of this life. He had tried everything he knew since his mother had died and his father had abandoned him, not far from here, at the age of twelve. How many years ago? Twenty?

He had even lived for a while as a *chapero*. But he couldn't deal with being a whore for homosexuals. He wasn't like that.

He straightened, looking at the tennis shoes, tied together, dangling in his left hand. Useless, grayed, full of holes. Not even good for replacing Francisco's taped-together cowboy boots. He tossed the tennis shoes away, muttering, *"No tengo ni un puto peso . . ."* He had found nothing, had not a fucking penny.

"Ay, Francisco! Mi hijo. ¿Que pedo?" That was Herve, a squat, rag-clad older guy, mostly toothless—maybe not so much older, it was hard to tell, with his hair so patchy, his skin reddened from days outdoors picking through the dump with the other scavengers. He'd had a bad glue-sniffing habit, too. He might not really be much older than Francisco but he acted like his old man. Nothing but a *sanguijuela*. A leech.

"I'm not your little one, Herve, and where's that dope you promised me when I gave you that radio?" Francisco asked, in Spanish.

"It's coming, my boy! Hey—you see that old church across there?"

"Church?" Francisco squinted through the swirls of dust at the horizon. He could just make out a cross, crooked against the sky, not much else. Maybe a quarter mile off, maybe more. "Nothing but a hole where there was a church."

"I heard there was a man asking about it—asking

over at the village who owned the land. He said he was a professor, some kind of history thing, he thought there was something there to find. If we could go there before he buys it . . ."

Francisco was intrigued—but suspicious. "Why do you ask me about this? If you think there's something there"—he approached Herve, lowering his voice so the others wouldn't hear—"why wouldn't you go alone?"

"Oh—because, like you say, I owe you something . . ."

Herve looked vaguely at the sky. Francisco scowled, thinking that Herve wasn't likely to be concerned about paying a debt. There was only one explanation: Herve was scared of the place. He was superstitious, even more so than Francisco.

"You're afraid of something, Herve . . . the place is supposed to be cursed?"

Herve shrugged. "Some say. Not me. It's like I say. You're like my son. I want to share . . ."

"Mi madre!" Francisco snorted skeptically. But he gestured sharply to Herve, nodding toward the church.

He led the way across the rubbish, climbing over a rusting refrigerator, circling a rotting sofa, kicking a crow out of the way that pecked at something bloody wrapped in toilet paper. Francisco thought he saw a tiny little fetal hand, blue and delicate, protruding from the tissue, and he looked away, fixed his attention on the church. It was a good long walk.

~

The dusk had come, and with it the wind had picked up by the time the two scavengers got there. Just the crust of a church was left. Some of the walls stood, leaning, supporting random sections of roof; some walls had crumbled. The doors had long been carted away. Sand duned against the walls, blown inside the church itself.

There was a great heap of trash here, outside the door. At some point someone had used even this church for a dump. That was sacrilegious, wasn't it? But what did it matter? If God had ever been to this part of Mexico, Francisco figured, he'd left.

"Hey—there's stuff dumped here no one's picked through!" Herve said, bending over a pile of random, rain-rotted clothing. "*Ay!* It smells bad! But look, here's a nice pair of shorts, not much stain . . ."

Francisco was stepping deeper into the church, where part of the roof remained over the nave. He let his eyes adjust to the dim interior. The floor was covered with junk, partly cloaked by blown sand. Most of the junk was without value—he could tell at a glance. An old, broken cross leaning against the wall was half buried in the sand.

But there—something shiny, picked out in a ray of light. Maybe an old rosary that could be sold. It might even be silver.

He took a step toward it . . . and stopped, feeling a strange chill, as if he'd stepped through an invisible wall into someplace cold. His mouth was dry. He wet his lips and called, "Herve—why don't you come in here, too?"

"Yes, yes I will. I've found some copper . . ."

He could tell by the older man's voice that he was making excuses, Herve was reluctant to go inside. He'd heard something about this place, all right.

"Huevon!" Francisco shouted. *"Carapecha Boun!"* No response, except a clattering noise.

Francisco shrugged, and muttered, *"Melo paso por los huevos . . ."* He pushed into the interior of the church—that's what it felt like, as if the air itself was resisting him. Or warning him.

The shiny thing—where was it? He'd lost sight of it.

A crunch underfoot—his boot had gone through something. He pulled it free and bent to look. He'd stepped through the dry-rotted wood of an old crate. It looked as if it had been buried under the tile of the floor, and someone had dug up the tile recently. But they hadn't touched the crate. Why?

He bent closer, and a sound vibrated the air in response: the sound of a million insects chewing at wood and quivering their wings. He imagined beetles and maggots chewing at human bones in a coffin, their sound magnified to a chittery background grinding, merging into a drone that rose and fell . . .

But the sound couldn't be heard with his ears—it was heard in his mind.

It's fear, he decided. Herve had awakened his superstition.

Ignore it, Francisco. There's something in that crate—maybe what the professor man had been looking for.

That suggestion came like a voice in his head. Even calling him by name.

He shook his head, amazed that his imagination was so lively for once.

He steeled himself, and reached down, slowly, into the crate, expecting to feel the sharp incisors of a rat biting into his fingers. Something he'd felt all too often in the dump.

The gnawing sound was louder as he reached into the crate, and wetter—like the amplified sounds of a feast . . . crescendos of gnawing . . .

The crate seemed empty, just empty space inside. But then his fingers closed over something firm, wrapped in cloth. A strange feeling shivered through him from the object: a feeling that laughed and growled and lifted him to his feet.

He drew the object out, straightening to hold it up in the light. The cloth was the decayed remnants of a flag, or might be. Wasn't that the crooked cross the Germans, the ones who hated Jews, had used in the big war?

Hands trembling, he unwrapped the object in the flag.

Within the cloth was a triangular spike of iron, rusty and stained brown, markings he didn't recognize incised on it: some strange language, or symbols. The splintery suggestion of a wooden shaft extruded from the object's flat end. The point was far from sharp, yet there was something about the metal spike—almost tooth-shaped, really—that suggested it could kill, and had killed before. It filled his hand suggestively . . .

He dropped the cloth, held the iron, and the strange feeling redoubled in him; it was like the hot, delicious sensation he'd had when he'd hit that *Cargador de Bandeja* when the man had tried to rape him—without even giving him the money. Francisco had hit him in the head with the big metal flashlight he'd found in the back of the man's car. Maybe he hadn't died: he had grabbed the wallet and run, and he'd never found out. But what a feeling it had been, to hit that *pendajo* in the head, again and again—a sweet release, like a rush on *caballo*. The very same feeling, but subtler, seemed to course from this old piece of iron itself, right into his hand, and from there it coursed all through him, shimmering in his spine with a soft purple light. But . . .

Someone was watching him. Not Herve—someone in the shadows.

Francisco turned quickly to glare that way . . . and saw no one. He could have sworn someone was there, but he was alone in the ruins of the church. Except, were you ever alone, really?

Nothing else here, Francisco. You already have the great find. This thing of iron! This is power! Take it away from here!

There it was again. Was it a voice in his head, or was it merely his own thoughts?

He shook off that notion. Imagination again. But this spike of iron—this was real. Some marvel of antiquity. It must be what the professor had been looking for. He could find the man and sell it to him. He must get it away from Herve, and quickly.

He hesitated . . . looking around. Surely there was more of value, here?

No. That cold, pushing sensation redoubled—and he only wanted to get away from it. *Get out* . . .

He put the thing of iron in his shirt, against his belly—he wanted to keep it in touch with his skin. He wasn't sure why.

And he turned and picked his way out, into the failing light, the mounting wind.

"Francisco!" Herve called out from somewhere behind him as he strode for the old pockmarked concrete road near the church. "What did you find? Francisco!"

"Chinga tu madre!" Francisco replied, cheerfully, not even turning around. He was feeling good. He hadn't felt this good since the last time he'd gotten high. It was like he had new strength in his limbs, and a new sense of destiny.

He walked out of the dump near the church, toward the sound of trucks and cars on the road. There was a whole world out there . . . and here he was scrabbling about in a dump!

Herve was shouting something after him. He couldn't make it out.

Fuck him. Here was the road!

He stepped onto it, feeling that this cracked, potholed, sand-strewn road would lead to glory. He would never turn back. He would go north. Yes . . . he had always wanted to go to the United States but had never been able to afford to pay the *coyotes*.

He looked north, distantly aware of a roaring behind him. Someone honking a horn. It didn't seem important. A truck screeched around him, and roared past with a receding blare.

Yes, to the north, Francisco . . . To Los Angeles . . . That's where the money is. Money and beautiful women who spend all day in bikinis. And the best dope. Not the shit you get here. . . .

Women and dope. And power—

That's when he heard the squeal of brakes, and then the car struck him . . . at sixty miles an hour.

~

Mendez and Rodriguez, two *federales* driving an old Chevrolet Impala, pulled up at the wreckage, both of them hoping no one was alive. It would be a pain in the ass if they had to take anyone to the hospital. But then, Mendez decided, maybe they could ask the survivor for money before they got the ambulance. Or there could be a wallet or two—though it was hard to imagine anything surviving that wreck, flame licking up through black, billowing smoke. . . .

What kind of car had it been? It was hard to tell now; it was accordioned around whatever it had struck; the driver, bloody and cooking on the burning hood, surrounded by broken glass. The car had struck—

Mendez looked at Rodriguez. Did he see it too? Rodriguez nodded, gaping. There was a man, standing there, unhurt. A skinny, ragged, hollow-eyed man of indeterminate age, probably one of the scavengers who picked through the dumps by the look of him. But the car was twisted around the man . . . just as if he were a column of the hardest steel.

An illusion, it must be. He had just walked up to the car that way, surely.

Mendez shrugged and got out of the cruiser. "You—did you find anything in the car? Have you been robbing the dead?" he demanded, in Spanish.

The scavenger just stared back at him. Glowering. Unafraid.

That would not do. You couldn't let the local scum think they could look you in the eye.

Mendez drew his gun. . . .

~

Francisco looked away from the *federales*, then back to the wreckage of the car. Had it really struck him—and not hurt him at all?

Yes, Francisco. Do you see your power? Take your power north!

The cops were snarling something at him. One of them drawing his gun. Going to treat him like a dog, as they always did.

Not this time.

That swarming insect sound again. It seemed to urge him on.

And something caught his eye. His wrist had been freshly scarred, a symbol burned there in puckered red. A strange circular symbol . . .

The two cops came closer.

Francisco snarled and raised the iron spike in his hand and ran toward the startled *federales*. They fired their sidearms. The bullets whined harmlessly by. It was as if he had slipped into a kind of indefinable sideways-place where the bullets couldn't touch him.

And then he was upon them, slashing with the iron spike. Their heads exploded under its impact like eggs struck by a hammer. Their headless bodies staggered and fell.

Whistling a song, he dug through their pockets. Not carrying much money, for cops.

"Francisco? What have you done?" It was Herve, his eyes big and round, hands shaking, staring from the side of the highway. Herve had seen him kill these men. Francisco charged him. Herve turned with a strangled sound and tried to run, and immediately stumbled, falling among the rocks beside the road.

It was the work of but a moment to kill Herve.

Run, Francisco. More will come. If there are too many . . .

He went to the old patrol car, found the keys in it. He had had one legitimate job in his life, taxi driver, till cops like these had told him he had to pay them a great bribe in order to keep his license. Money he didn't have. Then it had been back to the gutters.

He drove the car down the old highway headed to the nearest town.

Abandon the car, Francisco. It is a police car. You will be questioned . . .

Here, the edge of town, seemed as far as he could safely take the car. He left it by the side of the road, engine running, and trotted across the highway and into the labyrinthine warrens of plaster and baked clay and brick, past startled faces, deeper into the ghetto of the poor.

Not everyone here is poor, Francisco. There is money. A man who loans money, there up ahead, with only one handgun to protect him. Kill him and take his money and his clothes. You must go north. You will find a way across the desert . . .

The voice seemed to come from all around him and from within him at once. But as he stopped for a moment to catch his breath, he felt that someone else was there too. He looked around.

No one was there. Watching.

Francisco felt that "no one" distinctly. Invisible, but somehow Francisco felt him there.

It does not matter, Francisco. Go north. Trust me. Trust the spike of iron . . . It protected you from the car and the police . . . Anything is possible!

So Francisco started his journey north . . . to Los Angeles.

TWO

Los Angeles, California

Little Consuela had a cold, that was all. Her mother, Dierdre, pouring hot water into the mug containing the powdered flu medicine, was quite sure it was just a cold, had convinced herself that it was just a mild delirium from fever that had made the child say those horrible things; had made her throw that lamp.

Dierdre would give her the children's aspirin, some TheraFlu, and take her to the doctor. Hard to get her an appointment at this hour of the morning, but the pediatrician had finally agreed on ten A.M. Consuela would be fine.

"Mama . . . MAMMMMAAAA . . ." A frightened wail. Well, she was only seven. The delirium would naturally frighten her. Still—there was something in her voice that wrenched Dierdre's heart.

"I'm coming, baby. I've got your medicine. . . ." She really should be at work, but there was no taking a child this sick to kindergarten. This was yet another time that asshole Fred could've been of use.

Maybe I should've given Fred another chance, she thought, carrying the tray down the hall of the two-bedroom West Hollywood apartment. *Maybe he'll grow up eventually and stop trying to boff everything in—*

The thought simply snapped off by shock as she stepped into her daughter's room.

Her little girl, Consuela, was clinging to the wall near the ceiling, defying gravity, insectile and inhuman, angled so her head was aimed toward the floor. Her face was whipping back and forth, in shadow, so fast her features couldn't be made out.

And the sound from her throat—the sound of a thousand souls merged in torment—

Distantly Dierdre heard the tray crash on the floor, the mug shattering. Then all sounds were swallowed up by her screaming.

~

A dirty Los Angeles sunset. Sun blazing all sickly as it sank into a band of smog. As the taxi pulled up in front of the apartment building, Constantine gazed at the sullen colors of the sunset between the silhouettes of palm trees on the western horizon.

All that color in the smog, Constantine thought. *Funny how poison can be so pretty. Reminds me of a girl I knew when I was in the band. Now what was her name....*

Constantine—a lean man in a long, shabby black coat, stub of a cigarette between nicotine-yellowed fingers—got out and signaled Chaz to wait. Chaz was getting out, too: A young man in casual LRG hip-hop regalia, with a very non-hip-hop artifact in his hands: a book about Martinist symbology, written in French. Getting the signal to wait from Constantine, Chaz sighed, and nodded, leaning against the car.

One of these days, Constantine thought, going into the building, *I'm going to take Chaz in with me. What's the use of an apprentice if he doesn't back you up? But I'll probably regret it.*

He tried to draw on the cigarette, saw it had gone out, dropped it into the gutter, ground it out with his boot. He went into the apartment building, patting his coat pocket for another cigarette. He lit a Lucky Strike with his ornate lighter figured with spiritual symbology.

Father Hennessy was waiting in the foyer. A stocky, sweating, heavy-breathing middle-aged man with broken veins on his red face, a priest's collar. "I think . . . I think I found you one," Hennessy said.

Hennessy still had his collar, Constantine observed. So the Church hadn't given him his walking papers quite yet.

"I . . . I'm going to rehab, John. In a month or two.

They're giving me another chance. Listen, I found you one—here."

Constantine just stared at him. Poor Hennessy. Damaged goods.

"Look, I called you, right?" Hennessy said, hands shaking as he wiped sweat from the tip of his nose. "Soon as I couldn't pull it out myself I called you, John."

Constantine just shook his head and went through the door to the staircase. At the next landing he came to a small crowd of gossiping neighbors—Mexican, some Asians, a few Caucasians, all standing around— and two people seated on the stairs: a white-haired black lady with her arm around a plump, tanned, shoeless bottle-blond in a suit dress, shivering on the stairway and hugging her knees, shoulders twitching at every sound from that apartment upstairs. The distant shouts from up there, the agonized squealing sound, the sudden bangs. Constantine knew this was the kid's mother. Nothing he could do for her here.

"It's okay," one of the women said to the mom. "You had to tie her down. It's okay. . . ."

He walked past her with barely a glance, continuing up toward those sounds. The exercise sharpening the burning pain in his lungs—pain that never completely went away. Knowing that the craving for cigarettes and the pain went together: one more in an endless parade of ironies in his life.

Hell. Was there any point anymore in following the doctor's directions?

Even as he thought this, he had begun to do what he'd come here for. It was second nature to him by this time, almost instinctive: reaching out with the part of him that couldn't be touched by sickness, extending supremely fine feelers from the field that surrounded him—like the unseen field that was around everyone, except that his could be controlled. Extending feelers from his lifeforce-field upward, right through floors and walls, toward that room. And drawing back a bit at the furious response. That thing up there felt his psychic groping—and resented it. But then, it resented everything: all human existence.

He suspected it hadn't identified him yet. It didn't know who it was dealing with. He followed the feelers up to the apartment. The door stood ajar. He'd have known it anyway—he could feel fury as pure energy coming from it in waves, like heat from a house fire.

Constantine put his hand on the apartment doorknob—and the thing inside sensed him. . . .

The building was quiet for a pregnant moment—and then *THUMP. CLANG. ROAR!* And the sound of shattering glass.

He entered the apartment. Stepping into the waves of demonic energy was like stepping into a sauna. Par for the course. But there was something unusual about this emanation. It was more intense, clearer, the wavelengths crystalline-sharp. Powerful.

He stepped over a broken chair, a shattered television set, and went down the narrow apartment hallway. He felt like he was moving upstream against an unseeable current. His gut wrenched as the diabolic stench hit him. Like burning shit and sulfur and rotting blood, only it wasn't really a smell in the air but in the mind.

The girl's bedroom was beyond wrecked—everything was rubbled, smashed into small pieces. The bedposts were snapped off; a toybox was kindling, dolls ripped to pieces; the dresser was splintered, its clothes shredded. There were several small puddles of blood. Some was the girl's, judging by the state of her fingers, the red hand-marks smeared on the wall.

The girl was tied to the remnants of the bed. She made a repugnant rattling noise, like a hateful comedian imitating the last sound of a dying man, over and over. . . .

She glared at Constantine. Her face seemed to shift within itself—

He had to look away. He'd glimpsed something he didn't usually see in a possession, and he had a gut feeling it wasn't smart to look at it directly, not for long. Constantine understood exactly what gut feelings were, and why you never, ever ignored them.

The creature in the little girl's bruised, rag-fluttery body seemed to tense, as if about to tear itself free and leap at him—and then hesitated, sensing . . .

Recognizing Constantine, knowing how many of its kind had been repatriated to Hell, the dark spirit quivered in fear and fury both . . . and a wind exploded toward Constantine, generated by demonic energy, making him sway, nearly fall. He held his ground, and pulled back the sleeves of his coat and jacket to show the tattoos, the sigils on his forearms that seemed to writhe in anticipation of his retaliation.

The demon looked away at the sight of the tattoos, gathering its strength for a killing assault.

Constantine checked his watch. Then he strode across the room to the window—deliberately showing no fear, not watching his back. It was as much about the psychological as the psychic, and even demons had a psychology. He had to be in charge here. The demon would resist it, but Constantine already had the psychological leverage he needed.

Disliking daylight, the demon had left the curtains intact, and closed. Constantine drew them open with a sweep of his hand, and the room flooded with the amber light of sunset.

The light struck the girl—the demon—and she made that sickly rattling, that polyglot muttering, deep within her. Then, head shaking in a blur, she went to moaning, and the moan sounded like a little girl's voice for a moment, before the seething voices, the roaring rattle returned.

Constantine kept his hands extended, letting the psychic energy flow through him—a particularly fine grade of energy called *astral light* by the hermeticists. He drew it from above him, into the back of his head down through his spine, out through his arms, so that the "feelers" with which he normally tested the psychic air became channels for divine power—which closed around the demon, contracting to hold it pinned. . . . He didn't trust those improvised straps. There. That would hold her . . . it . . . just long enough.

He lowered his arms, squinted against the smoke rising from the cigarette in his lips as he removed his coat and laid it aside. He coughed, took the cigarette out long enough to spit a little blood, and then took another drag. He laid the butt on the remains of a table, then took a key chain from his pants pocket. On it were house keys, keys to a car he couldn't legally drive anymore, a Ralph's Supermarket swipe card, and a set of small, very old silver medallions, each with an image of a saint. When Constantine got to Saint Anthony of the Desert, standing with one foot on the head of a gorgon, the demon reacted with a wet chattering glossolalia.

Ah—that's the one, is it? Constantine thought, stepping onto the bed, squatting to straddle the girl.

Sending his field energy out along his arms, into his fingers, Constantine raised his hands, making the passes, the runic shapes, that directed the energy.

Then he snarled at the demon, so that its master—who heard whatever the demon heard—would know: "This is Constantine. *John Constantine*, asshole!"

He pressed the medallion against the girl's bruised forehead. The metal began to glow red-hot, and smoke rose from burnt skin. The child—and the demon—screamed and convulsed.

All the time, Constantine was careful not to look directly into the child's face as it flickered in and out of shadow—but seeing out of the corner of his eyes, he had an impression of the girl's face alternating with another. One that should not be visible at all in the world of men.

The girl jolted on the bed, the bonds cut into her wrists and ankles, and then her eyes snapped open and Constantine found himself looking into them as the demon in her snarled, *"Vamos juntos a matarla!"*

The pot calling the kettle black, Constantine thought, holding her down with one hand while he pressed the medallion with the other as the girl's body shimmied on the bed. . . .

And then suddenly she went limp. Lay still, as if dead.

"What the hell?" It should not have killed her. The thing should be fighting for a while yet.

He leaned forward to look at her face—and something jumped beneath the skin of her neck, up into her face, distending abruptly malleable jaws so that they jutted forward, as if trying to gnaw its way free from within . . .

Constantine recoiled—and the demon kept coming at him, lifting the bed frame off the floor telekinetically, arms outspread in the now-upright frame like a mock of the crucifixion; like a wolf dragging its cage, it came snapping at his face with its unnaturally outstretched jaws.

The demon roared and foamed at the mouth and contorted, beginning to shake the bed frame apart . . .

And Constantine, swearing—old-fashioned obscenities and not incantations—stepped in and punched the girl hard in the side of the head with his right fist.

She gasped, her eyes rolled back—and the girl, bed frame and all, fell backward, out cold.

Heart thumping, dizzy, Constantine became aware of voices behind him. He turned to see a small crowd at the half-open door. Several men and a woman, mouths and eyes wide open, staring.

Constantine hoped they'd seen more than him punching a little girl. But if they had, there was no condemnation. Just horror as they stared at the unconscious child.

Constantine knew how to take control of dazed people when he had to. "I need a mirror. Now!" He turned to look at the girl. "At least three feet high! Move!"

The three men looked at one another, murmured, then ran down the hall. They ran to the nearest apartment, didn't find a suitable mirror, hammered on another door, and thundered inside, making an old woman shriek as they tore a big floor mirror from its stand and raced puffing back up to Constantine with it.

Distantly aware of all this, Constantine went to the window and shouted down to his apprentice, still leaning against the cab.

"Yo, Chaz!"

"What?" Chaz shouted back.

"Move the car! Your cab, move it!"

"What? Why?"

"Just MOVE THE DAMN CAR, CHAZ!"

"We got your mirror!" shouted the burliest of the onlookers as they wrestled it through the door. Constantine turned and took the big oval wall mirror.

~

Down on the street, Chaz glared up at the window and then snorted, shaking his head. "Park the car, move the car."

He got into the car, shifted into reverse, moved it a few feet backward, parked it again.

"There, fuck it, I moved the damn thing."

He turned the engine off, and went back to his book.

~

Constantine had the heavy, wood-framed mirror tied with drapery ropes to an inert ceiling fan so that the mirror dangled above both him and the twitching, semiconscious girl. She was lying there with her eyes shut, the demon dormant within her but coming to life again. The mirror hung glass-downward, parallel with the bed. The other men stood nervously to either side, steadying it.

"Close your eyes," Constantine told them. "And whatever happens, do not look at her. . . ."

Constantine put his hands over the girl's eyes just as they began to flutter open. He intoned in a rapid whisper, *"In nominee Patris et Filii et Spiritus Sancti extinguatur in te ominis virtus diaboli per . . ."* He could feel a change under his hands. The girl was coming to.

*"Impositionem manum nostrarum et per invoc-
tionem gloriosae et sanctae dei genetricis virginis
Mariae . . ."*

Someone whimpered close by—not the girl. He
turned to see one of the tenants, a middle-aged man
staring straight at the girl's face.

"No!" Constantine barked.

It was too late, the man backed away, wide eyes filling with tears, sobbing. "Oh no . . ."

Without him holding it, the mirror tilted. The men
moved to reposition the mirror, but the damage
was done. She began to wrench about under Constantine, her face writhing under his fingers. She broke
free of the straps, snapping them like strips of cardboard. She began to levitate and he just managed to
keep his hand covering her eyes. The demon grabbed
Constantine around the throat, squeezing, fingers becoming talons. But Constantine was thinking about
those miraculously distended jaws and what they'd do
to his hand. He felt her jaws swelling . . . then his
breath shut off.

Okay, it has to be now, Constantine thought, *or
you're going to be choked to death by a little girl.*

"Smile pretty, you vain prick," he said to the
demon, and slid to one side so he didn't block the mirror, whipping his hand away from the girl's eyes. Mentally, he commanded the demon, *Look!*

The girl's eyes fixed on the reflection in the
mirror . . . and Constantine looked too.

What was reflected in the mirror had nothing to do
with a little girl. It showed a head whose most promi-

nent feature was what it was missing: The top of its skull was sliced away at the eyes. Demons had no need of brains; they took orders, and they were pure instinct, pure *appetite*, driven by the lower-body impulses; it had distended jaws bristling with needle teeth. Gaunt, scaly limbs . . .

And the little girl suddenly sagged back, panting with relief: The demon was now trapped in the mirror glass. Trapped but not surrendering yet—it thrashed and clawed to escape the reflection, heaving its force against the mirror from the looking-glass world, the frame and glass beginning to crack. . . .

The demon was starting to come through, fighting to get its body into the material world. And that, Constantine thought, was against the rules.

"Pull that rope, *now!*" Constantine shouted.

One of the men jerked the dangling rope end so that the mirror swung toward the window—and instantly got stuck in the jamb.

"No you don't," Constantine snapped.

He jumped up and pushed the mirror free, shoved it out the broken window so that it fell free of the rope, plummeted toward the street, turning end over end.

He had a glimpse of the demon staring out of the cracked glass at him as it fell away, and Constantine flipped it the finger. "For your boss!"

And then the mirror fell directly onto the hood of Chaz's cab, denting it deeply, the mirror glass shattering on impact, showering into countless glittering pieces. A repellent rattling sound reverberated away from the fragments . . . carrying with it a reptilian stench . . . away, away, the demon's astral form flitting invisibly into the city's gathering night.

In the cab, Chaz stared at the broken glass, the smashed wood—and his dented hood.

In the girl's bedroom, Constantine was untying the bloody remnants of the straps when her mother came in.

"Mama!" Her mother gathered the child up in her arms, rocking her.

Constantine checked on the man who'd looked into the demon's face: he was lying on his back, staring, twitching, muttering. Something broken in his mind.

Hennessy had crowded in, too, and was clearing his throat. "Ma'am—about the money . . ."

Constantine picked up the stub of his cigarette, no longer burning. Feeling like he might fall over if he didn't keep moving, he put on his coat and went into the hallway, to the kitchenette. His stomach was churning, seething. He hadn't eaten today. Just something, anything, so he didn't throw up.

There, a quart of milk in the fridge. He sniffed at it, drank deep. A soothing hand covered the interior of his stomach. He put it back, closed the fridge, and found himself staring at children's drawings held by refrigerator magnets. All the same. A crude figure, arms outspread, another figure poking at him with a stick. Stabbing him in the side. More on the walls. The mother, though she must have been puzzled, had put the child's obsessive art up as a point of pride. He pulled one of the images off the wall, tucked it in his coat, and pushed past the tenants again, out to the corridor, coughing as he went.

Downstairs, Constantine leaned against the front wall of the apartment building, watching the scene: Chaz, cussing a blue streak, cleaning off the dented hood of the cab; people staring and pointing at the apartment window. Weak though Constantine was, his feelers were still out, and his perceptions heightened—he could see ghosts among the crowd. He didn't like seeing ghosts. At least, not the ones trapped on this plane—the ones who hadn't even made it to purgatory. Like that pasty-faced old man with the torn-open throat, his wife beside him, still clutching the butcher's knife she'd used to cut that throat—and the bullet hole the old man had put in her forehead as he'd died. The two ghosts gazing mournfully at Constantine. Condemned to stick together, Constantine supposed. As he watched, a cop walked through the old man and his wife, oblivious to them.

And that one, near the fire hydrant—Constantine nodded to the specter of the greasy-haired thin man with the pockmarks on his face. He tended to follow Constantine around. Probably because Constantine was the reason he was dead.

The thin ghost nodded gloomily back and melted away, as Constantine made the effort to shut off his psychic vision. It was best to keep it shut down, most of the time. Sanity had to be protected.

He lit the stub of the cigarette as Hennessy joined him.

"Like I said, John, I found you something, didn't I? Well, didn't I?"

Constantine shrugged and looked around for ghosts. Didn't see any. But he knew they were there.

"What happened up there?" Hennessy asked.

Constantine just shook his head, coughing a little and trying to keep it from becoming a fit of hacking, and rummaged through his coat pockets.

"Inside pocket, on the left."

Hennessy was right; that's where the cough drops were. "Save your little psychic gimmicks for the customers," Constantine said, popping a lozenge into his mouth.

"Sorry, sorry. Right. Sorry."

Hennessy took a half-pint bottle in a brown paper bag from his inside coat pocket, glanced around, then took a long pull.

"Going to a lot of meetings, I see," Constantine said dryly.

"It keeps them out. So I can sleep. I have to sleep."

Constantine knew just what he meant. "I need some help myself, Father Hennessy."

"You do?" Hennessy blinked in surprise. "From me? What kind of . . ." Instinctively, Hennessy touched an amulet around his neck.

Constantine looked at it. The four intersecting crosses . . . Yes.

Seeing the direction of Constantine's gaze, Hennessy groaned. Constantine didn't need a confession. "Oh. That. Oh, John, no, listen, I can't—"

"Padre, that exorcism just wasn't right. I need you to do some . . . research."

"I just don't like to do that anymore. . . ."

"Come on, surf the ether for me. A few days. You can do that for me. Anything unusual—anything—let me know."

Hennessy's hands were shaking. He looked like he was thinking about bus tickets. Escaping town.

Constantine put his hand on Hennessy's shoulder. "It'll be like back in the day." He reached around and unclipped the amulet from Hennessy's neck. . . .

"No, John, I need that—"

"A few days. . . ." If Hennessy was going to quest for him, he'd need to keep the amulet off to get full access. He dropped the amulet into Hennessy's coat pocket.

Hennessy looked at him a moment, chewing his lip. Maybe there was a flicker of friendship there. Memory of the days they'd worked together—before Hennessy had started to crumble. Not too many could look Hell in the face, more than once, and just keep on, ignoring the fact that life was under siege by the demonic; that the world was like a fortress surrounded by an enemy horde, just waiting for a crack to open, a chance to get in. When you really realized that, it could break you.

Hennessy swallowed and said, "Okay. Okay, for you, John. Like . . . back in the day. Right."

Hennessy took another swig.

Constantine felt a tingle on the back of his neck. Someone was watching him, from up in the apartment building. Someone who flipped a gold coin, a very old gold coin, from finger to finger. . . . Someone . . .

Sensing the peculiar metaphysical quality of that scrutiny, Constantine turned and looked that way—but that someone had gone.

~

Constantine found Chaz punching out the dent in his opened hood, hammering it from below. Not improving it much.

"John, it's not my cab. What's wrong with you?"

"I told you to move it."

"Well, maybe if you'd told me you were dropping a fucking three-hundred-pound mirror with a pissed-off demon in it, I would have moved it further. . . ." Chaz slammed the hood shut and got into the car. Constantine got in beside him.

"What you think they'll call it this time?" Chaz asked, hearing the sirens approaching. "PCP? Crystal meth?"

"They'll call it something. They always do." Coughing, chewing up another cough drop, Constantine poked a finger through the litter of books on the dashboard. Aleister Crowley. Eliphas Levi. Dion Fortune. Manly P. Hall. "Los Angeles . . . never ceases to entertain."

Chaz started the taxi and drove into the street, the sudden motion making books fall on Constantine's lap, just as the cops and the ambulance arrived.

"Take Alvarado . . ." Constantine said.

"I know how to go, okay?"

THREE

❧

Echo Park, Los Angeles

Detective Angela Dodson, LAPD, was running, gun in hand, and she hated to do that. Hated to run with a gun, worse than running with a knife. You run with a knife, you probably only hurt yourself. Run with a gun and trip and it goes off, you might kill anyone. She wore flat shoes with her civvies, with her suit—skirt, white blouse and purse—but she could still trip.

No time to worry about it. The guy who'd just shot three people at random, including her young partner, Xavier, was somewhere up ahead, she was sure of it—though she wasn't sure how she knew. There—Xavier—she'd heard him right on the walkie-talkie: he was lying on his back in a pool of blood, near the base of a tree.

"Get away from here!" Angela shouted at the on-lookers, running toward the fallen man. She pulled the badge from her purse and waved it. "LAPD! Get out of here!" Xavier gasping, pale. Wounded in the left shoulder. "Get down—get under cover!" Angela shouted at a family gaping at her as she knelt.

Where was her backup? There were supposed to be two bicycle cops in this neighborhood.

The shooter, serial killer, whatever he was—had he shot the bike patrolmen, too?

She pressed an improvised compress against Xavier's wound, and with her free hand reached to take away his gun. He wouldn't let go of it.

"You're down," she said. "Let go."

" 'Cold dead fingers', Angie," Xavier said hoarsely, ruefully quoting the old NRA slogan, fingers tighten-ing on the .44.

She nodded, scanning the crowd. Checking out the faces. Feeling that the shooter was still here. She stood, drawing her badge, on a slender strap, from under her shirt. "LAPD! Get down!" she shouted.

He's here. The shooter's still here, Angela thought. She was sure of it. Xavier was still alive. And she could feel it: the killer wanted to finish him off.

Turning around, looking at the faces around her, muttering, "Where are you? Where are you?" Most of the people nearby on the pier had run off at her warn-ing, but there were still gapers: a pleasant-looking blond man in a gray suit and a puzzled smile, stand-ing behind a woman and her two children, near a vendor's cart.

Angela heard Xavier catch his breath at the pain and Angela realized—caught up in the sense that the gunman was still at hand—that she hadn't called an ambulance yet. She got her little walkie-talkie from her purse. "Officer down. One shooter. Officer down, need assistance . . ."

The man with the pleasant smile, his hand moving below her line of sight . . .

"Officer down . . ."

And suddenly she was spinning, her gun up and aiming. Firing before she could think.

All in a split second as some part of her was silently shouting: *I can't do this! Stop!*

But she felt something more powerful than instinct: a primal certainty and a conviction, from way down inside, that if she didn't do this then she and Xavier and others would all be dead, before another word could be spoken.

And so she shot the man with the puzzled smile right through the forehead.

Have I shot the wrong man? Mary, Holy Mother of God, have mercy on me. . . .

The other people around him screamed and ran to the right and left—like a curtain of people parting to reveal the man sinking to his knees . . . with a silenced 9mm pistol in his hand.

He flopped forward, facedown, not even twitching. Quite dead.

Lowering the gun, she glanced down at Xavier, who was staring up at her, grimacing. "You scare me," he said.

Didn't sound like he was kidding.

She looked at the gun in her hand. She closed her eyes . . .

It had happened again.

~

"You know, Angela, this is starting to make a few people nervous," Captain Foreman said, scratching in the short bristles that passed for his hair. He was an ex-Marine and he'd kept the haircut. He looked at her with his small, blue eyes, and the lines on his tanned face deepened with his frown. "Shooting four people in six months—doesn't happen too often, *Dirty Harry* movies aside."

"Yes sir, but uh—it's not as if any of it's my idea," Angela said.

"You know, you can sit down in that chair there."

She was standing almost at attention in front of his desk, in his downtown office. Pictures of his kids on the wall, framed certificates of commendation, a smell of pipe tobacco. "No thank you, sir."

She knew she was being petulant, acting the martyr by refusing to sit, but she felt like she was being hauled on the carpet for just doing her duty.

"You're thinking you should get a medal and not a hassle," Foreman said, leaning back, his chair creaking.

She felt her face redden. "Not a medal, sir—but, maybe, not a hassle."

"Tell you what *I* think. I think it bothers you, too, all these shootings in a short time."

She let out a long breath. He had her there. All four shootings had been instinctive. All four had been one-shot-one-kill affairs, instantly lethal. All four had been people no one mourned, no one complained of losing. Murderers, every one. A child killer, a vicious enforcer for a drug gang, a bank robber who'd already killed a hostage, and now a lunatic, a random shooter.

And in every case she'd just *found herself* in the vicinity. Just following a feeling. And every time she'd been right.

She tried not to think about her sister. How what had happened to Isabel could be happening to her. She tried not to think about the voices she'd heard, the ghosts she'd seemed to see as a child. She couldn't let herself believe all that was coming back. Because that had been madness.

But how could this be madness? She'd been . . .

". . . right every time," the captain was admitting. "That's the damnable thing. They all checked out to the bone. You probably will get a commendation, when things quiet down. But we still have to suspend you pending investigation. It's just routine. I'm sure it'll be fine."

"I know, Captain."

"Dodson—there's nothing you want to tell me about this?"

"Like . . . what?"

"I don't know. Just . . . next time you have one of these, you know, these hunches, call somebody before you . . . follow up. I mean—not if there's a shooter right there, but . . ."

"I know what you mean, sir."

"Okay. We'll see you in the morning at the inquest."

She nodded, and walked out, thinking, *He's right. I'm scared by this thing, too.*

~

Chaz had just pulled up in a discreet, shadowy corner of Twenty Lanes' parking lot. He took Constantine's bag from the trunk of the taxi, followed him toward the door of the bowling alley. "Ever think if you told me more now and then, maybe I could help you out?" he asked Constantine.

"Nope," Constantine said, without so much as a glance at Chaz, as he led the way inside.

Anyplace else, this much noise and clatter, the sounds of things crashing down, would be a sign to take cover from a landslide. But in a bowling alley it was normal. Most of the lanes were going strong at the Twenty Lanes as Constantine and Chaz crossed the lobby, walking past the pimply young man renting shoes, past rows of the house balls in cabinets, all in bright primary colors.

"Bowling shoes—what a scam that is," Chaz remarked.

"Just get me Beeman, now please," Constantine said, looking down the lanes at somebody curving a ball in for a perfect strike. He could shoot a gun straight as Buffalo Bill, he could punch like a son of a bitch, he could summon fire sprites and wind elementals, he could trap a demon in a mirror, and he could see the astral world—but for the life of him, he couldn't roll one of those hooks to get a strike. Bowling technique was an esoteric mystery to Constantine.

Drive me here, get me Beeman, blow my nose, Chaz thought. Aloud he said, "Question: How much longer do I have to be your slave?"

"You're not my slave, Chaz, you're my very appreciated apprentice. Like Tonto or Robin or that skinny fellow with the fat friend from the old movies." They'd crossed the bowling alley to the exit on the far side.

"When do I apprentice something besides driving?" *And,* he thought, *signaling eccentrics who hide out in the back of bowling alleys?*

But Constantine had already slipped through the exit door.

Chaz growled to himself. "No. Really. Great. We'll do lunch."

He sighed, went to the ball rack for lane thirteen, as always, and ran his fingers across the house balls. Only one was bright pearly white. He held it in one hand, took a grease pencil and wrote *NEW GAME* on the overhead, then stepped onto the polished wood, prepping for a bowl. He winked at a pretty brunette girl watching from the next lane. Her buff young boyfriend didn't like it. Chaz bowled, and the hook was perfect. The strike was a mathematical inevitability, every ball going down just when it should. The brunette grinned.

He returned the smile and, resignedly, went back out to the cab.

~

Constantine's apartment was small—but not as small as it looked. He pulled a chain hanging down the right-hand wall as he came in, and the far wall shuttered open, revealing a farther room and making the whole as long as a bowling lane—and indeed, it used to be one. The rumble of the pins came steadily from next door. At the far end from Constantine was a bed enclosed by a metal cage. Mostly to keep things *out*.

On the floor along all four walls were lots and lots of big Sparklett's bottles, each adorned with a small hand-marked cross. Holy water. It discouraged certain entities. Others didn't give . . . a damn.

Constantine checked the seals on the window. No indication of invasion, material or astral.

He grunted to himself and took a small black box from his jacket, set it carefully on a little shelf made for it, near the window. He looked around, thinking he'd settled for too little.

"Home sweet home," he murmured. He lit a cigarette, took off his coat, and sat down at the table to wait for Beeman. Didn't take long. Maybe a quarter-inch of cigarette.

" 'New game,' John?" Beeman said, coming into Constantine's apartment without knocking.

Constantine inhaled cigarette smoke, and almost immediately suffered a fit of coughing.

"The big one, the mother lode—the one you've been waiting for?"

Constantine managed to get his racking coughs under control. He spat blood into a tissue and said, hoarsely, "Humor me."

Turning to glance at Beeman: A small man. Prissy. Arch expression. Clothes as neat as Constantine's were rumpled.

"Don't I always?" Beeman said as he set his custom bowling bag on the counter of the kitchenette near the front door.

John gestured to a small can with the image of a cow on it, waiting on the table. Beeman picked it up. The novelty can went *mooooo*.

Something Beeman had requested. Taste is relative.

"Much obliged," Beeman said, putting the moo can in his pocket. He unzipped the bag, took out some water balloon–like ampules of holy water and a couple packs of Lucky Strikes, put them on the table. Constantine scooped them up, tucked them into his coat, which was lying over the chair. "How you feeling, John?" Meaning: Been back to the doctor? Diagnosis?

Constantine didn't want to talk about it. He nodded toward the bag. "So—what's new?"

Beeman began pulling things out of the bag. "Stone fragments from the Road to Damascus, bullet shavings from the assassination attempt on the Pope. And—oh, you'll love this. . . ."

He took out a little matchbox with a homemade smiling bug drawn on it.

"A screech beetle from Amityville."

He shook the matchbox and the beetle fluttered and clicked inside. Its wings whirred with an unnatural high pitch, like a muted scream.

Constantine chuckled.

"Yeah, funny to you—but to the Fallen, it's like fingernails on a chalkboard," Beeman remarked.

"What is it exactly with you and bugs?"

"I just like them."

"Yeah, who doesn't." Constantine smiled. He liked Beeman.

Beeman took a set of brass knuckles from the bag. It was solid gold and engraved with Catholic insignia. John tried them on—and they fit with an improbable snugness.

"The gold was blessed by Bishop Anicott during the Crusades," Beeman said, offhandedly.

Constantine pocketed the gold knuckles, spotted something odd in Beeman's bag, took out a foot-long copper tube, gripped the bulb at one end. "What's this, a bicycle horn?"

"Easy there, hero—"

Constantine squeezed the bulb, and a ten-foot-long flame belched out of it. Constantine blinked, wrinkled his nose. The air stank of sulfur and reptile gut.

"It's dragon's breath."

"I thought you couldn't get it anymore."

Beeman shrugged modestly. "I know a guy who knows a guy."

Beeman reverently laid out what looked like an old, frayed rag. Constantine started to put the dragon's breath tube down next to it.

"No, whoa, John—boom! This is a piece of the robe Moses wore to the mountain. Very, very flammable."

Fire-from-the-burning-bush flammable?

Constantine picked up the rag. Had Moses really worn this? Not all relics were what they were cracked up to be. But he did sense something. . . . He looked at Beeman inquiringly. Meaning: This for real?

Beeman nodded. "Yes. And yes. So, what's the action?"

Constantine held the rag up to the light. What was he expecting to see? "I just pulled a soldier demon out of a little girl. Looked like it was trying to come through."

Beeman stared at him. Constantine couldn't mean come through—physically?

"I know how it sounds. . . ."

Beeman snorted. "We're finger puppets to them. Not doorways. They can work us but they can't come through onto our plane. You know that."

"Check the scrolls anyway. See if there are any precedents, will you?"

Beeman nodded. Constantine suspected he was being humored.

"Sure, John. Anything else?" Beeman asked.

Constantine coughed. "You wouldn't happen to have anything . . . for, uh . . ."

Beeman nodded sagely and reached into the bag. Pulled out a bottle. Vicks Formula 44.

"On the house."

"Thanks, B. Hard day at the office." Constantine toasted the air before taking a long pull on the cough syrup.

~

A building stood in the midst of Los Angeles, a spired hulk that seemed out of place in the sunny L.A. after-noon—it looked like something from thirteenth-century France more than twenty-first-century Sherman Oaks.

The sign on the building had once said CATHOLIC THEOSOPHICAL SOCIETY. But the Cardinal had got-ten wind of it and made them change it to CATHOLIC THEOLOGICAL SOCIETY. The difference between mysticism and religion.

Angela looked at the large gothic structure, once a seminary, attached to the church, and thought about going to one of the more conventional churches for confession instead of the Theological Society.

But Father Garret had been a friend of her family's for years. She trusted him.

"Bless me, Father, for I have sinned," she mur-mured, a few minutes later, in the confessional booth. It was quiet and cool and private here and smelled faintly of wood polish. "It has been . . . if I told you how long since my last confession, you'd probably throw me out. And . . ." Her mouth was dry. She wished she had something to drink. She didn't want to tell him . . .

On the other side of the confession booth screen, Father Garret just waited. His silence was question enough.

"And I killed a man today. Another one."

"I'm so sorry you had to do that, Angela."

"I didn't even see his face. I just pulled the trigger and he went away. Just like all the others."

Father Garret considered, and cleared his throat. At last he said, "He was the shooter you were looking for?"

"Yes. He needed to be stopped. But most cops go twenty years without firing their gun. Much less killing anyone. They have names for me at the precinct. They think I don't hear. Sometimes I wonder if there's something wrong with me. Something . . ."

"Angela . . . no."

"Maybe there is, Father. Maybe I'm . . . damned."

~

That evening, after a day of keeping herself busy with shopping and errands—and of waiting for the decision of the inquest—Angela came home, locked her door, and looked around at her neat, carefully furnished apartment. She waited . . . and then it came:

Her cat, gray and nondescript. They passed the time of day. Mutual caresses. The cat trotted to her dish and Angela poured cream for her, remembering the conversation in confession.

I'm struggling with my faith, Father. What kind of God wants me to be a killer?

These feelings are natural in your line of work, Angela. I'd be worried if you didn't have them.

She kicked off her shoes, let down her hair, and lay back in her recliner. The cat jumped up in her lap.

Angela sighed. She was so tired. Her eyes felt heavy. . . .

But you have to be strong, Angela. God has a plan for you. He has a plan for us all. You mustn't allow your faith to be overshadowed by guilt.

I'm trying, Father. I'm trying real hard.

She was so tired . . .

She closed her eyes. Sleep came. A troubled sleep. Sleep that carried a message. . . .

~

Night at Ravenscar Hospital.

Angela . . . can it be Angela, here, now, in a hospital-issue nightgown? Her eyes bruised with sleeplessness, her face glossy with sweat? And the fear—has Angela ever shown so much fear on her face? That's not something a cop is supposed to do, is it? Who surrenders to a terrified cop?

But here's Angela peering around the corner, seeing a nurse pinning something to a bulletin board down one wing of the hall, a janitor with a floor polisher working the other. She darts past the cross-hall and down toward the stairway, finds the door to the stairs slightly ajar and up she goes, two flights, to the metal fire door with its broken lock, and through it to the roof.

In a moment she's out and running barefoot across the tar roof. She steps up on the aluminum-trimmed rim of the roof and looks down. It's many stories to the roof of the hydrotherapy center below.

A cool breeze flutters her gown and alters the tracks of the tears streaming down her cheeks.

She looks at her hospital bracelet, grimaces, and tears it off with her teeth, pitches it into the air so it falls far below.

She gazes at the matrix of city lights. . . .

But she sees something else. She sees flames leaping up over those lights. She sees the red flames engulfing the city. She sees the skies black with flying demons and the screams of innocents; the screams of those who had known, had been absolutely sure, that such things could never happen. . . .

She rubs her wrist—the mark there, the strange circular symbol that burns there . . . and she knows in her heart what it means. It means she's been chosen. And she can't let that happen. . . .

So she makes up her mind. She steps off the roof. And she falls and she falls . . . and she hardly feels the impact as she crashes through the glass of an atrium sun roof, smashes down, slashed by broken glass, into the hydrotherapy room's shallow pool. Water, swirled red with her blood, gushes up as if in protest. Her body bobs, faceup, oozing blood. Wounds fletched with broken glass like feathers from some inhuman being. Her eyes staring, dilated, looking into the infinitely deep well of death.

Now she feels nothing. She's simply falling through space to . . .

Oh, no.

~

As Angela sat bolt upright in the recliner, screaming at the morning light that streamed through the window, the cat leapt yowling from her lap, startled.

The nightmare was like a living thing in the room with her. Like that painting by Goya of the creatures looming over the bed—she could feel the nightmare's hot breath on her neck.

She got unsteadily up, realized she was sweating, shook the vision off.

Just a dream. It wasn't as if it'd really happened.

The hospital. Ravenscar! Oh, Mother Mary— don't let it be. . . .

~

That same morning light. Another kind of nightmare. The waking kind.

Constantine spat blood into the bathroom sink. And then a little more. And then a long hacking cough—and more blood came up and he spat that, too, and washed it down the sink with water. *There goes my life, bit by bit, down the drain.*

He was pretty sure it was going to be a rough day. Because the morning sucked big-time. *Today's the first day of the end of your life. . . .*

He looked in the mirror and he knew the oncologist had been right.

He shouldn't be afraid of death. When he'd been a kid, troubled by visions, by seeing unseeable worlds, he did have one edge that other people didn't have: He *knew* there was an afterlife. He knew it for sure. He'd seen it. Windows into that world opened to him all the time. Not just windows into the bad places, either.

So things that scared other people didn't scare him so much. Not then. Why be afraid of death when you didn't really die? He'd been pretty sure he could manage to go to one of the better places after his death. It wasn't all that hard. Just don't screw up too badly. Give a damn and you won't be damned.

It hurt to remember the way his life was then. Being a kind of freak. His parents. The streets in those days.

He learned to fight—in both worlds. *Master your gift*, a magician had told him, *or your gift will destroy you*.

He'd sought mastery of the arts, black and white. His wasn't the way of the ascetic; he was not much into self-denial. But he was strong and determined. He'd studied hard to learn to control the voices that taunted him, the unseen forces that roiled around him like a whirlwind; studied with low teachers, who took the money offerings he brought to get their fix before a lesson, and higher teachers, who looked at the anger in his soul with pity.

And he read every book on the occult: on Fludd and Flammel, on Paracelsus and Plotinus; on the ancient initiates and on the Golden Dawn; on the Mysteries of Isis and Serapis and the secrets of the Theosophists. He'd learned Latin and Greek and Sanskrit so he could read the sources—and find the truth behind the legends. And he'd been careful.

But then things had gotten worse in his life—and worse yet. And he'd made a terrible mistake, and . . .

And now was not a good time to die. He hadn't found a way out of what was going to happen to him after that.

He coughed and spat blood in the sink. "Screw the Indians," he said. "Today is not a good day to die."

FOUR

Outskirts of Mexicali, Mexico

The old Ford pickup rattled through the cool early evening, along a potholed road between the warrens of dun colored, tile-roofed houses crowded together at the edge of town. The truck soon left the houses behind, came to a thinly populated region of warehouses, shanties, gas stations, strip joints, cantinas.

In the back of the pickup, among cardboard boxes and gunnysacks, Francisco savored the evening air. He savored even the truck's exhaust, the pluming dust. A new life. The north.

There! The crossroads.

The shape scarred into Francisco's wrist seemed suddenly to burn and quiver.

That way, Francisco. Not this way. The border guards will stop you. Head east and then north.

But then again, why not use his new power in Mexicali? He could take over every gang, with this kind of power. He could gather money, and purchase a false identity, a passport—

But the emblem on his wrist burned hot. And again he heard the buzzing, the gnawing . . . the ten million mouths chewing, feasting . . . then the whisper . . .

No, Francisco. No delay. America—as quickly as possible. Los Angeles . . . glory awaits you there. Glory and power . . .

But after all, why bother with Mexicali, or even Calexico? Why not a fresh start in the north?

The truck barreled and jounced past the crossroads.

"Pendajo!" Francisco shouted in Spanish, pounding on the roof of the truck. "The crossroad! Stop here—or go east!"

The driver's reply was hard to hear from within the cab. "First we go to . . . my cousin . . . you must pay more . . ."

"I will pay nothing!" Francisco snarled, realizing he'd fallen in with a man who was going to hold him hostage. It happened often to people; his new clothes had given the impression he had money tucked away somewhere.

The ratchety chewing, the droning, feasting buzz roared ever louder as Francisco drew the iron spike from his coat and smashed through the back window of the truck. The glass parted for his hand like paper. He grabbed the bearded, shouting driver by the throat from behind and with a single sharp pull smashed his head against the metal frame of the back window.

Francisco held on as the truck swerved out of control, spun around once, and stalled. He climbed down, went to the driver's door, pulled the dead man out and dumped him on the ground, then climbed in and started the truck. And he drove back to the crossroads, and to the east. He needed to find a way through the desert—to the north.

Los Angeles, Ravenscar Hospital

Angela felt the dread rising in her like hot bile as she walked through the hydrotherapy center, past the little spas, toward the shallow pool. Beside the pool a group of cops milled, uniforms mostly. They stood around two male nurses kneeling by a body.

Detective Xavier was there, his shoulder and arm bandaged, watching her arrival. She moved past him, not wanting to talk.

"Angie . . ." Xavier said. "You don't need to see this. . . ."

Angela ignored him, thinking, in a distant sort of way, that really it was Xavier who shouldn't be there. He should be convalescing, but it was like him to push the envelope.

She walked over to the body. It seemed to take a

strangely long time to get there. The coroner was hunkered by the covered shape. He was an older Chinese guy in a white coat, the pens clipped in his pocket leaking ink stains: a doctor, name of Zhem. He glanced up at her, hesitated, then lifted the tarp.

"No, no, no. No . . . ," Angela heard herself say. "No, Isabel . . ."

She knelt by the body and her tears fell on her sister's pale, bruised face. Her twin sister, Isabel, in a bloodied nightgown. The dream had been with her all morning and she'd known, even before hearing about a suicide at Ravenscar, that the dream had been real—had been about Isabel, not Angela. But then again, Isabel owned a piece of Angela's soul. That's just how it was with twins.

Sobbing without sound, she found herself looking at Isabel's wrist. She was expecting something more than just a patient ID band. In the dream, there had been an insignia there, marked in a welt on her wrist. It wasn't there now.

She felt she might crumble, looking at her sister. Death was so absolute, so without mitigation. She would never be able to comfort her sister now. She'd put off a visit to the hospital that week . . .

Angela felt Xavier standing at her elbow. She had to get control of her voice, swallowing a few times before she could manage, "She . . . fell from the roof?"

Xavier hesitated. Then he admitted, "She jumped."

Jumped? No. Isabel wouldn't do that. Not with her beliefs. No.

"I know it's hard to accept," Xavier said gently. "But she was sick . . ."

Isabel wouldn't kill herself.

"Angie . . ."

"She wouldn't. Period."

"Detective," Xavier said. Reminding her, with his emphasis on that single word, to be objective. "There was surveillance . . ."

She looked at Isabel's face, and then signaled the coroner to cover it again.

The job, she told herself. *Hang on to that. You're already under scrutiny for the shootings. Don't fall apart now.*

"Surveillance? A security camera? Then . . . I want to see that tape."

Xavier sighed. "You sure you want to put yourself through that?"

"Just arrange it. Please. Do that for me."

"All right. We can do that right away. Security's on the first floor, behind the foyer."

Angela turned away and forced herself to leave her sister's body behind.

But she couldn't abandon her sister. Alive or dead.

~

Ravenscar had a comprehensive "mental hygiene" facility, where Isabel had died. But the rest of the hospital was devoted to cardiology and to oncology; to cancer and chemo and little rooms where terminal patients withered away, like waiting rooms for that final physician, Death.

Constantine walked past one of those rooms. Through the open door he glimpsed a gaunt, bald woman propped up in bed, gazing sightlessly through a fog of heavy medication at the wall-mounted TV.

Once it was terminal, why couldn't it just take you? he wondered. *Why does God have to drag these miseries out?*

He realized he'd unconsciously taken a cigarette from his coat. He was flicking it unlit from finger to finger in his right hand. It wouldn't do for Dr. Archer to see that.

He put it away and went into the examination room to wait.

~

In another part of the hospital, the Security Suite, Angela sat in a swivel chair staring at a video monitor. Wishing she were heavily medicated.

She watched as the black-and-white tape from the security cam showed her twin sister stepping up on the rim of the roof. Looking around.

Throwing the patient's bracelet. Gazing out into the night. Shaking her head. Glancing over her shoulder. Stepping off the edge—quite deliberately. Pitching forward. Tumbling. Gone.

The breath Angela had been holding forced itself out as she blurted, "Oh!"

A shudder went through her as a hand, intended to be comforting, settled on Angela's shoulder.

Xavier said, "Hey, Angie? Talk to Foreman—he'll

tell you to take a few days off. . . . Hell, a few weeks . . ."

Angela shook her head and brushed the hand off. Then she turned—and saw that Xavier was on the other side of the room with two security guards. He'd spoken to her from there. So whose hand had been on her shoulder?

~

Constantine's death was a black splotch in a glowing white box, like a spider waiting in its webby den.

The light boxes illuminated his chest X-rays with a ghostly objectivity, and a dark mass spread in both lungs. Constantine stared at it, and thought it was in the shape of a rune he could almost remember.

It occurred to him, not for the first time, that he might be the victim of a psychic attack. One of his old enemies might've cursed him with this sickness. It could be an even more direct attack than that: an assassin spirit hidden away in his flesh. He protected himself, yes, but spells and blessed amulets were like computer firewalls. There was always a way to "hack" them.

But he'd sense it, if it were an attack. He'd know. And he felt nothing like that. All those years of smoking was explanation enough.

"I wish I had something more encouraging to show you, John," Dr. Archer was saying. She was a no-nonsense woman in a white coat, a longtime acquaintance of Constantine.

"Things I've beaten," Constantine said, slowly, looking at the X rays, "things most people have never heard of. And now I'm going to be done in by this?"

"You wouldn't be the first, John."

"Come on. You saved me before. You can do it again, right?"

"This is . . . aggressive."

Meaning it was just too late. Constantine sighed. "Not that simple, huh?"

Aggressive. Interesting term to use, considering Constantine's life.

Maybe related to why, Constantine mused, his own magic could not save him. He kept himself walking around by drawing life energy from on high—but that would carry him only so far. To really destroy the cancer would take a miracle—and he was not on the right side of the Lord's ledger, the side that gets the occasional miracle.

He had thought to feel a kind of barrier, when he'd tried healing himself through magic. But he'd thought the obstacle might be psychological—the sorcerer's psychology was a constant problem in magical workings. You had to have your mind in precisely the right state to make magic. And he had been in a self-destructive mood for a long time. Too many people had died around him. He thought of that lean, pockmarked ghost on the street. He'd failed him. And all the others who'd died. Feeling like a failure made him depressed—and that left him with his guard down. Vulnerable.

But maybe it wasn't that. Maybe the dark powers

couldn't attack him directly—but they could block the spirits who healed, once he got sick.

And he had every reason to believe Hell wanted him dead. Hell hungered for John Constantine. It owed him an eternity of torment for frustrating so many of its plans. . . .

He stared at the dark mass in his lungs, until Archer switched the light off. Then the diseased lungs vanished. He just sat there, on the edge of the exam table, staring into space.

"Twenty years ago you didn't want to be here, Constantine," Dr. Archer said, smiling sadly. "Now you don't want to leave. You should have listened to me."

Constantine lit a Lucky Strike. If Archer was going to needle him . . .

Archer snorted, glaring at the cigarette. *That's* a good idea."

A long vengeful drag of smoke. It felt good—and it spurred him to an ugly wet fit of coughing.

He found the Vicks bottle in his coat pocket, swigged right from it, twice. The coughing eased. He took one more drag, blew a plume of smoke at the ceiling, and stubbed out the cigarette on a stainless steel instrument tray.

Archer waved the smoke away, coughing herself. "John—you need to prepare. Make arrangements."

Constantine managed a dreary chuckle as he got up and headed for the door. "No need. I know exactly where I'm going."

~

Angela strode through the hallway, looking for the elevator. She just wanted *out* of the hospital—if she could only find the way. She'd been here many times, but now it all seemed strange to her. The fluorescent lights overhead buzzed—they seemed so horribly loud. One of them flickered, in a kind of semaphore. A steel table on wheels, covered with a white cloth, waited beside an operating room door. She had a feeling if she looked under the white cloth something terrible would be there.

Ridiculous.

Where were the goddamn elevators? She couldn't get oriented. She forced herself to stop and take a slow breath.

She remembered when her mother had died—she'd felt nothing at first, or so she thought, but for weeks afterward she was clumsy, forever dropping things. Forgetful, distracted. At last she had realized that she'd been caught up in high emotion all along—and that trying to stop it had overwhelmed her, so that she couldn't live an ordinary life until she faced her grief.

It was happening again—lost in the hospital because . . .

Isabel was dead. She was really gone. She'd heard the coroner say, *It was the glass that did it, really. It cut her throat. She bled to death in the pool.*

Angela shuddered. God, but she wanted out of this place.

An elevator door chimed, and Angela dashed around the corner, looking for it. There it was—a man was stepping into the elevator, a pale man with a rumpled black coat, two days' growth of beard, a haggard, inward expression.

"Wait!" she shouted. "Hold the door!"

She was a few steps away. He just stared at her, blinking. Put his hand to his mouth to smother a cough.

"You going down?" she asked, almost there.

"Not if I can help it," he said, as the doors closed in her face.

~

There was a drunk transsexual on Hollywood Boulevard that bright afternoon; and there were seven laughing Japanese tourists, a busload of German tourists getting out to take photos of the stars in the sidewalk, two punk rocker girls begging with their flea-bitten dog, a man juggling tied-off condoms filled with water, a young black man freestyling rap, teenagers from a youth hostel in JanSport packs sharing a pot pipe and not caring who saw it. And there was a blond, tanned, breast enhanced starlet-wannabe in hot pants and a belly shirt rollerblading in a graceful weaving pattern between all these people . . .

But it was Father Hennessy who was getting the stares.

The Mexican lady in the purple scarf, shooing her little boy inside her husband's souvenir shop, stared at Father Hennessy and crossed herself as he passed, and somehow he knew that if she crossed herself it was not because he was a priest—but because he was a priest who didn't seem *right* somehow. A Japanese girl took a photo of him. The drunken trannie staggered away from him, looking fearfully over her shoulder.

People know the cursed, he thought. *On some level, they know.*

He sighed, going up the narrow steps crammed between a souvenir shop and a discount electronics shop, that led to his studio apartment. He really should find somewhere else to live. But it'd taken him a long time to properly shield the place and they wouldn't let him do it at all in the priest's housing.

He heard his Filipino landlady talking in Tagalog to her husband on the flight above. He hurried to unlock his door and get inside his apartment before she should catch him out here and demand the rent. He was almost two weeks late again.

He intoned his usual prayers on arrival, but it was hard to concentrate with the noise from the television—he always left it on.

The television on the end table by the bed, surrounded by a litter of bottles, sizzled with a snowy image of the *Jerry Springer* show. People shrieking at other people for the camera, their fast-food-jowly faces contorted with rage. Those shows seemed to him as demonic, in their way, as any average possession case. But the case of the girl Consuela—that'd been something else again.

Funny that John Constantine, no priest at all, could succeed where he'd failed. But then few priests could have succeeded on that one. Constantine was right. Something had been even stranger than usual there.

He took out his carrying pint, found it empty, and dug another bottle from his dresser's sock drawer. He took a long pull of Early Times as he looked around the silvery, trashy box of a room, thinking he'd have to come up with the rent or his landlady would be in here again bitching about what he'd done to her property. Every inch of the walls was covered with aluminum foil, double thickness; the moldering, yellowed stacks of newspapers and magazines teetered at four and five feet high; the furniture was covered in crosses and mystical symbols he'd scrivened himself with a Magic Marker.

John would want him to remove the foil. It blurred the astral signals. It all had to come down.

He had a bad feeling about this. He should tell Constantine to go to—

Well, no, he shouldn't tell him that. But he should just say no to surfing the astral planes, scrying for occult significance in the papers—it'd bring the Snufflers down on him. And he was very much afraid of seeing the Snufflers again. . . .

"Got to do it," he mumbled. "Owe John. And he's gonna give me money. Pay the rent." There was another reason to. Low as he had sunk, Hennessy still sought ways to serve God. He suspected that Constantine was one of God's chess pieces—counterintuitive as that might seem at times.

Dreading the thought of removing his protections, Father Hennessy put his hand to the amulet around his neck—and then remembered it wasn't there. He took it out of his pocket, looked at it, and reluctantly set it aside, hanging it on the television's rabbit ears. He turned the TV off, took one last pull on the bourbon, then went around the room, tearing down the aluminum foil.

The voices of the damned began almost immediately.

FIVE

There's something about a Sunset Boulevard motel room, Constantine thought, sitting on the edge of the bed and taking a judicious swig from the Jack Daniel's bottle, *especially coming up to dawn: furnishing semiotics saying that life is short and everything is trash—except how you feel. That's what matters. So make yourself feel good and do it now.* He chuckled, feeling the sweat cool him as it dried on his naked flesh. How did he get all that from a cheap seascape, a chipped dresser, a TV set showing MTV without the sound on, a butt-scarred blue carpet, blue curtains, bedclothes in a rumpled heap? But that was the message.

"Oh shut up," he said aloud. "You're drunk."

"You talking to someone I ain't aware of?" Ellie asked, passing the cigarette they were sharing. She wasn't asking it jokingly. She looked like she was in her early twenties, though of course there was no telling what age she really was. Lying on her belly beside him, her big eyes reflecting the Li'l Jon and the East Side Boyz video on the wall TV, she was naked too, but more casual in it, like a cat comfortable in its fur. She was slender and curvaceous both; she was a vixen and a sylph both. She was tautly muscular and languid both.

He managed a short drag without coughing and handed the cigarette back. She got up on her knees and took the fifth of Jack.

"Lung cancer, huh?" she said. She drew deep, deep on the cigarette, and laughed softly—the smoke jittering out with her laughter as she exhaled. "That's funny as shit, John." She drank from the bottle and put it on the floor.

"Yeah. Hilarious. So, Ellie—you didn't answer me before. . . ."

"We got distracted. You seemed happy."

"Sure. But uh—any unusual soul traffic, maybe? New prophecies? Strange artifacts turning up?"

She put the cigarette in her mouth, squinting past the smoke, and began dragging her long fingernails up and down his spine, smiling maliciously—he could see her in the mirror under the TV.

Constantine thought: *Wall-mounted TV. Like in that waiting room for terminal cases . . .*

"Lung cancer, John! No wonder the Boss is in such a good mood."

Constantine grimaced. The Boss.

She rubbed and scratched, harder. "All those saints and martyrs slipping through his grasp. His own foot soldiers sent back to him in chunks . . ."

"Ellie . . . ?"

"He's going to take all that out on you, John. He's going to enjoy ripping your soul to shreds until the end of time."

"Ellie . . ."

"You're the one soul he'd actually come up here himself to collect if he could. And you know how much he despises this place."

"Ellie. A break here?"

Ellie took the cigarette out of her mouth and blew a smoke ring. Constantine could hear a cleaning woman pushing a cart by, outside the window.

Ellie considered. She shrugged. "No. Nothing out of the ordinary in my day-to-day." She reached down and got the bottle again, took a long pull. "And brother, that's saying something."

"Is he really your boss?"

"Not really—I'm more like a contractor these days. If he was my boss, you'd be dead by now. I'd have killed you my own self."

He nodded. It was true enough.

She tilted her head to listen. "Gonna rain."

"Weather report says no."

But then he heard it pattering on the roof. Pretty heavy.

"I take it John Constantine is still looking for the big score. To set things right."

"You got any better ideas?"

She tossed the cigarette into an ashtray, and found the pack in the torn sheets behind her. She tapped another out and lit it with a flame jetting from her fingertip.

"Anyway, Ellie . . ." He coughed, just once. Okay, twice. Well, three times. But short ones. "Just keep your ear to the ground."

"Most nights that's where it ends up anyway." She smiled wanly. "I do love it when you're feeling self-destructive. You know—I'm gonna miss having someone up here I can . . . relate to."

She scooped up the Jack Daniel's and passed it to him, kissing the back of his neck. Her tail switched behind her. He saw its serrated pink spike flashing in the mirror.

He drank deep from the bottle.

~

Chaz and Constantine sat in the cab, looking through the thin rain at the Theological Society.

"It's like that place grew there," Chaz said. "I can't see it being *built* here. Like with an architect."

"Plans were from a certain small cathedral in the South of France. Cathar country," Constantine said vaguely.

The rain had eased off some by seven A.M. John was still drunk, but that had eased off some too. Coffee and aspirin kept the consequences of excess at bay. He'd only thrown up once. The booze was in its nervous energy phase now. The fatigue would set in soon. He needed to get moving. "I'm pretty sure I can get you in here, Chaz."

Chaz looked at the Theological Society's gothic towers. "What? To see the Snob? Pass."

He shoved the meter down and it began its inexorable ticking. Constantine grunted in irritation at himself. *Everything* reminded him of mortality.

Pull yourself together, fool.

He got out of the cab and, only swaying a little, made his way into the building. The rain felt good on his forehead.

A priest was talking with a bishop in the vaulted chamber of the nave as Constantine walked through. Pausing at the holy water to take a splash, cross himself with it. And to light a few candles at the shrine to St. Anthony, the patron saint of the Society. Constantine wasn't Catholic, but what could it hurt?

In the library, he found two men standing at the big fireplace—it was big enough for a child of Consuela's size to walk right into. Constantine paused to look them over. One of them, anyway, was a man. The other only seemed to be. Constantine recognized him: his semblance and his spirit, both. The semblance wore a cream-colored Armani suit. He was handsome in a delicate way, with high cheekbones and a narrow chin, thick hair. Prettily pale, startling green eyes. Body as feminine as masculine. An androgyne. Constantine knew that this androgynous man, this being, had been aware of him the moment he'd entered the door—probably before he'd come in.

The other man at the fireplace, more rugged, was Father Garret.

A young servant—probably a priestly intern of some kind—appeared at Constantine's elbow. "May I take your coat, Mr. Constantine?"

"No thanks. I'm not staying long."

"How about you, ma'am?"

Constantine turned to see a young woman, lovely but with a grim purpose about her. Auburn hair, full lips, hazel eyes. Pretty enough to never bother with makeup. An air of strength, even danger, in a skirt, a white blouse. She seemed . . . he realized she was a cop of some kind. You didn't need to be psychic to sense that, only streetwise. And he'd seen her before somewhere. The hospital, at the elevator.

The vulnerability was there too—his feelers told him she was grieving. She'd lost someone recently. He suppressed the psychic contact, not wanting to intrude. Not unless it was needed.

"I'm not staying long either," she said.

There was something else about her . . . the field around her was strong, and seemed to cast about, almost without her intending it.

"I've got to talk to him," she said. "It's very important."

"First come, first served," Constantine said. Mostly to see what her reaction would be.

"So you're rude, no matter where you are."

She looked at him for the first time, sizing him up, and he was uncomfortably aware that his clothes were overdue for washing, his chin for shaving, his teeth for brushing, and he probably smelled of liquor.

He hoped he didn't seem drunk. *Why do you care what she thinks?*

It was odd. He usually *didn't* care what people thought.

Garret and the man with him shook hands—with just the faintest suggestion of a bow from Garret toward the other man. Acknowledging rank.

The woman went straight to Garret; Constantine went to the other man: Gabriel, who was now standing facing the fireplace—with his wings spread. You had to look close to see them; they were usually invisible, in this world.

The lady cop walked out with Garret, talking in low tones, as Gabriel sat in a large, high-backed wooden chair facing the fireplace; he sat on the edge of the chair, leaning forward, and watched the flames with unblinking eyes.

Constantine had the careful walk of a man not wanting to show he had been drinking. But of course Gabriel would know he was anyway.

Telepathically, Gabriel said, *Flame consuming wood. Time is fire, Constantine, for the mortals. Time consumes.* Aloud he said, "I know what you want, son." Gabriel's voice was silky—not a pleasant silkiness, to Constantine. Gabriel always seemed snobbish. Maybe he had a right, being divine.

"Still keeping your all-seeing eye on me, Gabriel? I'm flattered."

"I could offer how a shepherd leads even the most wayward of his flock, but to you it might sound disingenuous."

"So you're going to make me beg?"

"It wouldn't help. You've already wasted your chance at redemption." Gabriel smiled, though his eyes remained icy green, like frozen seawater. "You're not going to the fair, John."

"What about the minions I've sent back? Sending minions to Hell saved innocent lives. That alone should guarantee my entry—"

"Still trying to buy your way into Heaven, son? How many times must I tell you? It just won't work."

Constantine shoved his fists in the pockets of his coat—to keep from using them. "Haven't I served Him enough? What does He want from me?"

"The usual. Self-sacrifice. Belief."

"I believe, for Christ's sake!"

Gabriel shook his head gently, looking at Constantine. Who shuddered—feeling Gabriel's gaze on the soul within his flesh. "No. You know. There's a difference. As I have told you again and again, entry into Heaven requires *faith*. Meaning belief without proof. You believe because you have seen."

"A technicality. I never asked to see. I was born with this curse."

"A gift, John! One which you have squandered on selfish endeavors."

Constantine suddenly felt the fatigue catch up with him. He wanted another drink, maybe an Irish coffee.

"You're better off without another drink, John."

"I'm pulling demons out of little girls. Who's that for?"

Gabriel smiled with exquisite condescension. "All you have ever done, you have done for yourself. To try to earn your way back into His good graces. Simple commerce. So don't now come whimpering to me because you're scared of going to Hell."

Constantine lit a cigarette, eyeing a nearby Bible as he spoke. "I've read the manual. Ever consider you're the ones with the problem? Impossible rules. Who goes up. Who goes down. And why. Why? You don't even understand us." He blew a smoke ring at Gabriel. "You're the one who should go to Hell, half-breed."

Gabriel stood, a single fluid motion that was more a thought in action than the movement of a human body. He glowered down at Constantine. "I am taking your situation into account, but do not push me."

"Why me, Gabriel?"

Gabriel's reply was telepathic. *Why you! All mortals die and when they do they all say, "Why me?"*

"It's personal, isn't it? I didn't go to church enough? Didn't pray enough? I was five bucks short in the collection plate? Why?"

Gabriel looked into his eyes. "You're going to die because you smoked thirty cigarettes a day since you were fifteen. And you're going to Hell because of the life you took." He shrugged sadly, sweetly. "You're fucked."

~

In another part of the room, Angela, talking to Father Garret, looked over. "Who is that man, the tall one, Father?"

"Ah—I rather think you wouldn't believe me. Listen—about what's happened to your sister—you've got to accept the tribulations that come to you. Accepting our lot is what it's all about, Angela."

"You can do something, Father. She has to have a Catholic funeral. She has to."

"Angela—suicide is still considered a mortal sin."

"She didn't commit suicide."

"The Bishop believes otherwise, my dear. It's out of my hands. You know the rules, Angela."

She looked at him pleadingly. "Father . . . David. This is Isabel!"

He looked at the floor, not knowing how to answer.

Angela went on, "God was . . . I think God was the only one she ever believed loved her."

He just looked at her. Unyielding.

"Please, Father. . . ."

~

Angela's eyes were wet before she reached the rain falling outside the Theological Society. She stepped back a moment, under the eaves, to watch the rain come down. Thousands of tiny little splashes on the ground. Thinking of Isabel, hitting the water of the pool, oozing blood. . . .

She heard a cough and turned to see the rude man standing on the other side of the door, smoking a cigarette down to the filter, looking as if he'd been burned down to the filter himself.

He looked up at the rain. "At least it's a nice day."

She just looked at him. What an odd man. Something about him . . .

"God," Constantine said, "has always had a rotten sense of humor." He threw the cigarette into a puddle. "And His punch lines are always killers."

There was a taxi waiting nearby—the driver, a young man, leaning over to shout through the window as it rolled down. "Constantine? Come on, it's raining! Hey!"

So his name was Constantine. She watched as he ignored the taxi and trudged off into the rain.

～

The same downpour hammered the window of Father Hennessy's studio. Hennessy kicked restlessly through a litter of torn aluminum foil, Power Bar wrappers—they were mostly what he ate—Diet Coke bottles, and liquor bottles, to get to the small, listing brown sofa next to a stack of recent publications.

He sighed, a jelly jar of Early Times in one hand, and let himself fall back into the little sofa. Time to return to work.

The voices came and went, usually half heard, like angry conversations penetrating through the wall of a cheap hotel—but these came through the walls of the astral plane. They were the voices of the purgatorial dead, wandering between levels. Not quite in Hell—except the hells of their own making. Babbling, overlapping, each pressing to be heard over the others.

"... I knew they'd betray me, and they've put me in this place so they can get my money, but they will find out that it's all gone, and how I shall laugh.... Oh, why don't I have any hands ... if I could only see my hands...."

"Mama? I'm sorry, Mama. Mama? I'm sorry, Mama. Mama? I'm sorry, Mama. Mama? I'm sorry, Mama. Mama?"

"So he thinks we're imaginary, we're but characters of his invention, or some phantasm in a book he reads ... and all the while we stand just behind, waiting our chance...."

"What did he mean he was dying for nothing? If the fucking Reds take South Vietnam they'll take the rest of Southeast Asia and we'll have commies hitting the beaches in San Diego. Why did he say he was dying for nothing? Why'd that have to be his last words? I was following orders, goddammit...."

"Mama? I'm sorry, Mama. Mama? I'm sorry...."

Hennessy stopped listening to them. They were too random, there was nothing useful in them, and they rarely responded to direct questions.

He took a pull on the bourbon, put the jar down, and focused his attention on the newspapers and magazines stacked beside the sofa. He laid a selection out on the scarred coffee table, closed his eyes, and extended his hands over them, palms down, a few inches from the surface of each page, pausing now and then, without opening his eyes, to turn the pages,

then once more hovering his hands over them . . .
picking up vibratory associations . . . probing the lay-
ers of information. *Surfing the ether*, Constantine
called it. He went through one stack and was starting
on a second. . . .

Hennessy's left hand suddenly came to a stop. A
definite pull, an impulse of urgency. Supernatural
power had recently penetrated this world, with con-
siderable force—and it had entangled itself with the
subject of this newspaper article. . . .

SUICIDE IN PSYCHIATRIC WARD

Long-term psychiatric patient Isabel
Dodson jumped to her death from
the roof of Ravenscar Hospital on Tues-
day, according to the coroner's report
filed on . . .

~

Angela sat in her recliner, watching the tape from the
security cam over and over. It was as if she were trying
to share Isabel's hell.

Once more she hit rewind, and play.

There in grainy black and white was Isabel in her
nightgown, walking like she was already a ghost,
across the roof toward the mezzanine.

Angela was all cried out, her eyes aching with it.
But now and then a sob racked her, from deep inside.
She looked away from the image, fumbling with the
remote to turn it off. Maybe she should erase it.

Murmuring, "I'm so sorry, Izzy. . . ."

She heard Isabel's voice, then, crystal clear. *"Constantine . . ."*

Shaken, Angela looked at the TV screen. Isabel was ready to jump—but this time she was *looking right at Angela.*

Then she jumped.

The tape ran a moment or two more, on the empty rooftop, then went to snow.

She rewound it. She played it again, leaning forward in her chair. The whole sequence—

Isabel approaching the rim of the roof. Tearing off her bracelet. Looking at the city. Looking over her shoulder. And jumping . . .

But this time she didn't look at Angela. This time she said nothing.

Angela just sat there. *A grief hallucination,* she told herself. *It's a common syndrome.*

Only, she knew, somehow, it hadn't been. She had that same feeling she'd had when she'd shot the crazy in Echo Park. Uncanny certainty.

From somewhere else . . . from across the gulf of death—

Isabel had spoken to her.

SIX

The rain had stopped but the streets were reptilian with wetness as Constantine emerged from the Mobil station into the humid evening. His eyes burned; maybe the smog was merging with the rising mist from the asphalt. Maybe that was why he felt the coughing rise up in him again.

When it passed, he shook a cigarette partway out of his fresh pack with his left hand, popped a cough drop with his right, then lipped the cigarette from the pack, watching a surprisingly large rat scuttle by in the gutter. You didn't often see rats on Sunset Boulevard.

Constantine glanced up at a billboard across the street. It held his eyes for a moment. It said:

YOUR TIME IS RUNNING OUT

Seemed a message for him, even though below that in smaller letters it said, *To Buy A New Chevy.*

Constantine had to chuckle. Even as he wondered if the billboard had been put there to mock him—by some enemy who knew he was dying.

With anyone else, wondering something of that kind would be paranoia. Mental illness. Not with Constantine.

"Hey," said the man in the gas station booth behind him, in a Pakistani accent. "You don't please to smoke in gas station."

Constantine walked past the pumps to the sidewalk, where an orange flashing road barricade was set up next to a small gap in the concrete. Someone had been repairing a pipe. He looked at the flashing orange light and smiled, thinking of a time when he was young, still in college, and he'd swiped one of those things and brought it home, to flash and flash perpetually in his living room. He'd watched the light strobing for days, whenever he was home, waiting for the battery to run down. It had lasted a long time: flash flash flash flash . . . like a heartbeat. But eventually it'd stopped . . . like a heartbeat.

He shook his head. It was hard not to think about dying.

He'd gotten some sleep. Had just a little hair of the dog. Eaten some soup. Now mostly he felt numb. As he lit the cigarette, a couple crows flew by, low as if coming in for a landing; make that three, now five or six. And look at that, another rat. A real menagerie out here. What next, frogs?

Yep. There it was: a frog jumping by.

"Huh," Constantine said. Thinking about having one more drink.

A frog? But it was the crab crawling by that got Constantine's attention.

"Hey, buddy, you got a light?"

Constantine turned to see a man silhouetted against the light from the gas station. Unlit cigarette butt angling into the light.

The man coughed. "We gotta stick together, right?"

Constantine drew astral light into himself as he approached the man, taking a matchbox from his coat pocket. There was a strange scent off the man—many mingled scents. . . .

Constantine started to proffer the matchbox— then he shook it, hard, between himself and the stranger. The box jumped and vibrated in his hand and a high-pitched warbling screeched from inside it—too loud for so small a source. The stranger reacted instantly, staggering back two steps, his entire body quivering.

"Ugh—stop it! They . . ."

Constantine was sure now—the screech beetle Beeman had given him confirmed it—but he knew a moment too late. The stranger leapt at him, a single bound like an astronaut on the moon, carrying him seven feet over the asphalt to knock Constantine back with a swipe of one reeking limb.

The dark man's coat fell open, revealing that his body and face were an illusion, a shape hooked together of hundreds of small creatures: living rats and insects, poisonous snakes and frogs and crabs and scorpions, each a puzzle piece, all held squirmingly together, Archimboldo-like, in the outline of a man.

Constantine scrambled backward from the demon, inches from its outstretched grasp—its fingers of scorpion's tails. He shook the matchbox again, making the beetle screech even more loudly. The demon cringed—and its body fell apart, for a moment, the creatures tumbling away from one another, the thing's clothing flopping to the ground.

They slunk and scampered in circles, then coalesced, almost instantly hooked up again, like tumblers making a human pyramid, becoming a manshape.

"Nice trick," Constantine said hoarsely. Wondering desperately if he could outrun this thing.

What passed for the demon's other hand snapped out and wrapped around Constantine's wrist: a hand of rats and snakes.

Constantine backpedaled, stumbled, recovered, ending on his haunches with the demon looming over him. A crab ran down the creature's arm, up onto Constantine's wrist, to come snapping toward his face; it was followed by tarantulas and rats, running up Constantine's neck and onto his head.

Constantine managed not to scream and shook the matchbox violently with his free hand. It didn't respond this time.

So he smashed it on the ground.

The beetle let out a painfully high-pitched death

shriek that made blood start from Constantine's eardrums. The sound ripped into the demon, and the amalgam of small animals shuddered, the parts shivering apart. Constantine could see the street behind the creature through stretching seams of mucus.

He jerked his arm free, got to his feet, swiped the vermin off his face and head, and grabbed the nearest thing that could be used for a weapon—the road barricade. He swung the flashing barricade with all his might at the demon just as it was pulling itself back together. . . .

He struck hard in its squirming center and, caught in a moment of weakness, the demon flew into living rags, the shape coming asunder with a kind of chaotic finality, to become streams of scattering creatures.

Heart thudding, Constantine stomped the scorpions and let the rest scamper and scuttle into the city's shadows.

Trying to catch his breath, he took off his coat, checked it for bonus-sized spiders and other crawlers, put it back on, walked five unsteady steps . . . and threw up in the gutter.

On his knees, staring into a sewer grating, he thought:

That was no random attack. That was an assassin, sent from Hell. Someone suddenly doesn't want to wait for me to die of cancer.

Constantine stood up, feeling vaguely unclean, and was actually glad when the rain started again.

Angela typed in: *John Constantine . . . Los Angeles . . .*

She waited, staring into the police computer. She wasn't using it for an LAPD case search. She'd already tried that, and there wasn't much of a record on Constantine. Sure, dozens of parking violations, a number of speeding tickets, a few cases of reckless endangerment. His driver's license had been revoked. But nothing like real crime.

She'd shifted to the Internet, Googling him now. The search engine turned up a great many entries on a Constantine based in Los Angeles. Typical was the selection from a Society of Skeptics article:

CONSTANTINE, JOHN

. . . rumors of this paid investigator into the supernatural being a supernatural creature himself . . . supposed evidence of his psychic abilities . . . these hysterical legends were probably propounded by Constantine himself in order to promote his business, which is vaguely defined at best. . . . Like most charlatans, he . . .

Angela glanced at the precinct office window, hearing the rain starting up again, pattering at the glazed glass. It's not that it never rained in Los Angeles, but this much of it was strange. The soft sound seemed almost loud in the empty room. She looked at the other desks, each with its monitor and stack of manila folders. She'd chosen a staff room that wasn't being used much now, for privacy, but she almost wished someone else were here. She wasn't sure why.

She rocked back in her swivel chair and scrolled down through articles mentioning Constantine. They had headlines like:

OCCULT ACTIVITY ON THE RISE
and
CLAIMED POSSESSION REFUTED BY BISHOP
and
SATANIC CULT DISSOLVED

Some of the photos with the articles were disturbing. Patterns drawn in blood on a wall. Symbols burned into a ceiling. A crucifix burned to little more than ashes. And there was Constantine himself, in handcuffs and a rueful expression, looking at a mother holding her infant son in her arms. A man standing with them, unhandcuffed; caption said he was a Father Hennessy.

A line from the article struck her: . . . *insufficient evidence to prosecute* . . .

She scrolled down, seeing the variety of cities where Constantine had made waves. London, Paris, Rome, Budapest, Moscow . . . Los Angeles.

She went back to the LAPD case files, and scanned down . . . till she found Constantine's last known address. She highlighted it and told the computer to print it.

The printer started to hum, hissily shuffling paper inside itself. And then the phone rang—seeming so loud in the quiet room she jumped a bit in her chair. She picked up the receiver.

"Dodson. . . . Hello?"

No one there. Not even a dial tone. No sound of someone at the other end.

She hung up—and the phone on the next desk rang. She got up and put her hand on it . . . and the phone on the desk beyond that one rang. Then another phone, and another, and another yet, till every phone in the room was ringing.

She tensed, and then thought: *No. Stay calm. Stay calm and see . . .*

And as if in response to her refusal to be intimidated, the phones stopped ringing. All at once.

She took a long breath, looking around. But there was nothing to see.

She stepped to the printer, plucked off the page with Constantine's address, and left the building. Kind of hastily.

~

Chaz slammed the taxi's door and hurried after Constantine. Always trailing after. "It's usually the bear, right?" Chaz asked. "Or three ducks in a cloud?"

Constantine just shook his head.

The rain had eased to a drizzle by the time they got to the El Carmen. "So am I coming in with you?" Chaz asked.

"Give it a shot," Constantine said.

"Give it a shot? What does that mean?"

But Constantine was already on his way through the crowd outside the club. *Some very elegant people here,* Chaz noted.

Chaz heard a lady in a sparkly black gown say, in a sort of stage whisper, "I understand there's a kind of backroom club here that almost no one can get into. . . ."

"You wouldn't want to go there, from what I've heard," her handsome, tuxedoed companion said.

Constantine and Chaz threaded through the crowd and into the bar, where the sounds of a mariachi band pervaded the air like the flavor of pineapple. Chaz suddenly wanted a piña colada. But there wasn't time for that—Constantine was headed for the back, through a side door.

Chaz hurriedly followed, caught up with Constantine around the corner from the bathrooms, where a sizeable bouncer sat at a small table, looking uncomfortable on a small folded metal chair.

Despite his red blazer and tie—the jacket stretching tight for his massive chest—the bouncer had the look of a thug, but one who maybe knew more than most thugs do. He seemed to be blocking access to whatever was beyond the red velvet curtain behind him.

The big man sized Constantine up for one expressionless moment, then cut what looked like a tarot deck on the little table, and pulled out a single card. He held the card so that only he could see the front of it; Constantine and Chaz saw only the back, which showed an image of two dolphins leaping into the air.

Constantine looked at the card. He closed his eyes. After a moment he said, "Two frogs on a bench."

The card smacked down on the table, faceup. On it

was artwork showing two frogs sitting companionably on a bench. The bouncer gestured for Constantine to pass.

He sidled past the table and started through the curtain, which he left half-open, as if inviting Chaz to follow.

And Chaz started to follow—then was blocked by the bouncer's hand. He drew another card from the deck, held it up between them, face away from Chaz. It was Chaz's turn to take the test.

On the back of the card were the same two dolphins. Chaz said, "Two frogs on a bench."

The bouncer frowned, and slapped the card on the table faceup. It showed a dancing bear in a dress.

The bouncer wordlessly pointed at the exit, shaking his head.

"Hey, I'm with him!" Chaz said, shouting after Constantine. "Right, John? John! Come on, don't be such a dick!"

Constantine didn't even glance back. The bouncer got threateningly to his feet and Chaz backed away, thinking:

Someday, John. Someday.

~

Constantine pushed through a metal door, stepped out onto the landing over the cavernous room—a room far, far bigger than the nightclub upstairs. Impossible to tell, for sure, how far it was down to the floor. It was a vast chamber with many lights and other sorts of glows in it, yet dark for all of that. The farther wall wasn't visible at all—the light-flecked dimness might've gone on forever. The lights only dented the darkness, didn't illuminate much past their small circles. Smirking, thudding dance music played from somewhere within the walls.

He started down the stone stairway, cutting through level after level of tables and bars. At one table was a small group of businessmen in suits. They seemed ostensibly normal, but when one of them filled shot glasses from a bottle of Evian, another waved his hand over the water—and it turned instantly into what looked like red wine. And, Constantine knew, that's probably just what it was: a truly divine vintage.

At another table, two girls in their early twenties looked up at him—and their eyes began to glow as they watched him pass. He heard their flirtatious whispers, their giggles—and he felt a bit uncomfortably undressed. He sensed they had quite literally undressed him with their X-ray eyes.

Still Constantine descended. At one of the many bars set off to one side of the stairway, a young man, seated on a stool, extended his long tail to wrap around the waist of a girl sitting beside him: a girl with jet-black eyes. Just jet black, no whites. In that same bar a manlike being who was perhaps ten feet tall, or a little more, spotted Constantine moving down the stairs—and beat a hasty, nervous retreat to the exit, ducking to go out the door.

Constantine paused—not because of the giant; he was old news—but because Ellie was smiling at him, from a table near the edge of the bar's balcony. She was sitting with two men—one black, the other white. When the two men turned to glance at Constantine they showed just the flicker of halos. Ellie had no halo, of course.

Funny to see her with them—but not unusual in this club. That was the point of the Club Midnite: It was neutral ground for supernatural beings, and those who trafficked with them.

"Hey, John! Want to party?" Ellie asked, her tail twitching invitingly.

"I'm a little short tonight."

"I can fix that."

She was, after all, a working . . . creature.

Constantine shook his head and waved good-bye. She turned back to her demi-angels as he continued down the stairs, passing people and nonpeople; from the corners of his eyes glimpsing wings, tails, horns; turning a couple of times to look at some of the more distinct ones: a crookedly smiling man whose arms and legs and head were detached from his torso and floating in the air near the places they should be connected to but not touching them, the limbs sometimes spinning in place in a way impossible for people with joints; a man with a winged skull sitting on his shoulder, a sort of pet nuzzling his head like a cockatoo, now and then tearing off bits of a human heart and feeding them to the sniggering skull; a black woman whose gown seemed to be brilliant red rippling satin, till he saw that it was made out of flame, real fire that exuded from her unharmed skin; a prominent senator chatting up a creature with the body of a woman and the head of a large snake, the creature somehow seeming surprisingly pretty, for all of that.

At last Constantine reached the level he was looking for, and set off down a corridor cut into the onyx wall. At the end of the corridor, he found two imposing doors of some indefinable material that might have been frozen time.

He waited. Knowing Midnite was aware of him out here. Seconds ticked past.

A wave of dizziness swept over him as he stood there, till at last he gathered his strength and shouted, "Midnite! Come on, do I have to huff and puff here?"

Two long moments, as if the doors themselves were considering the matter, and then they groaned open. A tall man entirely covered with old scars emerged, and gave Constantine a wide berth, looking at him askance as he passed.

Constantine stepped into Midnite's office, a big room busy with masks, exotic plants, and a variety of phones and computers. Midnite sat at a table on which was a brass orrery, a scientific sculpture of the sort that displayed the solar system, except that this sculpture was frozen, unmoving at present, and it was an orrery of the primary forces of the universe—and these versions of the worlds were etched with sigils and ancient terminology, correspondences in Greek and English: *Material, Astral, Spiritual, Iconic,* and so on. The globe at the center of the orrery was labeled *Creator.*

Seated at a table, working over the orrery, was Midnite—which he was black as. At one time a Haitian witch doctor, he was rather more now. He still had his shamanistic chops, of course, but he had progressed into more sophisticated magic. He was also a savvy businessman, owner of this club and the one that concealed it, and more; and possessor of many very finely tailored suit jackets—including a silver pendant shaped like a scorpion. Constantine had seen that pendant come alive and sting people.

Midnite didn't look up from his tinkering as Constantine entered.

"That thing's never going to balance . . ." Constantine remarked.

"Ah," Midnite said, wielding a tool with the delicacy of a brain surgeon, "but it always does. We simply must learn to see how it balances." His Haitian accent was still with him.

"Somebody has been reading way too many fortune cookies."

Midnite looked at him with mild irritation. "You've been absent some time. Have you come here with . . . relics to sell?"

"No. I'm out of that now. I've been too busy."

"Or perhaps peddling forgeries has ended up being bad for your health."

Constantine stared. "You behind what's happened to me, is that what you're saying?"

Midnite shook his head, smiling faintly. "No. I don't know what's happened, but I'm not behind anything—not that's happening to you, anyway." His smile was an odd mix of joy and malevolence. "But whatever it is, I'm sure it's what you deserve. That relic cost me a lot of Krugerrands."

"Jesus, Midnite—I thought the thing was authentic. You can't still be pissed off about that. . . ."

They locked eyes. Testing wills. Constantine returned glare for glare—till he had to break off for a short fit of coughing.

Midnite sighed and shrugged.

"What?" Constantine demanded. "I didn't blink. That was a cough. You never cough?"

Midnite's eyes narrowed, seemed to look into him. And probably did. "Ah. I see now. Your health is bad for . . . other reasons. How long?"

It was Constantine's turn to sigh. He looked at the Creator sphere. "A few months maybe. A year."

"Yes. I *thought* I heard thunder last night. It must've been Satan's stomach growling. You're the one soul he'd come up here himself to collect."

Constantine managed a thin smile at that. "So I've heard."

"Well," Midnite went on, "I am most certain you did not come here for a sympathetic shoulder to cry on. And so?"

Constantine toyed with a cigarette but didn't light it. "A demon just attacked me—right out in the open, on Sunset."

"Not so surprising. They don't like you, John. How many have you deported back to Hell?"

"No, you don't get it—this was not some angry half-breed. It was a full-fledged demon. Here. On our plane. On Sunset and Crescent, to be precise. Here in person."

Midnite raised his eyebrows. "Clearly I do not have to remind you, that is impossible."

"And . . . I saw a soldier demon trying to punch its way out through a little girl. Scout's honor." He cleared his throat, wishing he had something to spit blood into. "I mean, if I was a scout."

"Or had any honor. But you must have been mistaken. Here we have only half-breeds and remote-control—what people call 'possessions,' John. Demons stay in Hell, angels in Heaven. The great détente of the original superpowers."

Midnite thoughtfully touched the orrery, just where the circles of Heaven and Hell intersected at the orbital plane of Earth. "Fantasies of savage, marauding armies from Hell are simply tales spun to scare schoolgirls."

Constantine dripped sarcasm. "Thanks for the history lesson. You've been a tremendous help."

Midnite spread his hands as if to say, *No problem.*

"Now, Midnite—I need to use the chair."

Midnite shook his head. "John. John. Forgetting the fact that it would almost certainly kill you . . . you know I am Switzerland. Neutral. As long as the balance is maintained, I take no sides. How else could I provide an establishment where my patrons can let their hair down, come in and feel free to be . . . themselves."

Constantine decided it was time to remind Midnite of old debts. "Before you were a bartender, you were the one witch doctor against, what, thirty Ashgar? And I—"

"You were Constantine," Midnite said, nodding, just a little. "*The* John Constantine." He looked at Constantine, then again at the sculpture. "Once." He smiled sadly. "Balances shift. Times change." He sat back in his chair. "And I have always been a businessman first. You know that."

"This isn't the usual game," Constantine insisted. "I can feel it. Something's coming."

"Ooh," said a voice from the doorway. "Spooky."

Constantine spun to the door to see a man there— lean, superficially human, chillingly confident. Young and old at once. Stylishly dark clothing.

"Balthazar . . ."

Balthazar smirked an assent, flipping a gold coin from finger to finger. "The expression on your face alone, Constantine, has made my entire night."

Constantine took a step toward him, and another, setting himself. Grinned at Balthazar. "I'll make your night. I'll deport your sorry ass right where you stand, you half-breed shit!"

He took another step, raised his hands to make the passes that would begin the deportation.

"Constantine!" Midnite barked.

Constantine stopped in his tracks, knowing. . . .

"You know the rules of my house, Constantine! And while here, you will abide by them!"

Balthazar hadn't bothered to tense himself. He just stood there in the doorway, smirking, rolling that coin . . . finger to finger to finger.

Finally Balthazar said, "Johnny-boy, you're not still sore? I just made a suggestion. She was free to choose, remember?"

He leaned into the room a little, and went on, the coin flashing in his fingers, "Word is, you're the one on your way down. Fresh meat!" He leered and licked his fingers with a flickering forked tongue. "Finger-lickin' good!"

Constantine turned a pleading look to the impresario. "Midnite—he practically fed her the pills. . . ."

Balthazar chuckled. "Temper, temper, dead man."

"We have a meeting now, John," Midnite said, shrugging. "He has an appointment. I'm sorry."

Constantine started to answer back angrily—but all that came out was a fit of coughing. He tasted blood.

Balthazar grinned. "What? I didn't catch that."

Constantine tried to catch his breath—and couldn't. A frisson of unmitigated fear ran electrically through him. Was this the moment? Was he going to die *now*, this instant, with Balthazar leering at him? Balthazar, who'd seduced and destroyed someone important to him?

At least he could die somewhere else. Not in front of this sneering son of a bitch who just might catch his soul as it left his body—and personally carry it down to appease Satan.

Still coughing, Constantine plunged past Balthazar, out the door, down the black corridor. He managed to catch his breath as he got to the stairway.

Said the words that would make it carry him up like an escalator. Managed not to fall off . . .

Just barely.

He spotted the sign for a bathroom, behind one of the bars. He stepped off the stairway and staggered down to the bathroom door. Once inside he just got a few strides into the room before the blood came up, a double mouthful staining the sink red.

Behind him: giggling, carnal laughter from inside a stall. He fumbled in his coat for the Vicks—which he'd topped off with Jack Daniel's—and chugged it, till at last the convulsion in his breast abated.

Breathing hard but shallowly, he looked in the mirror, past his pale face, to the reflection of the leather wings rising over the top of the stall door behind; to the barbed tail snaking out beneath it.

He looked down at the sink again. The blood had fallen into a shape he could almost read, like tea leaves. Yes: It was a cabbalistic sigil symbolizing . . .

Triumph through death.

SEVEN

The United States/Mexican Border

Francisco left the keys in the truck. He couldn't take a truck over that fence . . . and driving it across the desert to this spot had nearly wrecked it, anyway. Its radiator was steaming and the right front tire was flat.

He trudged to the fence and looked it over, shading his eyes against the baleful sun. The fence was high, chainlink, and topped with razor wire.

It cannot stop you, Francisco. It cannot hurt you.

But beyond the fence . . . desert, and bouldery, scrubby hills. The northern reach of the Desierto de Altar. A place where many would-be immigrants on foot had died, on a hot day like this. He had no desire to leave his bones to be cracked by the sun.

He touched the iron spike, which he'd tied to a

thin piece of rope hung around his neck. At his touch, the chorus of gnawing, buzzing, the seething of a million appetites was heard . . . speaking to him without words. Urging him.

"*Sí,*" he said aloud.

He smiled and he ran at the fence, jumped, caught the links in his fingers and began to climb. It was surprisingly easy. He grabbed the top of a post supporting the razor wire, gripped the links with the toe of his boot, and in a moment he was over the fence, dropping to the dirt on the other side. He was distantly aware that the razor wire had cut him, he was bleeding on his arms and one thigh, but it didn't seem to matter. He could hardly feel it.

He looked back at Mexico. Around here, anyway, it looked exactly like America. Brown and gray dirt on that side; brown and gray dirt on this side. But that side was Mexico. This was America. A marvel.

Francisco turned and, laughing aloud, strode north, one hand to the iron spike. The bleeding soon stopped and on and on he strode, till he could feel his boots falling apart under his tread. Yet still he felt tireless, impervious. Mile after mile . . .

He should be thirsty. He should be hot. But he wasn't.

At last, in the late afternoon, he climbed a stony ridge, and peered into the distance. Was that a road, there, a couple of miles away, rippling in the heat at the horizon? Yes. A semitruck flashed in the sun, just a toy at this distance. But that was a road.

Heading north.

What awaited him in the U.S.A.? He knew that many found the United States to be almost as hellish as the more impoverished corners of Mexico. Illegals in North America were often underpaid, exploited. A man picking through the dump, Victoriano, missing two fingers on his left hand, had told him that he'd paid a lot of money to *coyotes* to take him north. He'd made his way to a meatpacking factory in Texas, because recruiters had told him he'd get ten dollars an hour. They paid him six, and then took half of that for his "housing"—which was sleeping on the floor of a mobile home with six other men. The work had been so fast paced, such long hours—with no overtime—that in his haste and fatigue he'd ended up slicing off two of his fingers with the trimming knife. When he'd asked for some kind of compensation they'd turned him over to the authorities, and he'd been deported. Penniless, down two fingers.

That was not for Francisco. He was still a scavenger—and Los Angeles was a great heap of money and gold and diamonds and dope and cars to be picked through. . . .

Thinking all this, he trudged on, until finally, topping a rise, he saw the highway below—and a truck stop.

There was a drive-in restaurant with a gravel parking lot containing only a semitruck, a car. The truck was spuming blue smoke and pulling away. As Francisco trotted down the hillside, pulling the spike free of its thong, he saw that a man sat in the lone car, eating a hamburger, the front of the car nosed up to the drive-in. He had just started: there would be much left for Francisco to finish. And he needed that car. But he would have to kill everyone in the drive-in, too. They might call the highway patrol, otherwise, if they saw him take the car.

He rushed into the restaurant. Just two people: a *cholo* cook and a waitress, a middle-aged white woman. They both looked startled when he rushed them, and neither managed to make much noise before he crushed their skulls with the spike. Easy as smashing lightbulbs.

He scooped the larger bills from the cash register, then went out to the car, approaching it from behind. The man turned around as Francisco opened his car door. Hadn't even locked it. He stared, wide-eyed, his mouth open and full of half-chewed burger. Didn't manage to swallow before Francisco dragged him out by the collar, and crushed his spine under his boot.

The spike made it possible, of course. A piece of iron with the power of the old gods in it.

The old gods return, Francisco. Trust us! Now, take the car. Head north. Los Angeles . . . Don't drive too quickly. Don't attract the attention of the police. Just go the speed limit. It's not so very far to Los Angeles. . . .

Los Angeles, California

Constantine sat on the window seat of his apartment with a shot glass in one hand and a cigarette in the other. On the window seat was the little black box he'd taken off the special shelf on the wall. The box just sat there, unopened.

He poured another shot from the dregs of the Jack Daniel's bottle he'd been working on for a couple of days, then lifted the bottle to the streetlight shine coming murkily through the dirty window. The light colored itself amber coming through the bourbon. Just a few fingers left. "You're nearly dead, soldier," he told the bottle. He put it down and drained the shot glass.

A black spider, no bigger than a dime, ran across the window seat beside him. Constantine clapped the shot glass down, trapping the spider under it. He took a drag on his cigarette, bent, and tilted the glass to blow smoke inside it. The spider skittered about, looking for a way out of the poison air, hitting only invisible glass barriers. Trapped and dying.

"Welcome to my life," Constantine said to the spider.

"Mr. Constantine?"

He blinked, looked closer at the spider, then realized that someone at the half-open door had spoken. It was that woman from the hospital—and the Theological Society.

She looked down the length of his long, narrow, holy-water-lined apartment—its dim, protracted space shot through with light angling from the blinds. "I saw you at—"

"I remember."

"And . . ."

He nodded. "Regular kismet."

"I'd like to ask you a few questions, if that would be all right."

"I'm not really in a talking mood right now."

"Maybe you could just listen, then?"

"You're a cop, right? They never take no for an answer. I've noticed that."

"I'm Detective Angela Dodson." She drew her LAPD badge from under her sweater. "Please?"

"Always a catch. . . ."

She stayed in the doorway. Ran her fingers curiously over the carvings on the inside of the door frame. They were warding sigils that kept out only a few specific evil spirits. "My sister was murdered yesterday."

"Sorry to hear."

Their eyes met. Constantine found her gaze painful to hold. And there was something else about it too. . . .

He had to look away.

"She was a patient at Ravenscar," Angela said. "Mental hygiene wing. She jumped off the roof."

"I thought you said she was murdered."

Her hands fisted. "Isabel wouldn't take her own life."

Constantine snorted and said dryly, "What kind of mental patient kills herself? That's just crazy."

She looked at his bed. "She didn't sleep in a cage," she said between clenched teeth—and for a moment looked as if she was ready to cross the room and belt him. He could see her reassert self-control. "Look, I know I'm not making much sense—I'm not even really sure what I'm doing here. I just . . . I've heard your name around the precinct. The circles you travel in. The occult, demonology. Exorcisms. And . . . there were other indications you might be . . . someone I should talk to."

Constantine looked back at the spider under the glass. Was it dead? If it wasn't, it would be soon. It was trapped.

"Before she was committed," Angela went on, "Isabel kept talking about things. About angels. Demons. I believe someone may have gotten to her, Mr. Constantine. Brainwashed her into stepping off that roof. Some kind of secret society or . . . religious cult."

"Sounds like a theory." He got up, walked unsteadily toward her. He saw her drop a hand to her side, a little behind, where her gun was. "Good luck."

He walked up to face her, but had to put a hand on the door frame to steady himself. He was poised to close the door in her face, but he didn't want to do that unless he had to.

"I thought with your background," she said, "you could at least point me in the right direction."

"Yeah, okay," he said. "Sure." Not liking himself much, and not caring that he didn't like himself much, he pointed over her shoulder, toward the exit from the building. "*Out* is the right direction."

She didn't crack a smile. She also didn't give up.

"My sister would never kill herself, Mr. Constantine. She was a deeply devout Catholic. Do you understand what that means?"

He looked her in the eyes and said, "Her soul

would go straight to Hell, where she'd be ripped into bloody chunks over and over in screaming brutal agony for all eternity. . . ."

Constantine grinned. This was all coming too close to home. He had to protect himself somehow.

He coughed, adding, "That it? That about right?"

Angela's mouth had dropped open. Her eyes glistened.

He knew he should take it back. He should invite her in and apologize and offer her a drink or tea and advice. Normally that's how it would've gone. But after a long night of sliding down into the slippery, sucking abyss of self-pity, it was hard to drag yourself out of it.

She looked like she wanted to hit him again. Instead she chose her words carefully— with unerring instinct: "You scared of Hell, too?"

Then she turned and walked out.

Bitch, he thought. *She saw into me.*

He watched her walking away. Watching her move made him want to live again.

Fuck it. He slammed the door after her and went back to the window seat. Good riddance to her. Like he was in a position to carry the world's misery on his shoulders; to ride to the rescue of Fair Lady Detectives when he'd fall dead off the horse before he was halfway there.

Suddenly a blast of wind gusted against the window. There was something about it. . . . A resonance, a kind of diabolic susurration . . . a nasty creaking behind it . . .

After a lifetime of distinguishing the natural from the supernatural, Constantine knew instantly. Some malign visitor from the astral world was exulting. He'd missed his cue, and that *something* was glad of it.

He stood up, grabbed his coat off the hook by the window seat, and put it on. He looked at the spider. Then reached down and tilted the glass up.

The spider ran free, scuttling toward a crack in the window.

~

"Detective!"

Constantine ran wheezing along the sidewalk outside his building, into the damp L.A. night. "Give me a break, Detective, I'm not fit for running tonight. Don't make me chase you."

Angela looked over her shoulder, took him in trotting up wheezily behind. "Go to hell."

"You can count on it." He gave her what he thought was his most charming smile—actually something quite grim. "What if I told you that God and the Devil made a wager? A kind of standing bet, for the souls of all mankind . . ."

Behind him, the streetlights began going out as he caught up with her, began raspily talking away as he strode beside her. "Humor me. No direct contact with humans. That would be the rule. Just influence. See who would win."

She just kept walking. He managed to suppress a coughing fit. And noticed the streetlights going off, one by one, up ahead of them. He stared. . . .

"Okay" Angela said at last. "Humoring you. Why?"

"Why?" He looked up and down the streets. Was it just a power outage? "Why'd they make this 'bet'? Who knows? Maybe just for the fun of it. No telling."

Angela shook her head. "Oh. It's fun. So what should I do when a woman's murdered or a mother drowns her baby? Who should I go looking for? A devil with horns? I don't think so. *People* are evil, Mr. Constantine. People."

They crossed an intersection. Streetlights on the side streets to their right and left were cutting off too, Constantine noticed. Darkness was closing in on them, a snuffed light at a time, pools of shadow joining to flood toward them. And there was no traffic. Only parked cars. He saw no one around at all.

"You're right," he said, wondering which way the attack would come from. From the darkness, he guessed—and the darkness had them surrounded. "We're born capable of terrible things. Then sometimes something else comes along and gives us just the right nudge and we do truly evil things."

"What—demons? Ghouls?"

"Yeah."

"Wow. Thanks for sharing. Really. But I don't believe in the Devil."

"You should," Constantine said feelingly. "He believes in you."

The last of the lights near them went out, and they were in near-complete darkness. In the dim light from distant parts of the city, he saw her look around. "Power outage?"

"Not likely," Constantine said. "Not that kind. We should go. . . ."

Constantine made out just one light within walking distance. Distinguished by its shining alone out there, against the black velvet of the dirty night. A raspy guttural wind raced toward them. That malevolent gust he'd noticed earlier had been a kind of foreshadowing of this wind. The wind of dark, malodorous, crackling wings.

". . . Fast!" Constantine blurted. He grabbed her arm, jerked her along with him. "Come on!" And they ran.

Something soared not so very far overhead—Constantine could smell its reptilian soul. Could feel the icy bite of hatred in its shadow as it passed over them, blotting out what little starlight there was.

And that noise—a rasp of leather on leather.

"What is *that*?" Angela gasped, meaning the noise, as she trotted beside him toward the light in the distance. It hadn't been as far as it had seemed.

"Wings!" Constantine said. "Wings . . ."

Coughing, running and slowing and making himself run a little more, he reached into the inside pocket of his coat, found the piece of sacred cloth that Beeman had given him.

"And maybe talons," he added.

The light up ahead was an illuminated statue of the Virgin Mary, set up in the recessed poster window of one of the abandoned movie theaters that lined this decaying strip of downtown Los Angeles. Above the statue a sign read: UNIVERSAL MISSION—JESUS

CRISTO ES EL SENOR. The statue was a single beacon in the darkness, its shine setting off a kind of aura of silk flowers the local believers had lovingly arrayed around it. The old theater had been converted to a church for the local Chicanos.

But the light from the statue was fading as they approached it. And the sound of the leather wings was getting louder.

They came puffing up to the grated theater front, pinwheels of oxygen deprivation flashing in front of Constantine's eyes. He looked around, trying the grate. Locked solidly.

He stood there, puffing, thinking hard, trying to catch his breath. Only it wouldn't quite come back. His lungs felt like they were full of broken glass. Remembering the ancient gray cloth he was still clutching, he wrapped it tightly around his right hand, as Angela drew her gun, breathing hard herself as she squinted into the darkness. "What's out there?"

Something was out there—flapping around maybe a dozen yards away. Something big, in a roiling darkness of its own making, like a squid hidden in its ink cloud.

The light on the statue was fading, as if dialing down—but it was more like the darkness itself was thickening, to such an extent that it smothered the light, however bravely it tried to burn through.

"Did you say talons?" Angela asked. "From what?"

"Something that's not supposed to be here . . ."

Now he could almost make them out, like scraps of pure murder fluttering in the darkness. Leather-winged shapes, their brandished claws catching what little light there was, as if the light were their prey; flying predators from the astral world, gathering for the kill . . .

"Close your eyes!" Constantine said, taking out his lighter.

"What? Why?"

"Because!"

She merely stared at him.

He shrugged. "Suit yourself." He flicked the lighter on, a small flame flickering feebly against the congealing darkness, and lit the sacred cloth around his hand on fire—the cloth from the robe that Moses wore to Mount Sinai.

As he swung his arm at the restless darkness, the cloth ignited with an unnatural flammability, making a flash so bright Angela yelled and covered her eyes.

The strobelike circle of light lit up a dozen winged demons, a few yards away and coming right at them— shiny-black, reptilian, gargoylelike but sleek, jaws bristling with needlelike teeth; missing the tops of their skulls like most soldier demons, the brainpan scooped away; their bat wings bigger than a condor's spread; their talons lifted in front of them like the claws of hawks about to pounce on mice. The nearest was a split second from Angela's throat.

But the circle of light from the igniting cloth expanded instantly outward in a ring of punishing flame, consuming the demons. The flame swept through the air, sizzling the demons' material forms away, leaving little but malodorous wisps of smoke.

All but for one, farther off than the others, that flapped away into the night, screeching.

And as the demon flew off, the streetlights came back on in its wake. The light seemed bright, cheerfully technological, as if nothing had happened.

One of the demons had been not completely consumed; its body was a rubbery, smoking shell, lying in the street. Constantine nodded toward it, muttering, "Demons stay in Hell, huh? Tell *them* that."

Angela suddenly bolted for a corner of the building, bent convulsively over, and retched into the trashed-up alley.

"Don't worry," Constantine said, "it happens to everyone the first time. It's the sulfur."

As he considered taking the demon's remains for evidence to show Midnite, a semitruck turned the corner, roared past them—and drove right over the demon's husk, shattering it into featureless ashes.

Spitting, Angela returned from the alley. Constantine found a handkerchief in his coat pocket, picked some old food crumbs off it, and handed it to her. She looked at it suspiciously.

"My handkerchief's not especially flammable," he said.

She dabbed at her mouth. "I saw wings . . . and teeth. . . . They were flying. What the hell were those things?"

She blinked at him.

He shrugged. "Demons. Ghouls."

Constantine looked around. Wondering if another attack was imminent. "Seplavites, actually. Scavengers for the damned."

She shook her head. "You can't be serious. This is impossible. . . ."

"Yeah, so everyone keeps telling me. And you know what—I don't think they were after me."

He looked at her, suspicions beginning to coalesce. There were many forces at work in recent events. Powers of darkness and light both. Someone had tried to kill them—but someone or something had also brought her to him. It wasn't something Hell would have wanted.

He felt like a drink. But he also felt something else. Just a flicker of light, somewhere inside him. A chance.

"Why are you looking at me like that?" she asked, frowning.

"You really believe she wouldn't commit suicide? You sure about that?"

"Isabel?" Her frown became a scowl. She dug in her purse, found a breath mint and chewed it up meditatively, looking out at the night sky. Neither one of them was in a hurry to leave the comforting domain of the statue of Christ's mother.

At last she answered him. "Never in a million years."

Constantine made up his mind. "Let's be sure." He started off toward his apartment. They'd need a few things from there. He wondered if Detective Dodson would cooperate. "Let's see if she's in Hell."

EIGHT

First time in a couple of years I've been alone with a respectable woman in her apartment, Constantine thought. *And what am I here for? Only the last damned thing I really want to do.*

Sitting on the edge of the recliner, Constantine rummaged through a cardboard box of odds and ends from Ravenscar, while Angela, in the kitchen, filled a large plastic bowl with water.

She carried the water carefully in, trailed by her cat. "Was it supposed to be hot or cold?"

It didn't matter and he didn't bother to say. "Are these all of Isabel's things?"

"I can't believe I'm doing this. . . ."

Constantine straightened up from the box to look at the cat rubbing against his leg. "How about the cat?"

"Duck? Yeah, why . . . uh . . . ? "

"Duck?" He smiled and picked up the cat. "Cats are good. Half in, half out anyway."

Angela licked her lips. "So if this is some kind of spell or something . . ."

He sat back in the recliner and looked at the cat. Seemed to see something in its eyes that looked across the stream of time.

". . . don't you need, like, candles and a pentagram for this to work?"

Constantine looked at her, deadpan. "Why—do you have any?" He smiled to show he was kidding—and to hide the fact that he was scared. He was used to a lot of things. What he was about to do was something you couldn't get used to in ten thousand years.

Some had tried to get used to it for just that long and more.

He pointed, and she put the bowl of water down in front of him. He let the cat jump up onto an armrest as he removed his shoes and socks, then put his feet into the bowl of water.

"This is crazy," Angela said, staring at Constantine's feet in the water.

"Yes," Constantine agreed.

But he meant it differently. Feeling some surprise that he could be more scared in this moment than he had been in thinking about it earlier. He'd have thought that was as scared as anyone could get. Apparently there weren't any limits.

He cleared his throat. Made sure his voice didn't tremble as he said, "I need you to step outside."

She looked around—this was her apartment. Then back at Constantine. "I'm sorry?"

"Angela? Please."

She let out a slow breath, then nodded and went to the hallway door.

Constantine looked around. There was a TV and stereo in an entertainment center, against the wall to his right; potted plants dripping vines down between the TV screen and the shelves of DVDs; prints of paintings by Turner and Whistler. There was a pink ottoman on the light blue carpet; a cabinet of books, some of them from a classics book club, some best-sellers, a Bible, a Webster's dictionary, a few police manuals, and a slender book he recognized: *Time and the Soul* by Jacob Needleman.

He smiled. This was Angela's house, an accretion of her choices, and it made him feel good, somehow, to look at it. But in a moment it would all change. . . .

"God," Constantine muttered, "I hate this part."

He drew a deep breath and took the cat into his lap. It came willingly, seeming to sense it was needed for something special. Constantine gazed into its green-golden eyes . . . and there was a connection. It was as if the cat was a kind of booster antenna.

He reached out with the feelers from his aura, stretched them out, and tested the air, looking for a particular wavelength, his probing enhanced by the presence of the ordinary gray house cat.

Constantine was casting about psychically for a particular, sharply defined vibration: the one that was the key to opening the netherworlds. That wavelength was everywhere—that subtle vibration that quickened passion, made intense resolve possible; it was an energy that kindled revolutions, and fueled homicides. The ancients thought of earth, air, fire, and water as the basic components of the universe—and, yes, fire could be destructive. But the world wouldn't have been complete without fire. Yang would not be complete without yin. What he was looking for wasn't evil—but it was a key that opened the doorway to the plane where real evil dwelt: a realm shaped by the minds of the diabolic.

He summoned that vibration, found it, drew it through him, from top to bottom; from head to feet. All the time he gazed into the cat's eyes . . .

The water around Constantine's feet began to boil. He let the cat jump free.

The lightbulbs pulsated and flickered, their light replaced by another, a malevolent glow, a fulsome glare colored the deep amber of a forest fire. The room rippled and shifted . . . and then it was done.

Constantine got up and looked around. The room was the same—and yet very different: The TV was there, turned on, showing what appeared to be a tape loop of Nazi footage from Dachau. The paintings were leering clowns, painted in prison by the child killer John Wayne Gacy. The plants were dead-white, and restlessly stretching, snuffling. . . . The ottoman was what would happen if you could put a human being in a trash compactor and have something alive afterward. It wept and tried to creep away. The recliner was made of human skin . . . including living faces. The cat was gone now—but no, he could see its eyes, the entire orbs, floating in the air, blinking at him curiously. It wasn't in this place in the same way he was.

He felt a blast of hot air and turned a bit more to see that one wall had been mostly torn away, as if a bombshell had hit it. From beyond the gap came a sickly sepia glow. . . .

He walked to the ragged hole in the wall, hearing, as he approached it, a sound like a million tiny jaws chewing all at once . . . and grimaced, remembering that he was barefoot and the carpet had changed too, and he could feel tongues licking at the bottoms of his feet, and the tentative scrape of the edges of teeth. He stepped quickly through the gap in the wall— and paused in a mound of reeking rubble to gaze out at this particular category of Hell: It was Hell Los Angeles.

It was Los Angeles, but one that was worse than its worst; many of the familiar buildings were afire, filling the sky with ash. It was neither day nor night out there—he knew that if you preferred daytime it would always seem like night; if you preferred the cool evening it was a glare of daytime. Constantine was not "here" in this dimension quite as much as were those condemned to stay. Some part of him was still back in mortal Los Angeles . . . so he was spared some measure of the subjective experience of Hell. He could experience feelings native to Hell—

but more distantly than would someone who'd gone through the Gates the formal, official way. He wasn't in perpetual agony—just a kind of diffuse, general misery.

But being "here" in Hell even that much was quite enough. Human forms and otherwise squirmed and shuffled indistinctly beyond the field of rubble. That vast gnawing sound made him picture a cloud of disembodied human mouths coming the way clouds of locusts did, chewing everything endlessly as they came—it throbbed and receded and returned again, seeming a dull counterpoint to the ragged chorus of screams and pleading that was as common to Hell as crickets chirping in a damp earthly woods. Just what you'd expect in Hell, those cries, but there were so many that they merged into a kind of grim chaotic composition, reminding Constantine of Penderecki's *Threnody for the Victims of Hiroshima*.

He set off, trotting between moraines of rubble. To one side was a brick building, and he made the mistake of glancing at it, his attention snagged by a twitchy movement between the bricks, a continuous shrugging of the bricks themselves: Every one was held in place by a mortar of human souls, a red and bone-flecked mortar of crushed bits of living bodies; the bricks grinding them, grinding the faces, the fingers, the gibbering begging bleeding souls, forever and ever, people compressed somehow alive into inch-wide spaces, the bricks moving in place, grinding like ruminating teeth, the whole building shifting like the working of closed jaws—

Constantine looked hastily away, making himself ignore the hoarse and hopeless pleading of those trapped in the jostling stones. He came to a low, eroded wall, vaulted it, slid down a charred embankment, and stopped again to get oriented on an elevated fragment of abandoned freeway. An indeterminate stretch of the freeway was somewhat intact, like a giant shelf for the display of hundreds and hundreds of fatal wrecks, perpetually just-happened, still smoking.

He peered through the roiling ash at the decaying corpse of the cityscape. He did have a specific destination in Hell Los Angeles. But would he recognize it anymore? There it was—that building, though shattered and shuddering, was just recognizable, and not so very far off: Ravenscar.

He took a deep breath—and regretted it. So he balled his fists and set out, running now, along the freeway, between the hulks of cars, fast as he could go.

Get there, get it done, get out. Hell's curiosity about why you're here may overcome its restraint.

And there was another factor. He was not yet condemned—they had to kill his physical body to keep him here. But certain predators here were not bound by the rules that constrained the higher demons.

Even as the thought came, his peripheral vision—his psychic peripheral vision—warned him that something insatiably voracious was tautly coiled inside a burnt-out Ford Explorer to his right; and it was bored with the sickly soul it was feeding on. Wanted something firmer. Oh, glorious scent; oh, lip-smacking possibilities: Here was John Constantine himself . . . unique in Hell this endless day.

Constantine ran past the Explorer, going faster yet, even as the predator burst through a windshield, somewhere behind him, uncoiling through the toothy frame of broken glass to undulate across the crumpled hood, dropping moistly onto the oily concrete—something centipede-like but bigger than a python and with the head of a leering, giggling fat man, coming after Constantine.

But Constantine was focused on getting to Ravenscar. He reached the broken-off edge of the highway, looked down through a sudden blizzard of ash at the streets below. There, soldier demons, like the one who'd inhabited little Consuela, hunted the teeming damned, the crowds of the condemned—hunting and feeding, sometimes in murderous phalanxes and sometimes leaping randomly into the wailing crowd, to rend, devour: an endless bitter harvest. And Constantine knew there was no surcease in being devoured: you were simply "digested" down into a worse level of Hell. . . .

Some of the gangly demons turned their heads—heads that were mostly mouth—toward Constantine, up above them. Sensing him, they began loping his way. They knew instantly that he was different, more succulent than these who'd been devoured many times before. . . . He was *fresh* meat.

Constantine saw a spiraling exit ramp off to the right that would get him to the street leading to Hell's own Ravenscar. It was quite a ways off, but he ran toward it, thinking:

Just keep moving. You can stay ahead of them. Long enough . . .

But the demons clambered up onto the freeway and gave pursuit, one undulating, the others loping and leaping, still a good distance behind Constantine, but closing, ever closing.

~

On the roof of John Constantine's destination—the cracked, smoking, flame-licked roof of Hell's version of Ravenscar Hospital—the soul of Isabel Dodson stood on the rim, preparing to fulfill the compulsion to which her suicide had condemned her. She teetered there, an apparent human body in a hospital nightgown, the flames of Hell reflected in her eyes. She wept soundlessly, and her lips moved to form a name: *Angela . . . I'm sorry, Angela . . .*

Soon she must jump. As she had many times since coming here. As she would for all eternity, over and over.

There were screams from the hospital below her. She could hear teeth clacking, and demonic giggling at some damned soul's exquisitely futile pleading:

"Please, tell Satan I'm sorry, tell God I'm sorry, tell Jesus and Mohammed, tell everyone! I didn't want to starve my children to death, but it had to look like they were just dying from being sick, see, because Billy said he'd leave me if I didn't get rid of them, and when they put me in Ravenscar for the tests I knew I didn't have another chance, I had to escape before I was sent to death row, and I jumped out the window but I wasn't trying to kill myself, only yes I was, but I'm sorry, tell God I'm—*oh no please don't do that . . . !*"

But Isabel was only faintly aware of this cry, or of the next from someone else that replaced it, and the next after that; after all, hopeless contrition, flavored with hypocrisy, was a fundamental element of Hell, just as muddy murk is fundamental to the environment at the deepest sea bottom. Futile pleas for mercy were elemental here.

Now Isabel felt the compulsion coming upon her. It was time. She tugged at the hospital bracelet on her wrist. . . .

~

Constantine was running, running, down a highway toward the looming Ravenscar building—he could see Isabel poised up there, silhouetted against a sky the color of a jackal's eyes. He felt no physical exhaustion, because he wasn't really here physically, but there was a down-tugging on his spirit, an ever-increasing existential gravitational pull from the sheer mass of spiritual misery that was Hell, and it threatened to drag him down. He imagined himself melting like a figure of wax, his soul turning to filmy liquid that would run into the cracks of the street he was pounding over, to be sucked into the living hate that was the fabric of Hell . . .

He tore his mind from that image. He must be goal-oriented, second by second, or he'd never make it. He mustn't let himself look at the faces in the windows of Hell's Ravenscar as he ran up to the building.

Don't look, John, at those screaming faces slammed over and over against meshed glass. Gnashing teeth and splashes of blood—here, blood was really soul-stuff in liquid symbolism, for everything in Hell was a concoction of the mind, the great dark Mind that encompassed it all: Lucifer Rofocale's mind, he who was called Satan and Shaytan and Iblis; who was the Supremest of Fallen Angels. All was contained within the ultimate demon's perpetually raging consciousness, since he had consumed everyone here.

Mind, Constantine knew, created subjective reality in the astral worlds. And it was mind that would keep him safe, if he kept on insistently visualizing his goal . . .

Ravenscar, and Isabel's trapped soul. Close, just ahead!

From the corners of his eyes he saw demons flanking him on the road, catching up to him and running just behind and nearly alongside, as they angled to come at him.

He could feel the hot breaths of hundreds of them reeking at him from behind. When they opened their mouths to roar, it was a sound composed of thousands of individual screams. . . . And now they roared in anticipation of fresh meat, John Constantine, fresh meat!

He knew if he looked over his shoulder he would

see the increasing, swarming mass of astral predators closing on him. A living avalanche of demons, snapping at his heels.

He ran round a crumpled VW Bug in which a hippie and a punk rocker strangled one another for all eternity, gnashing skin each from the other's face, just a short distance from the place where the Priests of the Inquisition were eternally tormented. . . .

Even as Isabel tore off her hospital bracelet and threw it from the top of the burning building. . . .

Constantine ran past a totaled Mercedes built for four passengers and filled with twenty-seven writhing, clawing trapped souls, squirming bloodily over one another, all of them drunk drivers who'd killed some innocent before smashing themselves to Hell after a night of *extremely important partying.* . . .

Isabel's bracelet falling . . . Isabel stepping out into space to follow it . . .

And with the demons reaching for his ankles, Constantine jumped onto the hood of the Mercedes, using it as a springboard to leap upward, straining, stretching out his hand, guided by a magician's finely developed intuition, to snatch the falling bracelet from the air—

While Isabel, above, pitched herself off the roof— and into the enormous jaws of a demon that swallowed her up, chewed her into shreds. It quickly digested her, so that a moment later she appeared on the rooftop again.

And once more Isabel was walking to the edge. She was taking off her bracelet, throwing it. She was jumping—into the enormous jaws of a demon that swallowed her up, chewed her into shreds. . . .

The same cycle for all eternity.

Constantine's own leap, however, took him not into the jaws of a waiting demon but—as his free hand made the mystic mudras, the signs in the air that opened the way—back into Angela's apartment, to the dimension of mortals.

~

Angela had just stepped into the hallway. Just closed the door behind her. For only a moment before, John Constantine had said to her, "I need you to step outside. . . . Angela, please . . ." She had just done these things, had only time enough to think: *He's sort of appealing, in a ruined, sad kind of way. . . .*

And then she heard the bowl smashing, the sound of something heavy falling in the room behind her.

NINE

Instinctively, Angela ran back into her living room, and found Constantine lying facedown in broken glass, coughing, malodorous steam rising from him.

Angela knelt beside him. Touched his shoulder, tenderly. "Constantine . . . what happened? Are you all right?"

He got up onto an elbow. Shaking, sweating. Looked around at her place. It was back to normal. Her selection of books, the ottoman just an ottoman, the TV turned off, the wall intact. But he was still carrying Hell with him, somewhere inside, in a memory he would always regret having.

"Constantine?"

His voice was hoarse as he answered the question that inhabited the air. "I'm sorry."

He had brought something with him from Hell.

Materialized it here. Something missing from that cardboard box of Isabel's effects. . . .

He opened his palm and showed her—a broken hospital band, delicately scented with brimstone. On it, the name: ISABEL DODSON.

"I've confirmed it," Constantine said, sitting up. "She killed herself. And she's damned for it."

She took the band from him, gripped it tightly, as if that would help her hold herself together. Tears streaked her cheeks.

Constantine caught himself wondering how he could help her.

Help her! Help a woman whose sister is trapped in Hell for all eternity! What an ego I've got!

Still—he opened his arms to her. It just felt right. . . .

And she tumbled into them, her shoulders shaking with sobs. "Not her," she wept. "Me! Not her—me!"

Wanting to take her sister's place, Constantine supposed. Only, if she knew what it was like there, what endless torture, perpetually renewed, really meant—what infinite hopelessness could be—she might not be so generous, sister or not.

But he simply held her, rocked her in his arms and said nothing. Feeling rather odd—he hadn't felt this close to anyone in a long time. Sure he'd had sex with people—and with semipeople. That got you physically close. But this was another kind of intimacy entirely. Something that reached deeper inside you. Touched something he'd thought had gone completely numb.

After a while, she straightened up and wiped her eyes. "How . . . ?"

He knew what she meant. How had this happened to someone who feared death by suicide, who renounced any possibility of it?

Constantine had no answer for her. He just looked into her eyes. Felt a shock, gazing into them. So he tried to look away. And failed . . . Her gaze effortlessly held him.

Finally, feeling a deep-seated physical weakness engulfing him from within, he said, raspily, "I . . . need to eat."

She nodded, and took a deep breath. "Sure. Let's get out of here." She helped him to his feet.

Really, he just wanted to get away from this room—and the pull of her gaze. Stop up that feeling of vulnerability. Get back to his fuck-'em-all Constantine persona. That persona, mocking and always ready to take aim, was what felt comfortable. It was like the butt of an old gun, molded by long use to his hand.

But the question still hung in the air.

How?

~

A bleak, almost featureless, cramped little office; a computer, several disused old filing cabinets, a calendar. A door leading into the morgue . . .

The lights were still burning here, even at this time of night. *Maybe they never turn them off,* Father Hennessy thought. Murder didn't sleep; why should the coroner's office? In the City of Angels, the Los

Angeles County Coroner was forever open for business.

The metal door of the morgue was open, suggesting that someone had just been here and was about to return.

Hennessy stood a good chance of being arrested, and spending at least a night with the DTs in a jail cell, if he went any further with this.

He decided to take the chance. He was onto something important. He didn't know what it was, but he knew it mattered.

And that meant that *he* mattered. It'd been so long since he'd felt that way. To feel like you were contributing something, that you were good for something more than a doorstop: That feeling had once been everything to him—and for a long time *everything* had been lost to him.

He wished he'd brought some liquor with him. He was going to be alone with the dead—and the voices were starting to come back, to nag at his inner hearing. He knew that some of the purgatorial dead hung around their bodies for a while before wandering on. Some of them dragged it out as long as possible, sucking every last drop of denial, before surrendering to the inevitable.

Stunned by death, identifying with their material lives, and without the reasoning faculties provided by an actual brain—since spiritual intelligence was something that had to be spiritually built up—the dead would gape for days at a time at their corpses, trying to understand, to grasp their separation from what was, after all, just a kind of garment. There were as many stupid dead people as there were stupid living ones.

You could, he reflected, actually fail at being dead. . . .

Some of these spiritual imbeciles were hovering near as he opened the shiny stainless steel door and stepped into the chill of the morgue, his breath visibly pluming the air, the telltale exudation of Early Times bourbon mixing prophetically with the smell of decay and formaldehyde. Just one of many such vaults, this was the one where intuition had led him.

It was an old-fashioned morgue, with shelves on the wall crowded by sheet-covered bodies. He raised a hand, extending his astral senses from his palm . . . thinking the name he'd found in the paper.

Isabel . . . Isabel Dodson . . .

He felt a tug pulling him across the room to a slim shape under a sheet—and then someone stood in his way.

It was a scowling old woman in her funeral best. One of those tediously stubborn ghosts. Her lips moved—but he heard the voice in his mind:

"Stay away from me, don't you put your rapist's hands on my body!"

"Lady," he murmured, "let your body go. It wasn't much to brag about in the first place. Just accept it—'cause you sure as . . . as the dickens can't change it. You're dead. Ask God for forgiveness and move on. . . ."

And he walked right *through* her—did it on purpose to discourage her from annoying him any further. He felt her prissy indignation as she vanished.

Hennessy stepped up to Isabel's body, pulled the sheet back. Bluing skin, sunken, closed eyes. Tag in her ear like an earring.

The poor girl, he thought. *So young. And here an old, walking booze-sponge like me is still around.*

He reached out, placed his hand on her forehead. He sensed nothing special. Just a husk, abandoned by a soul. He picked up some vague flutterings vibratorily associated with the body's life, but nothing telling. He did a series of passes over her body—and suddenly stopped over her right wrist.

There. Very distinct. Almost painfully sharp . . . a connection to Hell itself . . . a symbol. He saw it in his mind's eye. . . .

"Hey, what the fuck're you doing in here?" came the strident voice from behind him. "Get your hands away from that body, ya fucking perv!"

He turned to tell a ghost to fuck off—and saw a solid, living, breathing human being: a burly security guard. He smiled—then lunged for the door, shoving the man aside as hard as he could. Sprinting through the door and out.

The guard fell, striking his head. Just stunned.

For a moment the security guard seemed to see an old lady in her Sunday best, looking down at him and pointing at a sheet-covered body.

"He tried to rape me! Get him! I'm naked under this sheet, you know!" And she began to giggle. *"Naked! Quite naked!"*

Then she faded away. Funny the things you imagined when you got a knock on the head.

The guard got stiffly to his feet and went to look for the guy who'd broken into the morgue.

But by the time he was up and had called for backup, Father Hennessy was long gone.

~

Molly's Burger was unusually crowded, considering the late hour. Constantine and Angela sat on stools outside, watching people trail in and out of the place; people sitting at the outdoor tables; homeboys talking on the street corner nearby.

Constantine pushed the remains of his second burger away, feeling that he'd created an inner illusion of being filled; of being really here in this world, and far from the astral nightmare he'd just escaped.

He sat back, wanting a cigarette, but he decided he didn't want to subject Angela to the smoke.

So he coughed a few times instead and drank some tea and said, just loud enough for Angela to hear, "God and the Devil. Oldest bad relationship in history. Very, very competitive.

"Angels and demons can't cross over onto our plane. So instead we get what I call half-breeds. Say you were very good in life—or very, very bad—they wrap your soul up in human skin and send you back here on missions. Rest in peace, my ass."

He looked around at the people nearby. Most of them really were just people.

Most of them.

He lowered his voice even more, leaning toward her. "They look like us so they blend in . . . sent to dwell among humans. Those with the demons' touch, like those part-angel, living alongside us. The half-breeds. They can only whisper in our ears. But a single word can give you courage. Or turn your favorite pleasure into your worst nightmare. They call it the Balance." He drank some more tea. Was careful not to look at the thick-ankled lady with the fiery red hair, stumping past. Sensing she was one of *them*. He waited till she was out of earshot before continuing. "So when a half-breed breaks the rules, tries to control free will, or hijacks a soul, I deport his sorry ass right back to Hell. I don't get them all, but I've been hoping to get enough to ensure my retirement."

"Your . . . retirement?"

"I'm a suicide, Angela. When I die the rules say I've got just one place to go."

She stared at him. "Let me get this straight. You're trying to buy your way into Heaven?"

"What would you do if you were sentenced to prison where half the inmates were put there by you?"

Angela studied him. He felt like he was the madman, she the psychiatrist. But what she said next made her sound like one of the crazies. "How does someone escape Hell?"

He toyed with his Styrofoam cup of tea. "I have no idea."

She swallowed. Her voice was bitter. "Let me guess: God has a plan for all of us."

"God's a kid with an ant farm, lady. He's not planning anything."

"When we were little, Isabel saw things, too. Like you do."

He snorted. Wishing she hadn't reminded him. "When I was a kid . . ."

He seemed to see his younger self—about ten years old—walking by the counter, the boyish John Constantine in the room with them right now. . . .

He watched the boy Constantine, followed himself with his inner gaze, tracking this young apparition back into memory . . . explaining some of it to Angela as he took the journey.

"I saw things human's aren't supposed to see . . ."

And he remembered:

~

The boy Constantine, a lean kid in jeans and jacket too big for him, with an unruly mop of hair, walking down the hallway of his apartment building. Passing an open door where a nervous, wide-eyed woman with bruises on her face was handing money to a monster.

The monster gave her something back—a gun.

Not a figurative monster. A man-shaped freakish thing with all-black eyes, his entire body covered with crawling, gnashing shit-colored cockroaches.

The boy winced and bit his lips but just kept walking. Best he not say anything about this to anyone else. He'd learned that other people couldn't see the monsters the way he did. . . .

~

Now, Constantine closed his eyes. "I saw things you shouldn't have to see, Angela. . . ."

And he remembered:

~

The boy Constantine on a city bus that barreled through the streets, rocking as it went. Some of the passengers on the late-night bus were human. Most. But some of them . . .

There was an old woman, a baby, and two teenagers, a boy and a girl, sitting together—fine, except they all had leathery skin and tails that switched and twitched and mouths full of fangs.

The baby bared its fangs and grimaced nastily at him; the teens grinned and licked their filed incisors.

~

Constantine turned to Angela. Hesitated.

"Go on," she said.

She was listening raptly, but with a look on her face that made Constantine wonder if she believed him— made him wonder if she'd started to doubt what'd happened in the apartment. Did she think he was trying to con her? But then, she'd seen the flying demons; she couldn't rationalize those away. Though it was amazing what people could find "rational" explanations for . . .

"My parents did what any parents would do," Constantine said softly, "when their kid tells them that he's seeing the souls of sinners in the streets. Seeing demons disguised as people. Seeing monsters. They showed their great fucking concern for me—by putting me in the mental hospital."

And he remembered:

~

The two men in white coats—big, bored but implacable—were dragging the fourteen-year-old John Constantine onto a table, strapping him into the restraints even as he writhed in their grip, as he shrank from the straps they buckled onto his head, tried to shake off the electrodes that would give him electroshock "therapy."

The doctor approached him and the boy screamed, seeing that the doctor had no face, no face at all . . . just a mocking pink blankness and those horribly expressive hands, reaching for the equipment. . . .

~

"Electroshock therapy . . . ," Angela muttered.

He nodded. "Very . . . therapeutic."

She sighed. "They did that to Isabel, too. It never helped. But they kept doing it anyway."

"The 'therapy' made it worse." He smiled ruefully. And then remembered the last step in the creation of the man he was now: "The last place they sent me was run by the church. . . ."

~

The sixteen-year-old John Constantine in the small, nearly bare concrete cell of a rectory. Crouched in a corner, as far as he could get from the priest in a surplice who stood over him, performing the ritual of exorcism, incanting the words, and flicking holy water on him. . . .

"Reverend Father decided I was possessed. . . ."

A second priest came out of the shadows in the corner of the cell—as if bred by those shadows—and came closer, to watch with a secret glee, licking his lips, eyes bright . . . and covered with feeding bugs, something far worse than cockroaches, for each had a parody of a human face: thousands of leering insect mandibles chewing industriously at his soul. . . .

Constantine chuckled. A dry, toxic chuckle. "They exorcised me—like pulling a tooth that wasn't there."

The teenaged John Constantine writhed as the words struck him; they were words of power and he could feel them resonating within him, digging at him like a surgeon's probe—only there was nothing there to be exorcised. There was only the excruciating irony of the demon watching . . . standing carefully out of range of the flicking holy water.

The boy screamed in agony—of being unable to communicate the truth. The hypocrisy of the situation seemed to turn the holy water into burning drops of hydrochloric acid.

~

Now, Constantine rubbed his wrist. Feeling defenseless under the relentless grip of Angela's compassionate gaze. Knowing she was seeing—for a moment—the boy hidden underneath the man.

He shrugged. "I started to believe I was crazy. You think you're crazy long enough . . . you find a way out."

He realized she was looking at the jagged scar on his wrist.

"You tried to kill yourself. . . ."

Constantine had to laugh. "I didn't *try* anything. . . ."

~

Seventeen-year-old John Constantine on his knees in his bedroom. With a pair of scissors in his hands. And he wasn't there alone.

There were teachers, doctors, lawyers, garbagemen—you knew them by their work clothes, their affectations. But you couldn't normally see what Constantine saw now: their fangs, their tails, their horns and scales. The demons in human uniforms lounged on his bed, leaned on his bureau, against the wall, all of them smiling encouragingly, arms crossed, not trying to urge him on—just that friendly, passive encouragement. Waiting for him to kill himself.

It wasn't just entertainment. It was important to them that he kill himself. It would end his pointing them out to people. And it would put him thoroughly within the grasp of their Master—which was something that the young Constantine didn't understand.

Constantine grinned defiantly at them. He would go to the afterlife and he would escape them. . . .

Not knowing, really, or not believing, that suicide

was a one-way express ticket to eternal damnation. To Hell . . . and not figuratively.

He slashed his wrists, deep, and let the blood spurt; it came out to long, appreciative exhalations from the demons crowding the room.

And applause.

The cut was deep. His blood pressure plummeted. The room seemed to spin away into a streaked blur. . . .

~

"I didn't *try* anything," Constantine repeated.

"But you're still here. Alive," Angela pointed out gently. Sipping her tea. Quietly watching him.

But one of her hands was balled up so that her nail was digging into her palm. This story made her think of Isabel. Where Isabel was.

"It's not my doing . . . that I'm still here," Constantine said.

He remembered . . . and the memory nearly sent him into a convulsion right there in the restaurant decades later. His shoulders tightened, and he gripped the edge of the table. . . .

~

Sweat-soaked paramedics, breathing hard as they labored over the teenaged John Constantine on a gurney in the back of an ambulance. There was an IV set up, shaking with the vehicle's motion. They gave young Constantine a shot. He was unconscious, dying, but he was prescient enough to be aware of everything going on in the ambulance. The young Dr. Archer was there—before finishing med school, she was a paramedic.

The EMTs watched him, waiting. But Constantine didn't respond to the shot.

Archer had the defibrillator paddles poised over Constantine to try to jolt his heart.

Maybe too late: Constantine felt himself tugged from his body. . . .

And he flew up through the ambulance roof, his soul soaring out of his body—for a long, long moment feeling triumph, exulting in his release. He was going to be free of his earthly suffering at last! Perhaps he would meet God and God would at last explain . . .

Soaring on wings of hope—sure, because the Devil likes it that way. He likes them to think they're about to escape, going to go up that smooth tunnel into that loving, welcoming light. . . .

Let them kid themselves about that. So it can be ripped away from them . . . hope ripped away like a child struck by a car while rushing to her mother's arms.

And Constantine, spiraling up over Los Angeles, gazing in awe over the city, its millions of mortal lives . . . suddenly realized that Satan's little joke was reaching its punch line.

One moment he was gazing at the familiar city of palm trees and pale buildings and broad boulevards and thriving freeways; the next, L.A. was transfigured, or perhaps revealed: as Hell Los Angeles.

As suddenly, ushered in by a demonic laughter

that rang from horizon to horizon, vast curtains of amber flame licked up over the complacent city; the pillars of smoke rose, the blizzard of ash fell, the buildings collapsed with rumbles of despair. And the demons boiled up out of nowhere, seething rapaciously in the city's new wounds like maggots in gangrene.

You died in New York, you went to Hell New York. You died in Bangkok, you went to Hell Bangkok.

But this—a Los Angeles captured forever in the yellow of a jackal's eye; a Los Angeles where it forever rained ash, and only the demons thrived; where humanity was always dying, everyone perpetually dying: in crushed cars, in rubbled malls amid melting plastic, in the very mortar of brick buildings . . . or torn to pieces as part of a show that never ended in the Hollywood Bowl.

Constantine's soul arced over Hell L.A.—and he told himself he was escaping from it, he was flying upward, not downward. But the laughter was for his benefit. A kind of astral gravitation took hold of him. He stopped ascending. Stared with horror into Hell. . . .

And plunged down into it. The soldier demons were waiting for him with open arms, gaping jaws.

Can a soul feel pain? Oh, yes; and with exquisite nuance. It suddenly seemed as if there'd never been anything but pain. Ever.

"Time's relative?" Constantine laughed to himself. "Angela—Einstein didn't have a clue. . . ."

The young Constantine's soul was one moment in

Hell . . . then suddenly he was back in the ambulance again, jerking convulsively to sit up in the gurney— screaming—as the defibrillators that had brought him back from the dead were pulled away from his chest, smoking faintly.

"Easy, kid," the young Archer said. "You were dead—don't push it! Lay back and rest. . . ."

~

Constantine was poised on the brink of that smoking pit of memory. He recoiled from it—carrying with him a terrible knowledge.

Muttering to Angela, "Take it from me, two minutes in Hell is a lifetime. . . ."

He sat up straighter as he realized people were staring at him. He'd been bent over almost fetally on his stool.

Angela reached out and put her hand over his. He was amazed by how much that small touch conveyed. How much warmth and life and tenderness. And yet, he thought, she was a cop—and from what she'd said on the way here, one who'd been so willing to use her gun, it scared people.

He cleared his throat. "When I came back, I knew. All the things I could see were real. You know something?" He snorted. "Crazy was better."

Angela sipped her tea and waited.

"I learned to not see the demons, the dead"— Constantine went on, lowering his voice—"unless I made a certain, psychic effort. . . . And even then I pretended they weren't there . . . unless I was with people who knew. People who could teach me things—the kind of self-defense you need in the astral world. . . ."

Angela looked nervously around. "So if you can still see them when you want to . . . Uh—are there any . . . in here?"

Constantine glanced at her. "You sure you don't know?"

"Why would I?"

He shrugged. He looked around. He dilated his psychic iris. There—that couple in the corner. Yuppie woman and metrosexual man. Both of them admiring her new purse, his new Gucci shoes. The two of them glancing over at him—twitching their tails, snake tongues licking out, their dragon eyes narrowing warningly as they sensed him. They hadn't been sent here to take him out, he figured. They seemed surprised that he'd spotted them for what they were. But best to keep an eye on them. Remembering the vermin-formed demon, the attack from the winged things downtown. Another attack was sure to come. . . .

He became aware that Angela was nervously waiting for his report. "Nah," he said. "None in here."

He wanted a cigarette more and more and it was beginning to make his nerves taut and twangy. *Keep your mind off it, old boy.*

"Heaven and Hell are right here, Angela. Behind every wall, every window—the world behind the world. And we're smack in the middle. 'The Balance?' " He put his cup down hard enough to make the tea splash. "I call it hypocritical bullshit. . . ."

~

There—a pay phone, in front of the liquor store, half a long block away. Father Hennessy jogged down the street toward it, sweat already making his clothes stick to him.

Maybe this phone was working. Hennessy had gone to two pay phones on the street already; both were vandalized past use. He wished his cell phone were still working. Should've paid the bill. Should've known there'd be an emergency, with Johnny Constantine asking favors.

God, he wanted a drink. The voices of the dead seemed to be hinting; they seemed to be saying personal things now. . . .

"Father . . . aren't you thirsty? Something is . . ."

"Oh, he's fine, he's been drinking in the morgue . . ."

". . . laughing at us, ignoring us, turning away from us, when we beg him to intercede with his Christ, his Holy Mother, but none of them help, the Saints won't answer. At least the devils will speak to you; at least they will take notice. . . . My Katherine never took notice, just shut me out, and thought I didn't know about her little blond boyfriend, so I killed them both, and made sure she lived long enough to see me standing over her, saying, 'Take notice now, do you, Katherine, eh?' Do you see, Father, what happens when people don't take notice, eh?"

"It's snuffling for you, Father. It's snuffling nigh and nearer yet, Padre, you cowering hypocrite. . . ."

God how he wanted to shut them up.

Just to go home and put the aluminum foil *back up* on the wall and pour a tumbler of bourbon. Shut them all out. But there was no time to get back to his place, and his bottle; not yet. He had to get in touch with Constantine.

He got to the pay phone, dropped in a big handful of change, each coin seeming to take forever. The rain had almost gone from the streets; there was a deposit of wet trash in the gutter. Someone's inexplicable yellow knit sweater there too, looking mushy with water, and a disintegrating *Los Angeles Times* sports page.

The dial tone! Father Hennessy's fingers tapped at the pay phone buttons.

"Be there, John," he said aloud. "Please . . ."

He had to warn Constantine. He'd seen it—when the symbol had appeared on Isabel's wrist, a window had opened, into the deepest darkest realms. Something down there had looked back at him—and it had spoken Constantine's name. It had pointed a claw at him. . . .

They were after Constantine. They were after him, too, because he was helping Constantine. And only John Constantine would know how to call them off.

The phone rang in his ear, rang and rang. . . .

"He's not home, Father, and something's behind you. . . . It's coming closer, devilish close, Father. . . ."

He wasn't going to listen to the nattering of the dead, not now. They were petty and peevish and they tried to get at you and they were all liars.

"Can't you hear it? It's behind you, Father! You'd better turn around and look, you old fool!"

He wasn't going to give them the satisfaction of looking. There was nothing creeping up behind him. They were only trying to . . . to scare him, to—

"Father! You'd better run!"

—to warn him.

Now he heard something skittering behind him—and as he turned it reached him and whipped under the cuff of his trousers, wrapped itself around his ankle, its touch repellent and slick and many-legged. He shook his leg frantically, trying to dislodge it, but it gripped him like moss on a tree.

"Mother of God—Jesus—help me—get it off!"

And now it was climbing up Hennessy's leg, winding its way around, whipping toward his buttocks, to the nearest entrance—

Hennessy shrieked and dropped the phone's earpiece to dangle and swing, faintly ringing, as he clawed at himself. But it was already too late. Maybe a bungled lifetime too late.

He began to run—as if he could outrun something that was right then climbing his body . . . forcing its way into him and grabbing hold of his spine and his nervous system and his soul . . .

And turning him toward the liquor store.

~

"So when a half-breed breaks the rules," Constantine was saying, toying with a cigarette, "when it tries to commandeer free will or hijack a soul—"

"Sir—there's really no smoking here," the manager said as she passed, not unkindly.

"I'm just *holding* it in my *hand*," Constantine snarled. He closed his eyes. "Sorry. Anyway . . ."

". . . hijack a soul," Angela prompted.

Hearing that, the manager glanced at them from a rack of cups, raising her eyebrows.

"Yeah. They pull something like that," Constantine said, leaning closer to Angela, not quite whispering, "and I deport their sorry assess right back to Hell. . . ."

He wondered if he should go on. He was giving her false hope that he had the power to help—but it seemed important that she understood everything.

Somehow he knew they were in this together, he and Angela. He'd felt it on the street, with the winged demons almost within reach. And when she'd brought him the water, with barely a murmur. They both felt it. It was like musical notes converging to make a harmonious chord. And to a mystic like Constantine, everything was made up of vibrations. He and Angela harmonized on a vibratory level. Gut feelings again—intuition with a special crackle of something extra, a quality that seemed to resonate of destiny, and, just maybe, of help from on high. . . .

You didn't ignore feelings like that, any more than you could ignore the current of a powerful river. You paddled with it, angled to use it, and let it sweep you to the side that you wanted to go to. Life itself as magic.

How does someone escape Hell? she'd asked him. They couldn't, of course. He really ought to tell her . . . how very final it was. But could she bear to think of Isabel that way—forever?

"Angela . . ."

She looked at him attentively. Waiting. He cleared his throat. "Let's . . . take a walk."

~

Hennessy stepped over the body of the Pakistani man he'd knocked out, and over the broken bottle he'd knocked him out with, to get at the liquor behind the counter. He had an infinite thirst in him. Like the fires of Hell burned in him and only the liquor could put them out. Sure, liquor fed fire, everyone knew that. But it didn't matter—he had to drink, and drink.

He screwed the top off a Jack Daniel's bottle, sucked at the bottle's mouth, hard, hard, and for a moment there was a burning golden flow—and then it was gone. He frowned down at the bottle. It was empty. Couldn't have drunk it. It must've been empty all along.

"What the hell are you selling here?" he asked the man moaning on the floor.

He went to another bottle, twisted off the cap, tilted it back. Same effect. More and more and more . . . bottle after bottle. All empty!

But the thirst wasn't gone—it was redoubled, if anything. That arid pit was deeper and darker than ever.

Balthazar, in the champagne aisle, was watching with a faintly amused smile, his own bottle, expensive and sealed, in hand.

He watched as Hennessy smashed the top off a

J&B bottle, tilted it back, cutting his lips, so that blood flowed to mix with brown liquor overflowing his mouth. Red and golden brown, prettily intermixing on the priest collar. Most amusing.

But to Hennessy it still seemed as if every bottle was empty.

That's when he saw the angel. The God-slave, as Balthazar thought of them, was in the body of a young Hispanic stockboy coming out of the backroom to stare around at the wreckage, at his groaning boss. Rushing to Hennessy's side as the ex-priest—staggering, seizing, twitching with alcohol poisoning—grabbed a corkscrew and jammed it, twisted it, into his own hand. He must drink something . . . anything. His own blood if nothing else . . .

But before he could put his hand to his mouth, Hennessy collapsed, the stockboy catching him, lowering him gently to the booze-puddled, bloody floor. The stockboy glaring. Knowing.

The stockboy looked up, his eyes meeting Balthazar's.

Balthazar grinned. Unconsciously flipping that coin between his fingers. And hurried out the exit.

The stockboy turned to smile at the spirit that was rising from Hennessy's body. Nodding at the ghostly Hennessy, to confirm—

You made it.

Hennessy paused only once to look back at his ravaged body. Oh, what a relief to be free of it. The demon had, ironically, done him a favor.

One time, as a boy, he'd gotten lost in the woods,

and fallen among ants, and they'd worked their way under his clothes, along with the sweat and grit, stinging him. At last he'd found a cool clear spring, and he'd taken his clothes off and bathed in that spring, and what an unspeakable relief it had been. . . .

That's what it was like now. His body was that soiled, pestilential garment, set aside; and now he felt cleansed. The demon gone, the desire for liquor gone. Instead there was a feeling that desires were just a kind of background music for a dance he was only now learning.

He saw before him an emerald meadow, and beyond it an impossibly pristine lake reflecting a city of light. He saw old friends drifting near to him; family members, his grandparents. So many had made it here.

Hennessy praised the Highest, grateful that he had not surrendered his faith. He had made mistakes, he had fouled himself with alcohol—he had started to be a kind of parasite, for money. But he had never lost his faith; it had remained inside him, tinier than a mustard seed. Which was exactly big enough, when the time had come—he'd asked forgiveness and that seed had grown to fill the world, all in an instant.

TEN

Constantine noticed Angela glancing up at the night sky as they walked down the street together. She was half expecting another attack from the flying demons.

"They won't come at us the same way, Officer Angela. The Big Son of a Bitch doesn't like you to be prepared for his attacks. Whenever the old boy can manage it, it's always what you don't expect."

"So—should we even be out here, in the open, like a couple of targets waiting to be shot at?" She shook her head. "Should I be asking you if you slipped me a drug at some point? Was it all hallucination on that street downtown? Is any of this real?"

"You know it's real. You can feel it."

She looked at him. "What do you mean by that?"

"I mean—I think we have some things in common . . ."

He coughed—and blood came up this time. He spat into the gutter. A motorcycle cop rolled by, shot Constantine a glare from under his helmet. Spitting in the street—not something he'd stop for, but show some respect for the goddamn law.

Constantine waved cheerfully at him. "Kiss my ass, traffic cop!"

Angela elbowed him. "Stop that! It'll be embarrassing if I have to . . . Anyway, you're just resentful about all those tickets. Which were probably all deserved, judging by the way you were drinking when I came to your place."

"So you looked at my record. Big Brother is watching—or Big Sister. Sure they were deserved. We all get what we fucking deserve, right? Oh yeah. Right. Some lady gets her kid murdered by a psycho. She deserved that. Everyone in Hiroshima deserved what they got."

"Not the same. They couldn't choose being victimized. You can choose whether or not you weave down the streets like a drunken idiot."

"Can I? I can't choose my state of mind, most of the time. I never did drive drunk—sometimes I just drove frantic." He shrugged. "Most of what happens to us is random as an avalanche. Random allocation of misery. Random violence. That's the same every-goddamn-where."

"There must be a reason. For what happened to those people. For what happened to you. What's happening to us the last few hours. There has to be a reason. . . ."

Constantine wanted to say, *A good reason for what Isabel is going through?* But he liked Angela too much to say something pointlessly hurtful.

"There must be some kind of plan," Angela insisted. "We just can't see it from where we stand."

He sighed, and relented just a little. "Well. I'll say this much. God didn't create Hell. The pit of Eternal Damnation is a collaboration—far as I can make out—between us and the Devil. The inside dirt is, when people don't open themselves up to God—or when they break fundamental rules, like going AWOL on Him, you know, with suicide—that leads to their being excluded from the Big Light after they die. And if they're, like, excluded from the Big Light, they're, sorta, *outside* God's protective grace—there's something in the Bible about the 'outer darkness' where there's 'wailing and gnashing of teeth.' And out there in that Outer Darkness, see, the disembodied are in a kind of spiritual wilderness. Who else is in that wilderness? Ol' Scratch, that's who. Lucifer and his boys. Demons are the wolves that roam that spiritual wilderness. And they prey on you out there. So you've *put your own self* outside God's grace—this is the story I've heard, anyway—and God says, 'Sorry, nothing personal, y'all, I'd like to help, but—you're on your own out there, pal.' And since you're alone in the wilderness, you get eaten. But it's not like the Big Guy—or Big Girl, or Androgyne, depending on how you see God—it's not like the Big Cosmic Dude wrote a rule book and arbitrarily said, 'Die and you go to Hell for all eternity.' The consequence of suicide is just sort of built into things. It's part of the spiritual physics; just in the nature of the universe. But I'll tell you something else, Angela: It's not as if He—or She or It—couldn't come and *get you out* of the Outer Darkness, if He, She, or It really *wanted* to, and *that's* the part that pisses me off, because I never asked to be born into all these rules. . . ."

"People say that, about not asking to be born," Angela said musingly. "But actually—how do you know you didn't ask to be born? Where were you, before you were here—before you were born? Do you remember? Maybe you existed in some way. Maybe you *did* ask to be born."

Constantine grunted: close as he came to even provisional agreement on that issue. Thinking: *Hidden depths to this woman.* He started to comment—but the coughing interrupted him.

"How bad is it?" she asked after a moment. "I mean—whatever it is you're sick from."

He sighed. He'd been treasuring the notion that sometime before the end she'd somehow miraculously find him desirable and they might . . . get closer yet. The other kind of intimacy. But who wanted to get involved with a terminal cancer patient right before he goes down?

If she did—then it'd probably be for all the wrong reasons. But it was no good lying to her.

"It's bad," he said. "Lung cancer."

She didn't say anything for a while. They paused

on a corner to look around. They were outside what looked like a gay disco, with people just leaving after last call. Laughing couples—a few of them bickering—in skintight pants and muscle shirts, milling on the sidewalk. The music some variant of trance; through the open door, Constantine could see a mirror ball throwing off light, spinning like a planet designed by a god with bad taste.

"When we were little," Angela said suddenly, "Isabel saw things too. Like you did. And . . ."

Her purse started to chime. She dug through it, found her cell phone, flipped it open. "Lieutenant Dodson . . ." Her expression darkened. "I'm nearby. Yeah. Send a car over. . . ."

~

"Just a block or so away from here," Detective Xavier was saying, "there's a morgue. . . ."

They stood in the shambles of the liquor store, amid alcohol and blood and broken glass. Angela and Xavier were there, where Father Hennessy had had his rampage, along with three uniformed cops. John Constantine was leaning against the door frame behind them.

Mostly he was just thinking about Hennessy. Figuring this was his fault, somehow. Not liking the feeling.

"And this guy"—Weiss indicated Hennessy's body—"was also over at that morgue. Security guard was saying he was 'handling' a girl's body."

"What was he doing to her?"

Xavier just shook his head. "Comes in here, has a go at the entire stock. Alcohol poisoning. Guy drank himself to death in under a minute. Should have been in my fraternity."

Xavier noticed Constantine and snorted. "What the hell is he doing here?"

Constantine picked his way carefully across the floor to squat close beside Hennessy. Staring at the bloated body.

"Hey!" A uniformed cop noticing Constantine came over to intervene. "Get away from there—"

Angela stepped in between Constantine and the cop, flashing her badge. "Body's worked up and tagged, right? Just leave him be."

Constantine took in the gouge on Hennessy's hand; the blood on his face. He patted Hennessy's coat—found the protective amulet in a pocket. Drew it out, hefted it for a moment, thinking:

Would he still be alive if I'd let him keep wearing this?

"Shit," Constantine murmured. "Why didn't you call me. . . ." His voice was strangely tender as he added, ". . . you son of a bitch."

He looked again at the corkscrew wound in Hennessy's palm. A pattern in the blood. . . . Hard to make it out. . . .

He looked around, found some ice in the wine freezer, brought it back, pushed it into Hennessy's palm, wiping away dried blood. Not a random cut, no. It was a kind of bloody insignia.

Constantine found a paper bag, pressed it to the palm, looked at the paper. The residual blood had made an imprint. He'd seen this circular symbol before.

He stood and looked one last time at the remains of Father Hennessy—once a compatriot in battle, even a friend, before the booze took hold.

But all the while, even when he was grubbing for his next drink, he was a better man than me, Constantine thought. *And I've been treating him like crap. He deserved better.*

"I'm sorry, Father."

He turned away, suspecting—feeling it, really—that Hennessy was at peace. Maybe in a way that John Constantine would never be.

He turned to Angela. "I need to see where Isabel died."

~

"This part of East L.A. used to be kind of tony," Angela said, looking out at the vacant lots and decaying high-rises around Ravenscar as they walked out onto the hospital roof. "But when the economy went south . . ."

Constantine sensed that Angela was trying to keep her mind busy, by thinking about the neighborhood. This was a painful place for her to visit.

They reached the rim of the roof where Isabel had jumped to her death, and gazed out at the glimmering corpus of the nighttime city. The city pulsed with light amid swaths of velvet darkness, its energy only a little diminished so far past midnight. Constantine thought it was like a delirious fever patient in a dormant, semicomatose state, still twitching in its sleep, still sweating, soon to awaken babbling.

And Constantine could feel Isabel's suicide here—feel it like a recent, aching burn on his skin.

Terminal patients, he thought. *Isabel, Los Angeles—and me. One down, two to go: me next.*

Los Angeles gave off a background vehicular rumbling—softer at this hour but always there. Jets bringing in tourists thumped the air from LAX. A siren wailed from somewhere nearby. Was that a distant gunshot? Another? A drive-by, perhaps.

The city continued to mumble to itself: the screech of brakes, the grumble of a semitruck, a car driving nearby with its woofers booming out a hip-hop beat. Someone gets shot—or someone jumps to their death from a hospital roof—and the city shrugs and goes on.

"Let's go down to the place she . . . where she fell to," Constantine said gently.

They went back in, found the elevators, rode in silence down to hydrotherapy. Constantine thought he ought to say something to comfort her—only, he was pretty rotten at comforting people. She led the way to the pool. Police tape still around it.

Barely audible when she spoke. "I guess she was always trying to decipher it all. Make sense of it. Séances, Ouija boards, channeling . . . Our dad thought she was just trying to get attention." She took a long breath. Chuckled sadly. "She certainly did that. She'd tell everyone about the things she said she saw. Crazy things. Monsters. Like you saw. She'd scare my mother to death. Then one day she just stopped talking—for almost a year."

Constantine looked at her. Then away. It was so horribly inevitable: "So you had her committed."

Angela's outbreath was ragged. "The first time no one tells you. You don't know how to handle it. What are you supposed to do?"

"Show me her room," Constantine said.

~

A long, clinical corridor echoed with their footsteps. A black nurse came around the corner, walking with a little boy—shepherding him along, really. The boy fixated on Angela the moment she came into view—and bolted from his nurse, running to Angela with his arms outstretched. He flew into her arms, hugging her tightly. Angela was baffled, but she returned the hug.

"Barry!" the nurse said, trotting up. "Oh God . . ." She tugged the boy away from Angela. "No, Barry—that's not Isabel."

Angela squatted, eyes moist, to look into the child's eyes. There was nothing to say, but she was looking for the words anyway. Barry reached out, blinking in confusion, and touched her face with the tips of his fingers.

"Hi, sweetheart," Angela said, at last.

"I'm sorry," the nurse said. "They were friends. He kind of had a crush on your sister."

Angela nodded. The nurse led the boy away—looking over his shoulder at her as he went. Not taking his eyes off her till they'd turned a corner.

Constantine said, "You were twins."

Angela nodded, and led him into Isabel's room, flicking the light on.

"That poor little boy," she murmured. "There are so many like that. Lost children. No one really taking care of them. Get taken away from their parents and shoved into an institution somewhere—as if that's better. They're abused in the foster care system a lot of times. Even molested. Kids like that are something we see way too much of in the department. . . ."

The room was minimally appointed. Metal hospital bed. Dresser. Single window with wire mesh built into it.

"How long?" Constantine asked, looking around, extending his feelers. Not sure what he was looking for exactly.

"Two months," Angela said wistfully. "This time. She'd get better, then worse—recently, a lot worse." She chewed at a fingernail thoughtfully. "That symbol cut in the dead guy's hand—it have something to do with this?"

Constantine glanced at her, a little surprised.

"I'm a cop, John, remember?"

He shrugged. Pulled out a dresser drawer, and another, pulling them entirely from the cabinet to look at the bottoms.

"You know I already did all that," Angela muttered. Irritable with lack of sleep, and stress. She did have some ego about her job.

He ran his fingers under the steel bed frame.

Angela snorted. "Now you're just insulting me."

"You don't walk off a building without leaving something behind," Constantine said, thinking aloud.

Angela hugged herself wearily, swaying slightly in place. "You saw everything she left behind. In that box."

"Maybe she left something else." Constantine looked at her. "Something more personal. Just for you." He glanced at the window. The sky out there was going from blue steel to aluminum. Dawn was coming.

"You were her twin, Angela," he went on. "Twins tend to think alike."

"I'm not like my sister." She said it with a kind of cold insistence. As if trying to reassure herself as much as him.

"But you were once. When you were kids. When you'd spend every second with each other. You'd start a sentence, she'd finish it." Was she really going to deny this? "You'd get hurt, she'd cry."

"That . . . was a long time ago."

Constantine shook his head. Put his hands in his pockets. Chilly. He wasn't sure if the chilliness was a psychic or a physiological effect. "That kind of bond doesn't just disappear."

"There's nothing here," Angela insisted.

She seemed off balance. Increasingly defensive. And he wondered why. "She planned her death in this room. She thought it up right here, right where you're standing." He took a step toward her, prodding her with words and sheer presence. She took a step back as he said, "She knew you'd come. She counted on you to see what she saw, to feel what she felt. To know what she knew. *What did she do*, Angela?"

Her lips buckled. She looked like she wanted to hit him again. "How should I know?"

He took a step closer yet. "What did she do, Angela?" Another step, deliberately crowding her.

She backed up—against the wall. "I don't know!"

"What would *you* do?"

She looked away from him.

He went on relentlessly. "What would you leave her?"

He leaned close to force eye contact on her. They were a breath apart. "Where would it be?" he demanded. His voice getting louder. "What would you leave her?" Louder. *"Where would it be?"*

She shoved him away, hard, and strode to the window. Almost hyperventilating, her eyes squeezed shut.

Constantine just watched. Sensing something was emerging.

Her eyes opened, and the tension seemed to slip from her shoulders. She stepped closer to the window—and blew on it. Her breath misted the glass.

She did it once more, lower—and this time a shape emerged on the glass.

She surprised Constantine then: She turned, grabbed a floor mat, and began beating it hard against the steel bed frame, like a woman gone mad.

"When we were girls . . . ," she said.

Whap, whap against the bed frame. Dust was coming off it in clouds.

". . . we'd leave each other messages."

She struck the mat harder still; more dust flew.

"In breath—in light."

She struck it once more. Constantine was trying hard not to cough. It wasn't easy, but he managed to keep it down to a few wheezes.

"On the windows . . ."

She dropped the mat and went to the door, switched off the light.

The dawn light was coming through the window, outlining a shape written in finger oil, distorting the dusty columns of sunlight so that they projected a pattern, beamed by the dawn, on the wall of the room: **COR 17:01.**

"I need a church," Constantine said.

He struck out immediately, down the corridor, Angela hurrying to catch up.

"Corinthians," Constantine muttered.

"I know the Bible, John," Angela said, rubbing her eyes with fatigue. "There is no seventeenth act in Corinthians. I'm tired but—I was drilled as a kid on Bible stuff. I remember all the useless stuff . . ."

"Second Corinthians goes to twenty-one acts in the Book of Ethenius," Constantine said, shrugging.

She looked at him. "The what?"

"That's the Bible in Hell," he explained.

ELEVEN

C onstantine didn't explain how he knew about the Book of Ethenius. Or what a painful history he had with that particular "Bible."

Hurrying along beside him in the hospital corridor and down the stairs, Angela looked as if she'd had a little too much unique information in the last twenty-four hours. "They have bibles in Hell?"

"Satanic bibles. The Book of Ethenius paints a different view of Revelations. Says the world will not end by God's hand but be reborn in the embrace of the damned."

They were coming up to the swinging doors that led into the hospital's chapel. The sign CHAPEL looked as clinically institutional as a sign reading REST ROOM, say, or MORGUE.

"Though if you ask me," Constantine added, "fire's fire."

It was a small chapel. Dimness and a small stained glass window, pews and an altar with no definite image on it, all suggesting nondenominational plug-in-whatever-you-want worship. A pastor was comforting a man and wife. Constantine sensed they'd just lost a child here.

But he took this in only obliquely, on his way to the shelves of reference books off to the side.

Angela lowered her voice to a whisper. "And they're going to have this book in a hospital chapel?"

"Yes. And no."

Constantine stopped at a bowl of holy water, stuck his hand in it. "It doesn't exist on this side."

But Constantine had closed his eyes—and the water had begun to boil around his hand. He extended his feelers as he had once before—he didn't have the cat with him now, but his recent visit to Hell still clung to him, like the reek of sulfur, and he was still vibratorily close to it.

"Oh Lord . . . ," Angela muttered, seeing the water boil. "But John, what did you mean by—"

Constantine shushed her, and turned back to look at the chapel . . .

. . . which had transformed. It had become a church in Hell. The windows had gone slate black. There was a demon on the crucifix instead of Jesus, and a lunatic nun who giggled and capered, catching the blood dripping from the demon's fangs. There were different worshipers here too—Constantine saw them ethereally, shimmering in and out of physical existence, tittering and fornicating giddily on the floor beneath the altar, all the while clawing one another viciously: damned souls, who'd probably practiced sex magic as mortals, in the name of Lucifer; in torment, now, not in ecstasy, condemned to rend one another while copulating without pleasure. And that familiar multitudinous gnashing sound was as pervasive as the sound of the sea on a rocky beach.

The door to the Hell outside the chapel was closed. Sealed shut. But as Constantine glanced at the door something on the other side roared and the door shivered under a sudden savage blow from out there—something trying to break in.

They'd alrcady caught his scent.

He turned hastily to the books on the shelf: Where was it? The Book of Ethenius?

Another thud on the door—it splintered inward. Something was clawing its way through. Something roaring his name. Hungering for him.

There! That black and red book—he grabbed it with his free hand, and pulled his other from the holy water, turning to step back into . . .

. . . the chapel as it was in the human world.

As Angela finished her question, "—not on this side?"

He'd gone to Hell and come back in the space between two words in her sentence.

She stared at him, blinking, seeing he was now

covered in sweat, steaming, perfumed with essence of Hades. He was already flipping through the book, scowling over it, muttering.

Angela shook her head. "Where did that book come from?"

She looked at the shelves. None missing.

Constantine was looking through the "New Testament" correspondence in Hell's own bible. "Thirteen twenty-nine . . . thirteen-thirty . . . Here." He tapped the page, finding the entry he wanted. " 'The sins of the father would only be exceeded by the sins of the son.' "

"Uh—whose son?"

"That symbol on Hennessy's hand." He looked at her in sudden realization. "It's not a demonic sign. That's why I didn't recognize it. Could be something much more powerful than a mere demon."

"John—what are you talking about?"

Constantine mused aloud. "But he can't cross over . . . impossible for the son to cross over. . . ." Shuddering inwardly at the implications. *Soon it would be party time for devils.*

"Whose son?" Angela asked desperately. "God's?"

"No. The other one."

She looked at him, not wanting to understand. But understanding dawned slowly on her anyway. "The Devil had a son too?"

~

There was a reason Beeman lived in the back of a bowling alley, behind the lanes, at the end of that narrow strip of noisy corridor where the maintenance was done on the pinsetting machines. Back in the clatter and smash of the pins, most of the day and night. There was a bit of extra storage space at the end of that corridor.

Beeman suffered from a particularly nasty form of tinnitus—ringing in the ears, from the explosion of an alchemical beaker. He'd been a hair away from the Philosopher's Stone itself, working from the only known copy of the alchemical diary of Abremalin the Mage, and he'd put in a grain too much brimstone. The explosion had knocked him across the room—and consumed the book he'd worked from. He'd always figured that wasn't an accident. Something, someone—maybe the Angel Gabriel—hadn't wanted him to have the Philosopher's Stone. It led to immortality, and that led to cheating death, and that broke the rules for mortals. And Gabriel had warned him once. Maybe the tinnitus afterward was a cruel reminder. . . .

The constant buzzing in his damaged inner ear, the whistling, whirring, loud as a guitar amp turned two-thirds the way up—it made him nuts unless he was somewhere noisier than the buzzing. Something, anything, to mask that sound. And he'd always loved bowling.

So now he sat at his desk, talking by phone to Constantine and peering at a page of scrolls under the glow of a goosenecked desk lamp with the bowling pins clashing behind him—but only one lane going, since it was early morning: The manager always played a solo game or two before he started getting ready to open.

Beeman had a telephone—dialed to the absolute loudest setting—held by his shoulder to his ear. His neck ached from holding the phone there.

"16:19 . . . 16:30 . . . Yes, here we go," he told Constantine. "I've got it." On the page was an etching of that same damnably recurrent symbol. Underneath were ink drawings of a devil rising up through a human body.

Above the beast, a familiar figure on a crucifix, weeping, welcomed the beast into the human world.

~

"*Oh my,*" Beeman added, from the speakerphone in Angela's SUV. "*This is certainly not good . . .*"

She was driving, nursing a Starbucks coffee. Constantine was riding shotgun "This world has been invaded, all right," she muttered, "by Starbucks. And we all let it happen. . . ."

Constantine glanced at her, smiling, thinking she was getting punchy with fatigue.

"*As you know,*" Beeman continued, his voice as disembodied as any errant ghost's, "*the myth says Mammon was conceived before his father's fall from grace—but he was born* after."

~

In the storage area at the end of the maintenance corridor, Beeman seemed to hear something anomalous in a brief pause while the ball was rolling back to the alley's manager. A door opening?

He turned to look back down the alley: a long narrow strip of darkness with little pools of light coming from each lane, pacing it off. Nothing moved there, except the mechanical works of the pinsetter in lane seven, going up and down like the gnashing of a giant robotic jaw.

"Beeman . . . ? " came Constantine's voice on the phone.

"Sorry," Beeman said, turning back to the scroll. "Sorry. Right here." He forced himself to focus. But that uneasy feeling wouldn't go away. He glanced over his shoulder again. Saw nothing.

Well, he had various warding signs set up back there, to block whatever wanted to get in. Probably it was some irate elemental with a bone to pick—from the old days. Just hanging around. Let it hover. It couldn't get to him—he hoped.

He pulled the lamp closer to the scrolls. "Um . . . unlike Satan himself, Junior has never been in the presence of the Creator, so he has no fear of him. No respect, either. And that contempt goes double for us—God's most prized creations."

Beeman thought: *If we're "God's precious ones," as it says here, then God needs some higher standards.*

"Mammon—Satan's son—would be the last demon we'd ever want coming into . . ."

Was that another anomalous sound? Echoing laughter—echoing from far, far beyond this little mortal edifice?

". . . into our plane."

Something was definitely trying to get to him. Maybe something powerful enough to stamp over his warding sigils, the way a man in heavy boots might kick through a small campfire. He felt like he was over a slow flame himself. Sweat was breaking out on his neck, his face. It was strangely hot in here, where it was normally quite cool. . . .

But it was important to get this information to Constantine . . . important to far more than the two of them. And Beeman—though he dabbled in the black arts—had long ago chosen sides. He served the Light.

"But demons can't cross over," Constantine was insisting on the phone. *"Right? Remember? Beeman?"*

"Wait. . . ." The ancient text swam before his eyes. It was so hard to make it out in the heat waves . . . hard to concentrate when things were crawling on his desk. Scuttling across it. Bugs of some kind. Flies. He swiped haphazardly at them, squinting at the yellowing scrolls. Something alit on the back of his neck, crawling there. He shook it off but it only came back, to be joined by a companion, and another.

"Wait—John. Wait. I'm reading. There seems to be a . . . loophole. Very old. *Very* old. The translation is difficult. Conceived in Heaven, born in Hell—normal barriers might not apply. . . ."

He glanced up. Something was forming over there in the shadows, in the corner. Forming of thousands of tiny moving parts. But he had to finish telling Constantine about the scroll. This was the most important thing he would ever do. The agglomerate in the corner took on a vague outline—he wanted to scream but instead he managed to say, croakingly, "It says . . ." He looked again at the scroll. "First, Mammon would have to possess an oracle."

~

Angela pulled the SUV up at a stoplight. "That's a psychic," Constantine told her. "A very, very powerful psychic."

"I know what an oracle is," Angela said. Her voice distant. Thinking of . . .

Then she said it aloud. Making up her mind. ". . . Isabel."

"But that wouldn't be enough," came Beeman's voice. Sounding frightened even through the poor resolution of the speakerphone. *"To cross over he'd still need . . ."*

There was a growing background sound in the speakerphone. Noise from Beeman's—and not the usual noise. A kind of swelling buzz.

". . . he'd need divine assistance. To cross over, Mammon would need the help of God. It says—look for signs. Signs of his coming."

"What kind of signs . . . Beeman?"

"Minor demons. Trying to break through."

That buzzing noise . . .

"John," Beeman went on, his voice breaking. *"I know you've never had much faith. Never had much reason to . . ."*

Constantine looked at the phone. Something about Beeman's voice. Was he in danger—right now?

"Beeman?"

A certain resignation in Beeman's voice now. "But remember, John—that doesn't mean we don't have faith. In you."

The buzzing rose in volume—and suddenly cut off. There was no voice, no sound—except the dial tone.

Constantine looked hard at Angela. "Drive. Fast."

TWELVE

W hat's that smell? Sulfur?" Angela asked, as they stood outside the door to Beeman's peculiar little impromptu apartment.

Constantine sniffed—and winced. What *was* that smell? Raw sewage—and blood?

The door that led to the maintenance lane was closed, locked. Constantine hadn't been able to find the manager, though the outside door had been unlocked. A morning talk show played without volume on a TV set behind the main desk, above the shelves of bowling shoes. No other life visible.

"Beeman!" Constantine called. "Beeman!"

Angela stepped back from the flies slipping under the door, a stream of them darting past. That buzzing sound again, fluctuating.

Constantine felt something tickle his ankle—he

shook it, and several large houseflies flew loopily away. More were coming from the openings at the back of the lanes, and under the door, the air darkening with them.

He stepped back, and located the door's weak point, then kicked it—hard. He had a lot of practice kicking down doors, and it flew open immediately.

Inside the maintenance corridor, what should have been cool darkness was instead a sticky, buzzing heat. They hurried down the lane, past pool after pool of light, till they got to the area that widened for Beeman's little compartment.

The darkness seemed to thicken around Beeman's desk. To move there. . . .

Buzzing. Black buzzing.

"Do you see that?" Angela asked. Her voice taut.

Constantine pressed forward—and the flies swarmed up at him, as if warning him back, like bees disturbed at their hive. Angela kept up with him, covering her mouth, wanting to scream but only whimpering.

The swarm of flies had a locus, a thicker center. A solid mound of moving flies on the floor.

"Oh Jesus," Constantine muttered. "No . . ."

He took off his coat, flung it at the mound, and the swarming flies scattered, becoming a cloud over Beeman's body—or what was left of it. Mostly eaten away. Flies poured out of Beeman's mouth and ears.

"Oh God," Angela choked.

"*Who?*" Constantine demanded—of no one in particular. Who had done this to his friend?

The flies began to vanish into the shadows—were almost gone. He had to stop it from escaping. . . .

He pulled his shirtsleeves back, revealing two distinctive tattoos on his forearms that he used for conjuring; when he put them together they made one symmetrically complete image. He slammed the tattoos together and—drawing astral light to project the magic into the air near Beeman's body, visualizing the symbols—incanted, "Into the light I command thee!" He was having trouble breathing, the sickness in his lungs threatening to betray him at this critical moment. He might still be able to help Beeman, at least in the next world . . . if he could reveal the demon who'd destroyed him. "Into the light I command thee!"

Don't cough. Not now. Focus. The moment will be gone and it'll be too late. Don't cough!

"Into the light I command thee!"

The air around his outstretched arms seemed to warp as the summoning took hold. Angela stepped back, afraid. The flies buzzed overhead. . . .

"Into the light I command thee! Into the light I—"

And then the coughing fit came on. He couldn't breathe at all. His head swam with weariness, lack of oxygen—and despair, as blood erupted from his lungs into his mouth. He spat . . . and fell to his knees.

Angela knelt beside him, instinctively putting an

arm around his shoulders. The flies were gone. There was only Beeman's stripped body. And little spots of Constantine's blood on the floor.

The coughing fit stopped. But it was too late.

"This is my fault," Constantine said hoarsely. "A damned one-man plague."

"John . . . you need a doctor."

Constantine made a sound of disgust, deep in his throat, and shook his head. "I've seen a doctor."

He stood up—and the room seemed to spin. He was still having trouble getting his breath. He was afraid he was going to fall on his face. Put out his hands to try to keep his balance. Swaying. Angela stood and tried to help him.

"Stay away," he told her. Hoping she'd understand. He wanted to send her somewhere safe—away from him. First Hennessy, then Beeman. Maybe she'd be next. "Please . . ."

He looked at Beeman's desk—wasn't surprised to see that the scrolls were ashes now.

Angela sighed. She drew out her portable squawk box. "Ten-twelve to base. Office needs assistance. We've got a . . ."

She looked at Beeman's body. How did she classify this one? Which number was it in the manual?

". . . uh, officer needs assistance."

~

Constantine's apartment. He sat on his window seat, looking out at the street. Watching the police vehicles drive away from the bowling alley.

"It wasn't just Isabel," Angela said from the doorway. "I used to see things too, John."

He looked at her. Hadn't he told her to stay the hell away from him? Was everyone going to be stupid and walk in front of a juggernaut, whistling a merry tune as they marched blithely to certain death?

"But you knew that," she went on. "Didn't you."

He had suspected. But he said nothing. She took a step into his room. There was something about that step—like crossing a line. Coming over to his side, in some way.

"You see something in me," she said. "Something Isabel had . . ."

"Go home, Angela." Constantine looked at the cigarette in his hand. Almost burned out. The way he felt, he identified with the cigarette.

Angela came in, wandered around, looking at the oddities that constituted his "interior decorating."

"I need to understand, John."

Constantine just shook his head. "You don't want to know what's out there. Trust me on this."

"I'm not Isabel."

"No. She embraced her gift. You denied yours. Denial is a better idea. It's why you're still alive. Stick with me, that'll change. I don't need another ghost following me around."

Another ghost, he thought, *staring at me reproachfully, asking, "Why didn't you do something? Why didn't you save me?"*

Constantine got up, and started toward the door. If she wouldn't leave, then he would. Maybe she'd have a few more days before the end . . . if she stayed away from John Constantine.

"Dammit, John—they killed my sister!"

He stopped for that one. Sensing she'd go on without him, with that kind of motivation.

Angela continued, softly, meaning it: "I'd trade places with her if I could."

He just looked at her, waiting.

She went on, "I used to pretend I didn't. See things, I mean. By the time we were ten, they started forcing her to take pills, have treatments. They'd come for her and she'd look at me and say: 'Tell them. Tell them, Angie. You can see 'em too.' "

Tears were streaming down her face now. But her eyes had a hard gleam to them behind the tears.

"But I lied. I said I didn't see anything. And then one day, I finally stopped seeing. I left her, John. All alone." She turned away. Took a deep breath. And added, with finality: "I can't look away anymore."

She turned to him. It was there in her face: She was determined to go on, investigating this thing. And though she was clearly afraid to do it alone, she was going to do it, with him or without him. Either way, the Enemy would take notice of her. But if it took notice of her without Constantine around, she'd be a sitting duck. Defenseless. He sighed. He was left with no real option . . .

"You do this," Constantine said slowly, "and there's no turning back. You see them—they see you. Understand?"

Angela just nodded.

The car had broken down on a surface street, near the Los Angeles airport, and Francisco had flagged down a taxi, which cruised through the early evening past a row of high-rise hotels. The yellow taxi was driven by a rangy, wide-mouthed black man with a dollar sign shaved into either side of his head and a Raiders jacket that seemed three sizes too large for him. The man was listening to something on the radio. Talking rather than singing, but to a beat.

Francisco had heard some variant of this music in Chihuahua. Irritating stuff, but it interested him in a way. He touched the iron spike and listened. Something about slapping female dogs, and making them work as whores for him. *Ah! This word for female dogs must mean women.* Something about ruling the neighborhood, annihilating enemies, giving the biggest parties, getting two women into bed and putting money in their cleavage and kicking them out when you were tired of them. . . .

Francisco decided he was going to like America.

But the whispering cautioned him: *Francisco, you are in danger. . . . This man cannot be trusted. . . . Look at the photo on the dashboard.*

Francisco looked. The licensing photo on the dashboard was of another man entirely.

"Say now, man, you got American cash, right?" the taxi driver asked. "I don't want no pesos and with you not speaking English and the way you looking around, it's like somebody just got here . . ." And as he finished the sentence he pulled the car into a side street near a parking lot full of rental cars. No one was around.

Francisco had his hand on the iron spike, and understood. But he could not speak English, and he replied in Spanish. "I have yet to change my money."

The man shook his head. "Fool, I can't understand what you saying. You got . . ." He rubbed his fingers together in the universal sign for money. "American?"

Francisco shook his head.

"Motherfucker, that some scandalous shit you trying to pull. I don't wait around while you change your money. We going to see what you got on you and then you give all you got and you say thank you, Baley, for not shooting my motherfucking head off. Now get out the car."

He pointed at the door. Francisco shrugged and got out. The driver came around to his side, opening his coat to show a revolver in a shoulder holster. He put one hand on the gun and stuck the other one out. "I'm gonna kick your motherfuckin' ass anyway, wetback—you pissing me off, looking like that. Maybe we take you somewhere, find out do you got some relatives can pay your way, but there going to be big interest, cocksucker—"

"I'm no wetback. I came across the desert, not that river in Texas," Francisco said, in his own language. He pulled out the spike, and slashed downward with it.

Baley had drawn the gun, and the iron point smashed into his hand—shattering the gun and hand both, stabbing right through skin and bone, even though the point wasn't sharp enough to cut through paper, let alone flesh. The driver screamed and tried to jerk his hand away, but only succeeded in tearing it up more on the iron spike clutched firmly in Francisco's fist.

Francisco kicked out—angry now, wanting to feel some part of his body striking this lowlife. He struck the man's groin, hard, making him buckle over—as if the man were bowing to him. "Yes, bow to me!" Francisco shouted. "You should bow! You are scum! You dare to rob me? I will take all of this city for my own! I will be king of the thieves!"

As he spoke, Francisco raised the spike again, swinging his arm all the way around in a cartwheeling motion to bring it down into the back of Baley's head, and the spike seemed to carry a terrible momentum, as if energized by its own inner hunger, as it stabbed through the man's skull like a nail through a boiled egg.

The driver fell, twitching. Francisco examined the iron spike—and as he watched the driver's blood beaded like mercury and ran off it, as if in a hurry to be away. In a second the spike was dry.

He grunted in satisfaction and put it away in his pocket. He found a small roll of bills on the driver and got into the taxi, where he discovered the key in the ignition. He started it and drove away.

But where to? Anywhere! Perhaps a bank—the spike could break open a bank vault. . . .

*Plenty of time for that. First, follow your instincts.
You will be guided. There is somewhere else you must
go. . . .*

Yes, plenty of time for robbery later. He would just
drive to the east . . . that's what felt right. There was
something there, in the eastern part of this great
city. There was a place, someplace special, that called
to him.

~

Constantine and Angela slept for a murky, uncertain
while, fully clothed, spooning in his rumpled bed. He
was sorry he hadn't changed the sheets lately, but she
didn't seem to care. Later . . .

After he took some medication. After they ate a
spare breakfast. After what seemed like a gallon of
coffee . . . They talked. Made certain determinations.

They didn't have a plan exactly. But they had a direction. Like when you're lost in the wilderness, and
you decide to head downhill, following a stream, reasoning it'll take you to civilization. They'd follow
water down . . . to Hell.

So Constantine filled the old-fashioned porcelain
bathtub. The kind with clawed feet on it that looked
like they were going to run away with you once you
were in the tub.

Angela cleared her throat behind him. "Um—
John? Do I take off my clothes or leave them on?"

He smiled, making her wait.

"John?"

"I'm thinking. . . ."

"John!"

There, he almost made her laugh with that one. "On is fine."

She stood there chewing her lip as he turned off the water. Talking to keep fear from taking her over. "Why water?"

"Water is the universal conduit. Lubricates the transition from one plane to another. Now ask me if there's water in Hell." She didn't, so he said: "Sit."

She grabbed his shoulder for balance, lowered herself in the lukewarm water, fully clothed. Immersed all the way to her neck.

"Normally," Constantine said, "only a portion of the body has to be suspended, but you wanted the crash course. . . ."

"Couldn't you have made it warmer?"

"It'll be plenty warm soon enough."

"What will I see?"

There was no way to prepare her for that. But she seemed to get a glimpse in his eyes of what he might see. She swallowed.

"Lie down, farther," he said.

"Lie down?"

"You have to be fully submerged—you being an amateur."

She blinked at him. He could see the decisive moment when she decided to fully trust him. She nodded. "For how long?"

"As long as it takes. Here . . ."

He bent and cupped the back of her neck, held her face just above the water as she submerged herself farther. Breathing hard, through her nose. He could feel her pulse in her neck, thumping fast.

"Last chance," he said.

She just shook her head, once.

"Then . . . take a deep one."

She took a deep breath and held it. He pulled his hand away gently and she settled to the bottom of the tub, her eyes watching him from under the water. He kept hold of her arm, firmly gripping her bare skin just above the elbow.

He reached out with his psychic feelers and drew astral light down to him, transmitted it through his hand to her, helping her find the vibration that would unlock the gate to Hell.

He could see panic in her face as she started to run out of air. She started to come up but he shook his head at her, smiled reassuringly—and shoved her back under again. He could feel the key vibrations circulating in the water, enclosing her. Yet she seemed to be psychically resisting. . . .

Let go, he urged her, mentally. *If you're going—go!*

There—he felt the doorway begin to open, the room's lighting pulsating, each pulsation making the light dimmer.

The water began to boil, roiling and steaming.

His gaze caught a drop of water at the faucet, quivering, hanging there about to fall, then falling—and stopping in midair. From the corners of his eyes he saw a black mossy growth creeping up the wall; cracks forming, oozing blood and acid; from somewhere far away the sound of a million million chewing mandibles.

Time ceased, then gave a lurch. . . .

The drop fell.

Angela thrashed in the water, her eyes wide—screaming underwater. The water muffled the scream but the bubbles surged frantically from her mouth.

He pulled her to a sitting position. She coughed, and wailed, and coughed water again . . . and recommenced screaming, clutching at him, flinging herself from the bathtub, and knocking him back onto the tiled floor, water sloshing over them both.

Her screams became a wailing again . . . and then merely a moan. She lay there on him, trembling.

"Oh God, John. All those people. Isabel." She was sobbing now. "I've always known where the bad guys are . . . where to find them . . . where to aim, when to duck. . . . I can see. . . . I've always known. . . . And I sent them there! To think I sent them there!"

She squeezed her eyes shut. Her hands began to flutter at the air, as if conjuring—purely from some dormant instinct.

"Angela?"

She looked at him then. "Someone was here. . . ."

She jumped to her feet and ran out of the room. Constantine stared after her in surprise—then followed.

Soaking wet, she ran out of the apartment, into the parking lot, through the still-open side door into the bowling alley. Constantine followed, wheezing. "Wait, dammit! Slow down, tell me what—"

But now she'd gone through the door into the maintenance corridor behind the pinsetting machines. Constantine caught up with her halfway down the corridor.

"It was his, rolling—," Angela said, her eyes wild. "Not a ball—something smaller. Shiny."

She reached Beeman's little living area, cordoned off with yellow tape now. The outline of his body chalked on the floor.

"He's watching him die," she said, as if she were seeing it now. "Like eating. A kind of feeding. Good. Full. So good . . ."

She looked around, sensing something. Constantine almost picked it up too—but he let her have her head. She had let her talent out of the bag, and it needed freedom to blossom.

She was staring at the catch trough where the bowling balls would be caught up after striking the pins. She reached down, plucked up a coin. A gold coin. Moving it dreamily, now, across the tops of her fingers in a familiar motion.

Constantine stared at the cold coin.

"Balthazar," he said.

~

He'd found some dry clothes for her. One of his old button-up shirts, some jeans that more or less fit. Now Angela watched as Constantine took the Christian relics from a display cabinet in his apartment.

The pure platinum "Flask of Divinity" . . .

"They're all Christian relics? What about Islam and Buddhism? Don't they have any relevance?"

"Sure. But these work for me best because I come from a Christian culture." He held the ornate flask up in the sunset light coming through the window. Silver-tinted rose. "My understanding of their significance adds to their power—which is formed by their history in the struggle with darkness. But there isn't any one religion, one set of relics and rules, that decides things. And if you look close at them, all religions have certain basics in common. Stuff like . . . oh, you'll find some version of the Golden Rule in all of them. They all fit into the divine big picture somehow. Different symbols for the same kinds of things . . . and a Devil called Satan in our culture is called Iblis in the Muslim culture, or Shaytan— but it's the same guy. Gabriel's called something else by the Hindus. Of course, the Christians get some shit wrong—and so do, say, the Native Americans, and for that matter everyone else. Not that I have the inside track myself—I just know a little more than some. But you want to really know, you got to have *gnosis.* . . ."

"Have what?"

He looked wistfully at the golden, rose-tinged light that was turning the window into temporary stained glass. "Direct knowledge of the divine essence, girlfriend, the ground of being—you need to trust God for that, see. I don't trust anyone. Or anything. Not very far."

She didn't speak for a moment, as he put the petrified husk from the River of Life in his bag.

Then she asked, softly, "You think you could ever learn to?"

"Learn to what?" But he knew. He was just stalling.

"Trust. Someone."

"I . . ." He shrugged. "It doesn't matter now."

He didn't say the rest aloud: *Now that I'm dying*.

An uncomfortable silence, then. He felt he had to say something more. Bandage the silence. "I almost trusted Beeman. So of course I had to lose him. . . ." He felt the anger in him then. He remembered a line from a Public Image Ltd. song:

"Anger is an energy . . . anger is an energy!"

His smile made Angela shiver. "Damned right it is," he said aloud.

"So you're going to kill Balthazar? Can you just kill him? What about the Balance you told me about?"

"The half-breed tipped the scales when he started killing my friends. I'm just adding some counterweight."

He took down a finely inlaid Christian cross of silver and steel, oddly shaped pieces arranged symmetrically. He took it apart, and reassembled it in a new shape. The Holy Shotgun. What had been its base was now a drum for its ammunition. A crosspiece that had been the arms of the crucifix now projected at right angles from the gun barrel as an additional handhold.

"That's a gun of some kind?" she asked, with a professional interest.

"A special gun. Sort of like the Ace of Winchesters. Remind me to tell you about that sometime."

It was still cruciform in shape, but it broke down like a shotgun when he put the special round into it. He turned and fired it down the long length of the apartment; the gun roared and the shotgun pellets left a trail of flame before blasting apart a carton of Lucky Strikes.

THIRTEEN

ᔕ

F rancisco had decided to change vehicles. Someone would be looking for this one when they
found the body. Baley had probably used some
cousin's taxi.

Yes, said the whisperer. *That's wise. They're
searching for this vehicle. But make your change
quickly. The time is almost upon us.* . . .

He'd better do this fast. He had a sense of a mission to fulfill, though he wasn't quite sure what it was.
But had the iron spike led him the wrong way so far?
No. He was in America, where he'd always longed to
be. Here there were Chicano gangs, black gangs, Ital-
ian mafias, Albanian mafias, Cuban mafias, Russian
mafias; there were Chinese Tong, Armenian syndicates, Gypsy syndicates, and more powerful than all
those—the syndicates of the Rich White Men.

There was always room for another pig at the trough. And he would make himself head pig somewhere. . . .

There—a car lot. Somewhere in that glassy building to one side would be a rack of keys.

He abandoned the taxi in an alley several blocks away, walked over to the car lot—and immediately found the security guard, a chunky Chicano eating a Subway sandwich and watching a small portable television set behind the glass, with his back to Francisco. Like a gift, wrapped up and waiting for him.

Francisco looked at the glass, saw no alarm wires attached to it. They counted on the security guard. He smiled, thinking of the company counting on this oblivious, bored fat man to protect hundreds of thousands of dollars in merchandise. Like putting out a lapdog to protect against wolves.

The security guard turned, frowning, asking what he wanted in English, his voice dimmed by window glass.

Francisco grinned, and shouted, *"Ay, que pasa, cabrón!"* Then struck the plate glass with the iron spike, and the shards flew inward with such force—and such diabolic guidance—that they pierced the security guard a dozen times. He sat there in his chair, his mouth full of sandwich, spasming, blood runneling from the corners of his mouth to mix with mayonnaise, his eyes dimming—shards of glass, all of them roughly in the shape of the iron spike, transfixing his inner organs, some of them projecting from his neck in the front. He would be dead in moments.

Francisco scarcely glanced at the dying guard as he stepped through the broken window, his feet crunching on glass fragments, and went to the back room. Inside, he found a padlocked cabinet. The work of a moment to use the spike on the lock—it flew apart with barely a touch, and he reached for the keys to a fast sports car.

No, Francisco. Flashy would get you noticed. You would drive it too fast. The police must not delay you. No time to kill patrolmen. You need something more like the city's main fleet of cars. . . . That one—you feel the tingle as your hand brushes the keys? Take it, Francisco. . . .

Yes, it was better to have something a little understated, so the police didn't take notice, Francisco reflected.

Two minutes later he was driving a new van through the streets . . . but to where? Was he to wander this vast city with no destination? What was that? A whore? Perhaps he should take his pleasure. . . .

No time for that. Turn right, here, Francisco. Down this street. Left at this one. Now another two miles . . .

There, that building ahead.

It looked like some sort of hospital to Francisco.

He wasn't touching the spike in his pocket at that moment, so he couldn't read the sign that said: RAVENSCAR HOSPITAL.

~

The night hummed with engines, flashed electric light on chrome; neon signs blurred through car exhaust. SUVs and Hummers snorted, jostling for space on the streets like rhinos heading for a water hole. Angela and Constantine, driving through L.A., took it in the way leopards take in a jungle. Looking at very little directly—but aware of everything.

Angela's own SUV drew up at a stoplight near the BZR brokerage and public relations building. She looked up at the black, monolithic BZR offices. It was one of those buildings that seemed to suck in all the light that should have reflected from it; there were reflections of other buildings, but they were tinted, compressed, as if the building had eaten, absorbed their images; held them trapped.

She glanced at Constantine, grim and pale beside her, and thought about suggesting a SWAT team. She could find some excuse to make it happen. Tell the precinct a story. If it didn't work out, it'd ruin her career. But what did it matter? After what she'd seen, she believed that the end of the world was coming—unless they could stop it. Any risk was worth taking.

But she knew what Constantine would say: *Cops? They'll just get in the way on an operation like this.*

There was something she had to ask him, while she still had the chance. "John, if Isabel killed herself to save mankind, why is she in Hell?"

"Take your life in despair, you go down . . . rules. Spiritual physics. No grand plan. Just rules." He pointed at the entrance to the BZR parking garage. "There. On the left."

She pulled into the parking garage, wound her way through the spiral labyrinth that protects all such buildings, level after level, till she found a visitor's space. She parked—and Constantine turned to her. His eyes locked on hers. He reached into his coat pocket, then put his arms around her. They were cheek to cheek. For a moment sexual energy flickered between them. His arms went around her neck, teased at the nape.

Strange spot for him to pick, she thought. But maybe it was their last chance to have that kind of memory, before they both died in this cold steel and glass monolith. Maybe . . .

Then he drew back—no longer touching her at all—and she saw he'd clipped Hennessy's amulet around her neck.

She realized that she'd drawn her psychic field in again. Otherwise she'd have known what Constantine intended. But perhaps she had been right after all . . . in a way. It was just a question of timing. There was some kind of unspoken intimacy between them. She knew Constantine was afraid of it—but she also knew that it felt right. They fit together somehow.

He nodded toward the amulet he'd hung over her bosom. "Think of it as a bullet-proof vest," he said.

"I'm coming up there?" she asked.

"You're staying in the car."

She thought about that. Was this male chauvinism? Or was it about an expert taking over, like a homicide detective taking over from the uniformed cops?

Maybe he was right about that—maybe she'd put up with it. And maybe she wouldn't.

She let her psychic antennae reach out a little as he got out of the car. Questing . . . and she learned that there would be work for her yet.

~

Balthazar stood at the mirror in the BZR brokerage executive bathroom, adjusting his collar, his hair, his look. A squeaky-clean mirror. Stainless steel and immaculate tile and track lighting.

He thought about how different the executive washroom would be in its Hell version. He had grown to prefer Earth's version of things. Nice clean bathrooms, sometimes; gardens without human heads protruding from the ground; fountains that didn't spout slime; people not covered by insects and sores and infinite regrets.

He was becoming corrupted by being here, he supposed. The boss wouldn't like that.

Still, it was too bad, in a way, that this world would soon be just another level of Hell, and everything pristine in it would be soiled, damaged like a raped child.

Yet he would enjoy his part of the despoiling; oh yes, he would take great pleasure in it. . . . All that murder and violation and those great vast overflowing dessert bowls of suffering—it would be a great consolation to him.

He started to turn away from the reflection—and then turned back again. His image had distorted slightly, had it not?

Had it shown the demon he was within, for a moment? That would not do. That should not be the case. As he watched, his human face distorted even further—the demonic true-form beneath seeming to push out, like a man pressing his real face against the lineaments of a rubber mask.

The spell might be weakening. Now, what would cause that? Could it be a certain troublesome, arrogant, heavily tattooed human who should have been dead long ago, perhaps?

Balthazar did a vowel stretch, touching his face, leaning closer to the mirror. Perhaps he'd been mistaken. . . .

And then the skin of his face began to ripple, as if liquefying. The surface of the mirror too was blistering, quivering within itself . . .

And suddenly exploded outward!

The fireball from the mirror carried the glass like grenade shrapnel on its shock wave, slamming into Balthazar so that he was flung through the air to thud against the wall behind him. He slid to the floor, his earthly body stunned. Flames licked around him. Flames? *Fire?*

"*Fire!*" he raged, jumping to his feet. "I was born of this!"

He glared around him. Who dared?

And then he saw a shadowy figure through the

ragged gap where the mirror had been. There was an access corridor back there for plumbing repairs—and that's where John Constantine stood. Looking back at him in place of the mirror, some kind of shotgun in his hands. Constantine staring at him from the very place Balthazar's reflection had been.

For a moment it was as if Constantine were a photo negative of Balthazar's mirror reflection, mocking him.

"How's he doing it?" Constantine asked calmly. He kicked away a bit of the remaining crust of wall and stepped into the bathroom.

~

Constantine felt a short rush of satisfaction, seeing Balthazar with his suit ripped, smoking, in the wreckage of his smarmy executive bathroom. And pissed off. If you made him mad, that meant you were getting to him.

But it wasn't nearly enough—Balthazar had Hennessy to answer for; and Beeman. And how many others?

"How's Mammon planning to cross over?" Constantine demanded. Adding: "You half-breed piece of shit!"

Balthazar crouched to leap at him—but Constantine was already throwing an ampule of holy water at Balthazar, and it struck him square in the face. Most of that face burned off, the holy water melting away the spell of deception—for Hell's deceptions are innately unholy. The leathery, demonic face of one of the higher demons of Hell grinned sharp-toothedly back at him. . . .

Balthazar stretched his mouth to make more of the old, human face fall away.

"Ahh—that's better. *Au natural.*"

And then he leapt at Constantine—knocking the gun aside, body-slamming his human prey.

Constantine was propelled back into a wall, with the demon's clawed, leathery hand tightening around his neck, crushing his esophagus, spots flaring in front of his eyes so that all he could see was the demon's triumphant leer. . . .

~

Angela made up her mind.

And it wasn't just about chauvinism. She could feel that she was needed—had the "feeling of guidance from something higher" that Constantine had told her about. . . .

"I used to have it, once upon a time. Then I lost it. Maybe when I got depressed, and no help came, and I slashed my wrist and went to Hell—I got mad, and it can't get in past all that anger. Whatever guidance an angel like Gabriel offers, well, that ain't it. But I know it exists, kid. St. Francis, Ramakrishna, Rumi, Teresa of Avila—those guys were the real pros at getting that guidance. And I figure, maybe it's too late for me to get it. But it's not too late for you. It's . . . some kind of psychic opening, to the really high-frequency wavelengths, the highest astral light—it's all about energy

transmission, see. Some energies are intelligent, Angela. Find them and let them guide you. You know, after . . . whatever happens. . . ."

She'd been sitting in the car, trying to do just that. And getting a very distant sort of tingle, from somewhere, that came like a warm comforter on an icy cold day—just for a moment. And she seemed to hear . . . not a voice, exactly, not words, but a transmission of pure understanding, adding up to a sense of mission.

You must help him.

So she got out of the car. She checked her gun—fully loaded. She pulled off her jacket. Maybe with a little help from the Evil One, the amulet caught on a collar snap, and the chain broke. Stuck to her jacket, which she tossed in the car, the amulet was left behind when she headed for the concrete back stairs of the BZR building. She didn't notice.

She went up the stairs remembering. . . .

She and Isabel as little girls, playing in the park. On swings together, side by side, sometimes in tandem, sometimes together, higher and higher, till at once they'd both shout out, "Now!" and let go of the swing's chains, launching themselves into the air to come down in the sawdust, laughing. Liking it even better if they skinned their knees a little.

Isabel standing, turning—staring at someone. A man watching them. A squat, balding man in a trench coat. Staring at them with a kind smile and dead eyes . . . an expression so like that of the man Angela would shoot all those years later, in Echo Park.

Angela and Isabel looking at him as he hesitated there, seeming to be a fixture of the dusk, like a spider is a fixture of the amber it's trapped in.

Just poised there for a momentary eternity . . .

And then the spider came impossibly out of the amber, taking a step toward them. Angela saw the other one then—he hadn't been quite visible at first. Not a human face—saturnine, leathery, composed yet gleeful, like a greedy child with a big bag of sweets in front of him the morning after Halloween. He was going to feed somehow, if he could persuade this stubby little man with the dead eyes to do it one more time. . . .

Angela and Isabel both saw it then—a flash of what the man had done before. A thirteen-year-old girl strangled on a lonely beach in Maine. . . .

"No one's around," the demon whispered to the man. "I promise you that. No one but you and these two choice bits of stuff."

The man couldn't hear the demon the way Angela did—to him it was just an urge forming in him, the words somewhere in the backbrain, rising through the subconscious like methane bubbles. But Angela and Isabel heard the demon tell the man to kill them.

"Before they run," the demon hissed, urging the man on. And the demon frowned now, sensing that these two had the sight—that they were aware of him. "Get them!"

The man started toward them, reaching into his pocket for the ether and the ropes.

"There's a demon telling you what to do, mister," Isabel said. "He's standing just behind you—on your left side. . . ."

The man blinked, coming up short a moment—could not resist turning to look. Did he for a moment perhaps glimpse a snarling face?

His hesitation gave them their chance. "Run!" Angela shouted. She reached down and scooped up damp sawdust and threw it into the man's eyes—and the two girls bolted, dodging between trees and playground equipment, shouting for help.

The man yelled, clawing at his eyes—Angela saw it without having to turn and look—and then ran back to his car.

The girls had gone puffing home to their parents—white-faced and shaking but pretending that nothing had happened. . . .

"Should have given the police a report," Angela muttered now, going through the door to the stairs.

But there was a reason the memory had come up now. When she'd seen the demon, she'd felt like she'd been prompted, too, as the man was. By something else. Something she couldn't see . . .

It vibrated at too high a frequency to be seen.

Up the stairs . . . where was Constantine?

~

He was almost unconscious. Balthazar was taking his time, savoring Constantine's death, making it last a few seconds longer—and yet another few seconds longer. The demon was gloating about it, though Constantine could not tell if he was hearing it aloud or telepathically.

"Here, Constantine, have a little air—I'll loosen my hands a bit. Now I choke off the air again . . . but now here's a little more! Now I choke again, and this time . . . this time I'm going to finish the job!"

Constantine was so weak. . . . He was ready to give up. Maybe he was getting what he deserved for not being there to save his only friends.

That's it, Constantine, came the suggestion from Balthazar. Telepathic, definitely. *You don't deserve to survive. . . . Give up and take your medicine.*

That was Balthazar's mistake. His gloating infuriated Constantine anew—and a surge of fury brought strength with it, just enough so he remembered the artifact in his coat pocket, and clawed the relic out.

Coming up with that sacred gold knuckle-duster Beeman had given him, on his right fist—

He brought it hard to the right side of the demon's head—and the infusion of holy energies in the gold made Balthazar recoil more than did the force of the blow, the demon knocked rolling to the floor on Constantine's left.

Gasping for air, desperate to keep his advantage, Constantine rolled over and flung himself atop the demon, clocked him across the face with another enchanted punch, and another, each one sending a ripple through the demon's body, etheric force loosening his grip on the mortal world.

He hit the snarling hellspawn again and again, and with each blow Constantine shouted:

"Those—!"

WHAM!

"—were!"

WHAM!

"—my!"

WHAM!

"*—FRIENDS!*"

Constantine's right arm was sagging with fatigue, so he slipped the knuckle-duster onto his left fist and went on punching, slamming the blessed gold into Balthazar's head, over and over, with each punch feeling that he was striking deeper into the demon's spiritual core. He was striking spirit-stuff, rather than actual flesh—though his mind read it as seeing flesh and bone breaking apart, blood spraying—and it felt like trying to hammer a magnet into a repellent magnetic field, a sense of spongy, living resistance impregnating the very air under his punches. And he could feel Balthazar's spirit-substance diminishing, energy smashed off to spiral away into the universe, the demon becoming less material, more transparent, as Constantine slammed him to the brink of death.

At last he had to stop, winded, gasping for air, sweat dripping.

Balthazar himself seemed to strain for his final breaths . . . or so at least it seemed in the material interpretation of what was happening.

"I . . . will see you very soon," the demon rasped.

"Not really, no," Constantine said, sitting up. Feeling in his pocket for another kind of weapon.

"You can't cheat it this time," Balthazar growled. "You're going back to Hell, Constantine."

"True. But you're not."

The demon's eyes widened. What did Constantine mean by that?

Constantine took the small black box from his coat—the box that he'd kept on that special shelf in his apartment—and Balthazar watched, glaring through the wreckage of his face, gathering his strength for whatever Constantine planned. He tried to look unconcerned as Constantine unlatched the box and removed the one weapon he rarely used: the Bible.

"What are you doing?" Balthazar said, trying to get to his feet. Constantine thrust him back down.

"I'm reading you your last rites."

Balthazar licked his battered lips. "Your remedial incantations have no relevance to my kind!"

"Aren't you half human?" Constantine asked, mildly, as if politely inquiring of someone's ethnicity.

Balthazar just glared. They both knew. He was spiritually demon, physically partly human.

"You see," Constantine went on, as if in Sunday school, explaining to a child, "that makes you eligible to be forgiven. You do know what it is to truly be forgiven? To be welcomed into the Kingdom of God?"

Balthazar gulped: Constantine had just blithely articulated EveryDemon's worst nightmare.

Constantine chuckled.

"A demon in Heaven," he said musingly. Enjoying the thought. Real malice creeping into his voice now. "Love to be a fly on that wall."

"You're not a priest," Balthazar protested, his voice showing a very human terror. "You have no power!"

"No?" Constantine's smile was razor-thin. "I escaped Hell—who else do you know has the power to do that?"

Balthazar—stunned by Constantine's attack and on unsteady metaphysical ground—seemed to doubt his understanding of reality. Demons were hellthings and nothing else . . . weren't they?

Constantine hunkered by him, knuckle-duster at the ready, and looked him in his reptilian eyes. "Just tell me how Mammon is crossing over and you can go back to your shithole. . . ."

Balthazar's face hardened. Defy the son of Satan to please this ephemeral magician? He snorted.

Constantine shrugged, stood up, and opened the Bible to the place he'd marked ahead of time. "May God have mercy on you and grant you the pardon of all your sins. . . ."

He placed a hand on Balthazar's forehead. The demon glared as Constantine's voice rose with commanding authority.

"Whosoever sins you remit on Earth, they are remitted unto them in Heaven. I absolve you from—"

"It may not even work!" Balthazar interrupted,

frantic to break Constantine's assured, incantatory rhythm—the demon was already undergoing a sickening spiritual disorientation.

Constantine paused. Smiled grimly. Looked a warning at Balthazar. "How's he doing it?"

Balthazar's eyes rolled wildly as he looked for escape. But he was too battered to get away, too diminished in force.

Constantine nodded and went on reading:

"Grant your child entry into Thy Kingdom. . . ."

Balthazar was writhing now. Wailing to himself as he felt the Gates of Heaven start to swing open for him.

Persuaded by the sheer conviction of Constantine's invocation of the rites, the demon felt it just possible that he might indeed be forgiven—oh, the horror of being forgiven by God, and sent to a place of eternal peace, of eloquent silence, of that penetrating light that revealed every dank, guttering, shriveled corner of your soul!

Constantine continuing:

". . . in the name of the Father . . ."

No! The gate was opening! That light, the light that sees, was beginning to shine into him, probing—waiting for something!

The demon felt himself on the very uttermost edge of the universe, teetering on the verge of a cosmic precipice—but if you fell over that precipice, you fell up, instead of down. He must not fall up!

". . . and the Son," Constantine intoned, glancing at Balthazar. ". . . and the Holy Gh—"

"Sangre de dio!" Balthazar burst out, interrupting him. Anything to stop Constantine from saying those words. But what would Mammon do to him when he found out he had given Constantine the secret?

And Constantine was staring at him. Taking it in. As if wondering if he'd heard rightly. *Sangre de dio?*

Balthazar nodded. "The blood of God."

"How?" Constantine demanded. He made as if to recommence his reading, making a show of looking for his place in the book.

Balthazar groaned. " 'What killed the son of God will give birth to the son of the Devil.' "

Constantine finally put it together. The blood of Christ! From the Place of Skulls . . .

He closed the book. Looked blankly at Balthazar. "By the way—they wouldn't really have let you in. You have to *ask* for absolution—asshole."

Balthazar looked like he wanted to bend Constantine in half and feed him his own extremities. But then he looked past Constantine . . . and he grinned through blood and crushed fangs. "My work is done."

Constantine scowled. "What the hell are you smiling at?"

"Her," Balthazar said, staring at Angela. "You brought her right to us."

She was in the open doorway—gaping at Balthazar. Her eyes wide. The wrong kind of gun in her hand. Looking at the wreckage—the small fires remaining in the room, and Balthazar.

Constantine didn't want Balthazar aiming any curses at Angela. He picked up his shotgun and blew Balthazar away . . . quite literally. The demon's earthly body exploded under the impact of the shotgun blast, and his soul was torn free, to be driven down a long, long tunnel that appeared in the floor, down into the seething flame, the blizzard of ash, where Mammon's retribution awaited. . . .

A moment later the tunnel was gone. There was just what seemed like a shattered semihuman body on the intact floor.

Angela made a small sound in her throat, as if she might throw up. Without a word, Constantine turned and led her into the hallway.

There was no time for adapting to magical reality. He was armed with knowledge now. Which might be useless—because it might already be too late to use it.

~

Francisco stood over the body of the hospital security guard, shaking his head and marveling.

They were like little toys, these security guards in America. So easy to destroy. He had killed this one with his bare hands—just to see if he still had it in him, not even using the iron spike.

What was he to do here? He looked down the empty lime-green corridor. A light overhead was buzzing like an insect. . . .

Insects. He'd had a nightmare about insects when he'd pulled the car over to rest, on the way to Los Angeles. He had been a ghost standing by his own dead, naked body, which was lying on a metal table in an overlit room. There were men in white masks there, surgical masks covering all of their faces but their eyes, and they were laying out instruments. Planning to cut him open.

No, Francisco had said. *Don't cut that body!*

He had tried to hit them but his arms had felt like boneless things, rubbery, unable to exert any force. They didn't pay any attention to him. They simply selected tools and began cutting. He could feel the cutting as a thin distant sensation. Then one of them took out an unusually large surgical tool, made of steel but shaped like the iron spike. And he pushed it into Francisco's right eye, pressed down hard, and turned it exactly like turning a key in a lock. The top of Francisco's head flipped open, like one of those trash cans you opened by stepping on a lever, and inside it was overflowing with insects, crawling, chewing bugs. . . .

And the insects, all together, chewing and gnashing and swarming, were making that noise, that exact same collective eating sound that he heard in his mind when he touched the iron spike.

Just a bad dream, Francisco; it meant nothing. . . . Now hurry—to your right, down the hall, then down a stairs, to the left, and the first big door. . . . You will have to force the door—there's a heavy lock.

Francisco grabbed the security guard's body by the ankles and dragged him to a custodian's closet, wedged him in beside a mop and a bucket. Good thing he'd strangled the man; that left no trail of blood. He closed the closet door, putting a hand on the iron spike in his coat pocket—and paused, listening.

He heard it again, that swarming chewing sound,

as he touched the spike. He shrugged, and continued along the hallway, going down the stairs, to the left, coming to big double doors with a padlock on them. One hard swing of the spike and the lock burst, the doors swinging open.

He found himself in a big, unoccupied underground room containing many bathtubs. The tubs lined the walls; there were pipes everywhere, and still a lingering steam trailed near the mold-streaked green ceiling from the room's use a little while earlier.

How odd. Was this like the steam rooms, the homosexuals' baths they had in Chihuahua, that one of his customers had taken him to when he was a boy whore? He didn't like to think of that place, because the man had shared him with another, a fat sweaty bald man, and they'd used him till he'd bled.

The room made him shudder, but walking through it—and reflecting that it was a hospital—he decided that it was some kind of therapy room. He saw a sign, and touched the iron spike so he could read it. *Hydrotherapy.* Water therapy.

In the center of the room there was a big pool of warm water, like a swimming pool but not very deep. He walked toward it; looked into its chlorine-blue waters.

What was he doing here? He should be finding the dark side of town, where he could set up his syndicate.

You must wait here, in this hospital, Francisco. Glory is coming . . . A woman will come to you here. A beautiful woman. . . .

A mental picture came to him, transmitted, somehow, as clearly as an image from a television screen. Was this the woman? She was lovely. There was a strength in her too that he liked. So that was what the iron spike was bringing him here for? This woman? What was her name; who was she?

Her name is Angela. As for the rest—wait, Francisco. And all will become clear. Glory awaits you.

~

Her name was Angela. . . .

And Constantine was leading her toward the elevators, in the heights of the BZR building.

"He hurt you," she remarked. "Your neck . . ."

"It's okay now." Yet his voice was even hoarser than usual. "But you shouldn't have gone back in there again—just another delay. We can't afford any delays, Officer Dodson."

"I had to go back and put that fire out—there could be innocent people in the building. I don't understand why the sprinklers didn't come on. . . ."

"Because I found the alarm system and tore it all to hell, that's why. Including the fire alarm system."

The cop in her started to protest—but she broke off. Had to smile at herself. What did it matter, with the end of the world at hand?

"What happened to staying in the car?" Constantine asked, rounding a corner. *Where were the damn elevators?*

"You were in danger."

"Now *there's* a premonition," he said dryly.

"Does this hurrying mean you found something?"

He grabbed her wrist and pulled her around a corner, picking up his pace. "Jesus didn't die from being nailed to a cross—not exactly. He died after being stuck with a soldier's spear. A combination of factors, but the spear was important. It's sometimes called the Spear of Destiny."

"I'm Catholic, John. I know the crucifixion story."

~

Constantine was breathing hard; his lungs ached; his throat ached. He had to use all his capacity for drawing astral energy just to keep going. "Beeman said Mammon needed divine assistance to escape—how's the blood of God's only son?"

"The blood of Christ . . . on the spear?"

"That's it, Detective Dodson."

"So he gets the Spear of Destiny—he still has to locate a powerful psychic; you said that was part of the . . ." Her voice trailed off.

"Not really." He glanced at her.

And she understood then. Mammon had found another oracle. "Twins," she said breathlessly. She and Isabel had the same powers. In her, they'd been dormant, till lately. But the power was there. Mammon had lost Isabel—she'd sacrificed herself so that they couldn't use her to open the way for Mammon. But they had someone else. Someone quite handy.

Mammon could use Angela to complete the opening of the doorway; to populate Earth with the denizens of Hell; to make the unsuspecting world of men a literal Hell on Earth.

Probably, Constantine mused, *the flying demons hadn't been trying to kill Angela.* Him? Yeah. But they'd have just captured Angela.

"Where's the amulet?" he asked her suddenly.

She reached instinctively to her neck. It was gone!

They stopped, puffing, in the hallway. He looked at her with cool exasperation.

"I . . . it must be . . ."

She broke off then, a strange look coming into her eyes.

"What?" he asked.

"I don't know. I just feel—"

She broke off again, convulsively clutched at her middle—and seemed to stagger in place, then almost to "moonwalk" backward from him, as if doing a dance parody. She dragged her heels, stopped for a moment, gave him a wide-eyed look of desperation— seeming to struggle against something pulling invisibly at her from behind.

Constantine got over being startled and grabbed for her—but he was a split second too late.

She was smacked hard against the wall behind her—and it seemed to crumble as she struck it, as if deliberately buckling to make way for her as she was pulled backward right *through* plaster, wood, and metal braces.

Constantine leapt through the break in the wall— but saw her receding from him, pulled by some invisible force that seemed to warp matter behind her so that when she struck a wall, or furniture, it fell apart without doing her any significant harm. She flew through a row of office cubicles, through a conference room, right through the middle of a table—

Constantine was running hard to keep up, shouting her name, leaping over debris, vaulting pieces of table, lunging through smashed-open walls, never quite catching up with her.

Whenever she struck something, he could see the invisible shape that was dragging her, as it took the impacts on itself. An air elemental, maybe, slaved to Mammon? Some kind of man-shaped creature, but big. He could only make out an outline.

He heard her terrified yell: "Const—"

Crash, as she was pulled out through the side of the building.

"—antine!"

And then she was yanked bodily out into the air twenty stories above the street, paper and pieces of shattered furniture sucked by the slipstream out after her.

Constantine leapt over a wrecked desk, and came wheezing up to the hole in the side of the building. Metal braces and glass fragments lined the hole, the edges prolapsed outward; flames flickered up around the edges of the gap.

He was looking out of the big hole in the final wall, feeling the wind wash over him; coughing from the smoke and not caring.

He just stood there, one hand on a broken section of wall; gasping, blinking down at the debris scattered across the top of a low building far beneath. No sign of Angela's body.

No sign of Angela at all.

FOURTEEN

～

Chaz's taxi pulled up beside Constantine as he was standing on the corner, smoking a Lucky Strike and gazing blearily at the hole in the side of the BZR building, twenty stories up.

Constantine watched the cops milling around on the roof of the building, at the firefighters peering out of the gap, speculating—and a long way from the truth. All of it bathed in the red and blue whirling lights of emergency vehicles down below.

But no one had found Angela's body. No one's body had been found.

"Jeez," Chaz said, looking up at the smoking hole in the building, then down at the debris below. "That you?"

Constantine considered. In a way it was his doing. Obliquely. He'd forced them to do it the hard way.

"Yeah," he said, pausing to cough and blow a gray plume of smoke at the sky. "I guess so."

"Ever hear the word *subtle?*" Chaz asked.

Constantine shrugged, flicked his cigarette into the gutter, and climbed into the cab. Wondering as he got in if Angela was already dead.

But if she were, he reflected, there'd be a hell of a lot more chaos going down than one hole in a skyscraper.

He started to close the cab's back door after him—and someone grabbed it, held it open. LAPD Detective Xavier bent over to stare in at him.

"Constantine . . ."

"Xavier."

"Why am I not surprised."

They held each other's eyes. Constantine not giving an inch—or a word of information. If there was any time LAPD would be in the way, it was exactly right fucking now.

"I haven't been able to reach Dodson," Xavier said.

Constantine smiled sadly. "No. I imagine you wouldn't."

Xavier hesitated. Constantine didn't have to extend his psychic feelers to know what Xavier was thinking. He could guess.

Should I hold Constantine? Can I really prove he caused this mayhem at BZR? Can he tell me where Dodson has disappeared to, and if so, if I hold him to ask about it, am I interfering with him in a way that's going to cost Dodson?

The answer to the last question must have been

yes. Because Xavier finally said, "Do whatever you do, then."

Constantine nodded. Trying to look more confident than he felt. And there was a wide gap in between.

"That's the plan," he said.

He could feel Xavier watching him as Chaz drove him away. Probably Chaz figured the main thing was to get Constantine clear of the cops for now, before they changed their minds.

But where to?

Constantine needed another puzzle piece. He had to find the blood of Christ—which was known to physically exist only in two possible places. The Grail—and the spear that had pierced his side. Constantine was sure Mammon couldn't get hold of the Grail. That left the spear. So where was it?

There was one place he could go to find out, maybe. Only one anywhere near.

"So . . . where to?" Chaz asked, right on cue.

"Papa Midnite's," Constantine said.

~

Chaz and Constantine faced the bouncer with the peculiar deck of tarot cards once more. Chaz muttered something about not wanting to be left behind again. Maybe this time . . .

But Constantine had a headache and he wasn't sure he could get in himself this time. He was tired, his lungs were killing him, his head was full of psychic shrapnel, and he didn't feel up to reading the bouncer's mind right now.

He gave it a shot, as the bouncer at Midnite's club, at that secret door, held up a tarot card, showing Constantine only its back. But the telepathic image was blurred, uncertain.

"A bird on a ladder," Constantine hazarded.

The bouncer shook his head. "Sorry."

Constantine nodded, started to turn away, as if disappointed—and then spun back, and clocked the bouncer hard in the face.

He'd caught him on the cheek, instead of the point of his chin as he'd hoped, but there was enough force—and maybe a little extra telekinetic pressure—and the bouncer went down, eyes crossing.

Chaz stared at the guard. Shrugged. "All right!" He followed Constantine past the fallen guard and through the door.

And came to a dead stop on the other side of the door, staring.

They were standing at the top of the stone staircase. But this time, with the nightclub closed at the moment to customers, the interior of the space spreading out beyond the stairs was illuminated from a source Chaz couldn't make out. Below there were tiers on which were bars, tables, stools, doorways to secret places—but out beyond the edge of the landing the space stretched on and on, lost in mist, seeming infinite. It was a room that had no interior, because it went on forever.

"Wait here," Constantine said, descending.

Chaz just nodded. He was content to "wait here." He didn't want to go any farther. He definitely wasn't ready. Not today.

He watched Constantine descending, down and down, getting smaller and smaller in the distance, and finally vanishing.

Chaz felt a chill breeze lap at him from those impossible, infinite spaces. It seemed to snuffle at him, to taste him, to consider whether or not he might belong to the darkness it had come from.

Chaz turned—and found that the door was shut. And that there was no knob on this side. No way to open it.

The curious breeze snuffled at the back of his neck. . . .

Chaz huddled back against the wall, crouching, clutching his knees.

After a moment he called out, "Uh . . . Constantine? Hey, yo, uh—say, man, do I have to uh . . . I mean . . . Constantine?"

No response. His voice was swallowed up by the depths.

~

Midnite was wearing his black Borsalino hat with the wide brim; his shirt was open at the chest. Doing some last-minute paperwork at his desk, before going out somewhere, Constantine guessed.

At this hour, maybe he was going to the Special Stage, where his gladiatorial events took place—a highly secret and secretive show for Hollywood's most decadent elite, another unique entertainment project from the voodoo impresario. And its audience included many of Hell's half-breed Elite too—often as not they overlapped with the Hollywood set. The gladiators were zombies, usually, using knives and machetes and sometimes chain saws against clubs with nails sticking out of them. Convenient recruiting, Midnite being the master of a small army of zombies. In the old days he'd brought Haitian zombies with him to New York and L.A., but lately he'd been converting washed-up fashion models and former soap-opera actors and producers of failed reality-TV shows—people who'd gotten into debt at his gaming tables, on Level Seven; they seemed to convert to the Walking Dead with such ease it was like they were mostly zombie already.

"Got a zombie fight set up to regale L.A.'s royalty?" Constantine asked, marshaling his strength.

He ignored the cold fury in Midnite's eyes, but wasn't surprised by it. Constantine was not supposed to be here. If he was here without permission, then as far as Midnite was concerned, Constantine was a burglar. The bouncer had had orders to say that he was wrong about the card no matter what he said.

"Always found the zombie fights sickening," Constantine went on, lighting a cigarette. "Worst thing about them's when they tear each other apart without *feeling* anything. Made me sick to watch that. I mean, they're trailing entrails and brains and still snapping at each other's throats. Strangling one another with intestines—but feeling no pain. Seems like pain gives you some of your humanity. Lately I'm feeling human." He paused to reflect, glowing out a cloud of blue smoke. "The local movie agents seemed to enjoy watching numb mutual butchery, however. Old home week for them, I guess."

Constantine looked at the orrery, trying to misdirect Midnite's attention that way as he clamped the cigarette in his mouth and put one hand under his coat and around his back, where he'd hung the Holy Shotgun from a strap.

But Midnite saw the motion. "Have you lost what little mind you had?" Midnite demanded, rising from his desk. "Forcing your way in here . . . and armed!"

And his hands were moving, fingers spread open, at his sides, seeming to draw power from the air—Constantine could see the energies spiraling in, gathering for Midnite's attack.

"Don't!" Constantine said, snapping the Holy Shotgun up and aiming it at Midnite's head.

Midnite glared. But he knew they were at an impasse—that gun was made of a relic, and so infused with sacred symbols, divine energy, that if he tried to freeze its works or knock it aside, his own power would come back at him, rebounding violently: karma in its purest, most immediate form.

He lowered his hands. He waited.

"Where's the chair?" Constantine demanded.

Midnite let out a long slow breath, turning his body in the hopes of keeping Constantine from seeing the spell-casting movement of his right hand. If he could send a pulse of force against Constantine's body, missing the gun . . .

"I offer no aid to one side or the other," Midnite said, feeling the power build up in his hand. "The Balance."

"Screw the Balance," Constantine said simply.

Constantine, for his part, knew what was coming. He didn't want to shoot Midnite. But—

While Constantine was making up his mind about what to do, Midnite struck, flashing his hand out, sending a pulse of magical energy that struck the occultist, knocking him back into the wall to one side of the door, the impact sending the gun flying from his grip to clatter across the floor, shedding sparks.

Furious at himself for being caught off guard, Constantine fought to keep his feet, the wind knocked out of him.

Midnite vaulted the desk, coming at him like a runaway freight train. "You dare. In my house!"

Midnite slammed his hand hard into Constantine's chest, staggering him against the wall, power flickering between his fingers, power enough to pin Constantine against the wall or to reach inside him and stop his heart cold between one beat and the next.

Midnite was a man of power—and that power was about face and self-belief and respect, a *mana* that built up according to his psychological dominance of his territory. And Constantine had threatened that. Constantine had broken in, and worse, had drawn a weapon on him. This pale magician was making demands of him on his own power-ground!

Dissing Midnite had consequences—supernatural and physical.

"What do you know?" Constantine wheezed. "You can still do the right thing!" He held Midnite's eyes; their wills locked. And Constantine's was strong enough to hold Midnite in abeyance long enough to speak his mind. He caught his breath, and went on.

"Neutral, Midnite? Bullshit. You're the only one still playing by the rules. And while you've been imitating Switzerland, people are dying. Not zombies. People that matter. Hennessy. Beeman. They were your friends once too. Slaughtered. And there's so much more blood to come. Don't you get it yet, Midnite? We're at war! Nobody's neutral! Not anymore!"

Midnite just returned stare for stare. He was not going to let down his guard for mere rhetoric.

Constantine played his last card. "I need your help."

He smiled wryly—he knew it was absurd to ask for help after bulling his way in here. But they'd known each other a long time. And Constantine had once saved Midnite's life. "Consider it a last request, Midnite."

Midnite thought about it for a second or two that seemed to last a lot longer. Then he stepped back. "You play a dangerous game."

"Honestly," Constantine said. "What have I got to lose?"

They both knew what he meant. He was destined to go to Hell when he died. The suicide had worked—

even though he'd been brought back. What could Midnite do to him that would be worse than Hell?

Midnite shook his head, and fished in an inside coat pocket for a key. He led the way to a narrow side door.

Constantine followed, looking down at his shirt where Midnite's bolt of magical energy had struck him against the wall. It was singed.

"Two-hundred-dollar shirt, by the way," Constantine remarked.

They went down a hall, to the end, where Midnite opened another door. Midnite remarked musingly: "That little shit"—meaning Mammon—"has been trying to climb out of his father's shadow for eons."

Midnite flipped a switch, illuminating a high-ceilinged, dust-coated storage room—it could have almost been a museum except that its "exhibits" were so jumbled and cluttered together.

"Whoa," Constantine said, recognizing some of the artifacts. Some were Christian relics, some voodoo, some Ifa, some Santeria, some Hermetic, some Egyptian—and some unclassifiable.

Constantine looked at the body of a man—apparently sleeping, though his chest was motionless—in a glass case. He wore a coarsely woven robe with a hood, a rope around his middle, sandals. There was a scent of flowers around the case.

"A saint?" Constantine asked. "Which one?"

"I'm embarrassed to say I don't know," said Midnite. "But I know he was a saint because his body has never decayed, though he is quite dead, in this world. And that scent of flowers, of course. I believe him to be about, oh . . . thirteenth century of the Common Era, perhaps."

Constantine glanced at Midnite, then back at the saint. "You see the power of this Christian faith—but you don't consider, you know . . . ? "

"Converting? Vo'doun is a kind of amalgamation of Christianity and the magic of the old gods of Africa. . . ." He shrugged. "But it's true I'm no Christian. Still . . . it's all one in the end, as you know: The same rules apply. You can go to the hell of Vo'doun for the same things."

Looking around, Constantine shook his head in admiration. "Some powerful, valuable stuff here. I'm surprised you don't have it in a vault with like big combination locks or something. Laser movement detectors. Trapdoors with spikes."

"It is quite well protected. There are no fewer than seven murderous spirits guarding this room. Two of them are the spirits of Richard Ramirez and Charles Manson—"

"Waitaminnut, those guys are still alive."

"Their *bodies* are walking around in prison, yes." Midnite grinned wolfishly. "But I took their souls away long ago. And if you had not been here with me, within my field of protection, they'd have torn your head off your shoulders and sucked your spirit out the rag-end of your neck."

"About now, they're welcome to it," Constantine muttered. He felt like crap. The cancer was wearing him down again. His chest throbbed where Midnite had struck him. And worry about Angela was chewing away at his mind. He crossed the room, putting off his encounter with The Chair a few moments—it wasn't something he was eager for—and looked over a cross of silver that somehow he associated with St. Anthony, the great fighter of demons. Near it was a big jar with a bearded, shaggy, fairly well-preserved human head in it; the head turned to watch him as he went by.

"That is Blackbeard the Pirate's head," Midnite said, with simple pride of ownership.

There were human hands cut off at the wrist, with candles tipping their upthrust fingers—no ordinary voodoo artifact, they would be the hands of someone famous, some person of power. There was a jar full of what appeared to be miniature people, dancing around hysterically; there were several mummies, sarcophagi, a box of relics from assorted Muslim saints, and . . .

A set of Archie jam jar glasses. Constantine carefully lifted one up. "A full set?" he asked.

"No," Midnite said, with regret. "No Jughead. I've tried eBay. All the stores. No luck."

Midnite pulled a tarp off a humped shape in a corner. Dust flew. Somewhere in the room, a ghost laughed nastily as the chair was revealed: the electric chair from Sing Sing prison.

Constantine swallowed. "Forgot how big it was."

Midnite nodded. "Two hundred souls passed through this wood and steel at Sing Sing."

"Yeah." One of those souls, Constantine knew, had

dabbled in magic, and had tried to create a doorway of escape while in the chair. The spell went awry, crackled to another level when the electricity came on . . . and its effects still clung to the grisly artifact.

"You know," Constantine said, pondering the chair, "in the nineteenth century they thought of electricity as clean—it was hyped as a nicer way to kill something. Funny, eh? Considering how it fried people. Smell of burning flesh. Brains cooking alive. Thomas Edison started it—1887, I think it was. Edison electrocuted dogs and cats and once even a fucking circus elephant to demonstrate how deadly AC was—"

"You're stalling," Midnite interrupted. "You want this or not? I haven't got all night."

Constantine winced. Midnite was right. He was stalling.

He walked over and sat in the chair. Feeling a shock of sheer eeriness at the contact—his psychic sensitivity picking up residual emotions seeped into the very wood and metal of the device. Terror. Despair. A cry for help that no one would hear—all emanating from the chair as he sat in it, like a miasma of layered smells in a slaughterhouse.

He sighed and took off his shoes and socks.

"How many years since you surfed?" Midnite asked.

"Like riding a bike," Constantine said, feeling not a tenth the confidence he pretended to have.

"No. Not really," Midnite said.

The voodoo magician moved to a utility sink, filling a bowl with water.

He glanced at Constantine as he filled the bowl. "Tell me this isn't about the girl, Constantine."

"Definitely mostly not about the girl."

Midnite laughed. For a moment they almost felt the friendship they'd once shared, like a childhood memory stirred by a scent.

He shrugged, came to Constantine, poured the water at his bare feet. It puddled on the concrete floor.

"Cold," Constantine said. Mostly meaning the water. But also wondering how fast his body would get cold after he died—if this thing got out of control. The electricity would be modulated by Midnite's magic, and the spell on the chair, but who was to say it wouldn't kill him anyway?

Midnite grabbed a bottle of gin, already open, from a nearby shelf. Constantine took a swig—almost ritually—and handed the bottle back. It burned down into him; melted his icy nerves some.

"A little flavor," Midnite said. He swigged from the gin bottle, splashed the gin three times, in three directions. Set it down with a thump and stepped to a shadeless table lamp near the chair—plugged in for this reason?—and switched it on. He took hold of the base of the lamp and smashed the bulb on the table's edge. Sparks flew, and he held up the filament, still alive with electrical power.

"You sure about this?" he asked.

"No," Constantine said. No use lying to Midnite. He could smell fear through a steel wall.

Midnight shrugged and knelt, touched the puddle around Constantine's feet with the live filament of the broken lamp.

And Constantine was instantly electrocuted.

FIFTEEN

~

"P*ater de caelis, Deus, miserere nobis,*" Midnite intoned.

Constantine heard the words distantly, from a world away, as the electricity coursed through him. His body had gone rigid; his teeth ground on one another; the electricity snaked through him like a lash snapping along his nerve pathways. He smelled his hair beginning to burn.

"*Fili Redemptor mundi, Deus, miserere nobis. Fili Redemptor mundi, Deus, miserere . . .*"

The room seemed to recede from Constantine, the way the ground recedes below a rocket, and the electricity crescendoed to a searing flash of light that consumed all the world . . . and protracted into a single line of light that stretched out to an impossible attenuation, exactly equaling infinity. His soul was between worlds, hurled there, for the moment, by the chair and Midnite, but still connected to his body by the Silver Cord. That cord, he knew, could stretch across a universe, so long as the spell held; and the spell was held in place by a powerful will: Papa Midnite.

"Pater de caelis, Deus, miserere nobis. Fili Redemptor mundi, Deus, miserere nobis . . ."

The voice echoed between galaxies, from far away, from the beginning of time. It seemed to Constantine that he was at the end of time. It could have no end, and it had one, all at once. All paradoxes seemed to stand out here—finitude and infinitude, space that went on forever, yet curved; time and timelessness existing all in the same existential structure. Time . . . that's what he needed, to surf the stream of time, coursing the surface of it like a speedboat over a river—able to move against the current.

Here, he could choose the place in the time-flow he wanted to occupy. If he reached out with his psychic field and visualized what he wanted, he'd be drawn there, to a particular place—and time. Earth . . .

And he saw Earth turning below him. Now—he must move in time as well as space. Picture the spear. *Sangre de dio.* The bloodied spear of the crucifixion . . .

He reached out, visualizing Christ at the crucifixion. . . .

There he was. He was looking through time at the Man Himself. Ecce Homo: Behold the man.

Christ was a dark-skinned man, with long black hair dirtied by blood from the crown of thorns; he was lean, his nose hooked, his brow a bit heavy; his eyes, his black eyes, oh, his very black eyes—

—looked back at Constantine. That should not have been possible, Constantine should have been invisible. Yet Christ was looking back at him!

Constantine shuddered, feeling that gaze penetrate to his soul. He felt a vast pity wash over him from the figure on the cross. Strange that a man being crucified would feel pity for anyone else. A crow had settled on Jesus' shoulder and was trying to peck at his eyes . . . and yet Jesus pitied Constantine. He pitied all the world.

Was this an opportunity? A chance for redemption, a way to cash in his one-way ticket to Hell? Constantine wanted to ask the figure on the cross for help—but he remembered Angela and his mission. Whatever redemption Jesus might offer could require time. Midnite would not sustain the spell indefinitely. And as Constantine hesitated he saw the Roman soldier approaching Jesus, driving the spear into his side to speed his end.

Blood and water twined down the spear, just as the Bible had described, and a foxfire seemed to glimmer along its iron point. The sky beyond split with lightning; clouds black as judgment gathered; somewhere was the rumble of graves erupting their dead, and the cry of Pontius Pilate awakening in the night, in terror—without knowing why.

Constantine forced himself to focus on the spear

and followed it, as if fast-forwarding, pursuing it through time, strobing through scenes in the life of the Roman guard, who sold it to a Christian monk, from whom it was stolen; and again it was stolen, and kept in a dark place underground in Rome, and then a Nazi archaeologist exposed it to the light, and put it in a box, to be transported to their secret occult research team in Mexico. . . .

"Pater de caelis, Deus, miserere nobis. Fili Redemptor mundi, Deus . . ."

Constantine seeing the stream of time from a particular angle, time for a human being like a tunnel made of human shapes, a flow of endless buildings-up and collapsings, growth and death, lives passing in the flux of a single wave.

Whenever Constantine moved through time it was not just his point of view, not some distant "scrying"; his soul was actually time-traveling. His spiritual substance took the journey—a part of him that was ultimately more real, to an occultist, than his temporary mortal body.

Flash ahead decades, a spiraling meteoric journey through time to: Mexico.

To a ruined church . . . An emaciated man, a scavenger, kicking through the ruin, stumbling into a hole. Reaching down to pull something out . . .

Sangre de dio. The blood of God. The spear—only the point remained—that had driven into Christ's side. A relic impregnated with divine energy.

The scavenger turned—and seemed to see Constantine. No, he was looking past him. But he sensed him there, watching invisibly.

Constantine followed this scavenger. Watched as the car piled up on the man—and didn't hurt him. Only the spear with Christ's blood on it could explain that.

And Constantine watched the scavenger at murder. He was damaged goods, this man: He killed quite casually. With a sort of smugness, even glee at times. What would so powerful a relic mean in the hands of so nonchalantly murderous a man?

Constantine jumped ahead in time, followed the scavenger to the truck stop. Watched him murder a mother of two. Something in Constantine wanted to interfere—but couldn't. This had already happened; it was the past, set in stone, at least as far as a mere disembodied human spirit was concerned.

He followed the man to the car outside the truck stop's drive-in restaurant. And again the scavenger sensed Constantine, turned to look. And couldn't see him.

It was then that Constantine sensed another presence: A dismal, minatory presence, watching, whispering to the scavenger. It was a diabolic presence, equally invisible but far more powerful, and very much in control of what was happening. The puppet master, pulling strings.

Constantine thought about finding out who the scavenger was. Turning him over to the cops. But soon it wouldn't matter, in all likelihood. What was one murder more or less, now? When Mammon ruled, there would be no more police; there would only be criminals, and victims, and nothing else.

Constantine flashed ahead in time again to see the stolen minivan smoking and half crumpled in the broken back gate at Ravenscar. He watched the scavenger run up to a door, use the spear to effortlessly smash it in.

There was immense power in the relic, Constantine reflected—if a man who had no magical abilities could use it to break open ordinary walls, a magician or a demon could use it to break open the wall between worlds.

Would Mammon necessarily stop at Earth? Why not use his tools to spread Hell to the other levels of reality, to the astral worlds?

Could Hell be spread into Heaven itself?

The scavenger killed another guard, stuffed him in a custodial closet, found his way to a hydrotherapy room. He waited there awhile—seemed to listen, then, to someone unseen. A whisper.

Constantine could not hear what the whisperer was saying—probably because he was saying it within the scavenger's mind. He heard only distant psychic echoes, guessed at the message.

The scavenger was told to find a place to rest, he gathered: for he made his way into another wing, found rows of sleeping patients. And there, an empty bed. Exhausted, he covered himself well with the bedclothes, and seemed to fall almost instantly asleep.

Constantine approached the scavenger. Could he

somehow take the relic from him? He was not material enough to pick it up in the usual way, but as it was charged with divine energy he might use that to levitate it somehow, bring it away with him, since he was back in his own time. Transport it to a hiding place nearby, come back to pick it up, perhaps?

He reached out to the sleeping man . . . sending out psychic feelers. . . . Where was the spearhead?

The scavenger suddenly sat up and grabbed Constantine by the throat. Which was quite impossible.

Yet the scavenger began choking him—with his free hand, the other one on the spear, the contact giving him the power to grip an invisible spirit, to do the impossible: to strangle someone who wasn't quite there.

Constantine struggled but couldn't get a grip on the scavenger's hand, couldn't seem to find a way to prise him off—he was just spirit. His body back in the chair was reacting to the strangulation of the spirit. For it was strangling too, by extension, somehow, or by suggestion.

Even as he was choking, Constantine reviled himself for his amateurishness. He should have known better. The scavenger had been playing possum, sensing him coming closer. Perhaps the whisperer had put the idea in his head. *This could be Mammon's way of killing me through the scavenger.* Maybe he'd let him follow this long just so he could set him up for this moment. He thought he heard distant laughter from somewhere deep and dark.

This is bullshit, Constantine thought as that darkness seemed to close around his mind. *Don't give up. Make the body speak. The body in the chair. Control it.* It was choking, but if he could just get it to call out . . . He managed to sputter out the name:

"Midnite!"

And suddenly he felt strong hands pulling him free—as he came back into Midnite's storage room, dropped with a thud into his mortal body. Found himself still perched on the antique electric chair, gasping for breath. He nodded his thanks to Midnite.

"Any luck?" Midnite asked casually, looking at his watch.

Luck? "That's just the word for it," Constantine muttered dryly.

He felt strange, after the charge of electricity, and being out of his body. His physicality felt ill-fitting, awkward, and heavy: he was uncomfortably aware of the Earth's gravity on his body. He could smell himself; tasted old tobacco and coffee in his mouth; and every ache and pain had gone from a background grumbling to a shrieking. His clothing chafed on his skin. And he seemed to feel the tumor in his lungs quite clearly, as a defined shape branching out to eat him from within, like mold spreading in bread.

After a few moments he was nearly himself again. Massaging his throat, thinking that he had to get to Ravenscar. To the spear. But the *Sangre de Dios* would be damnably well defended.

"Cool," Chaz said, walking in, looking around at the roomful of artifacts—exchanging stares with Blackbeard's decapitated head.

Constantine and Midnite both turned and gave him a hard look—Constantine was merely annoyed, but Midnite's look was charged with warning. Chaz acted as if he didn't notice; he tried to blithely act as if it was perfectly normal and all right for him to be there, in Midnite's most private lair.

"You're Papa Midnite," Chaz said, blinking at the voodoo master.

Midnite scowled. "How did you get in?"

Chaz shrugged. "Found my way down. I got tired of waiting up there on that ledge. I felt like fucking Gollum on Mount Doom up there. It bit the big one. Besides, I think something out there wanted to eat me."

"Nonsense," said Midnite. "It would have tasted you, taken a small bite or two at the most."

"Oh. Well. That's so much better."

"I take it you're with Constantine?" He looked back and forth between Chaz and Constantine.

"My apprentice." Constantine sighed.

"When he lets me be," Chaz grumbled.

"Your apprentice? Really?" Midnite asked, eyebrows raised. "That the best you could do?"

"You work with what you have," Constantine said.

~

Midnite had delegated the running of his zombie gladiatorial show to an underling and allowed Constantine the use of his kitchen, under his supervision—theoretically. He had long ago learned that all supervision of Constantine was at best theoretical.

He watched, dubious, as Constantine cooked a pan of religious relics on the stove, melting them together. Small rosaries all of silver, a gold cross that'd belonged to Joan of Arc while she was still in the Dauphin's good graces, the very first St. Christopher's medal, a silver cross that'd supposedly belonged to King Arthur, the specific coin that Jesus had spoken of in the Bible ("Whose face is on it? Give to Caesar what is Caesar's. . . ."), an iron arrowhead that had pieced St. Peter in his martyrdom, a couple of Judas's molars . . .

On a counter nearby was a mold, something to pour the molten relic-fundament into—another loaner from Midnite.

Watching Constantine melt and grind relics together—things he himself would never have combined so haphazardly—Midnite shook his head and gave Constantine a look that seemed to say, *Only you would do it this way.*

The kitchen was big, set up for cafeteria-size crowds of employees, a thing of bright clean tile and stainless steel sinks and an enormous stove capable of unusually great heat. Chaz had a brooding air about him as he watched Constantine—the young man had been a bit disturbed by a curious peek into the walk-in refrigerator. Its frozen goods included some human body parts—*Well,* Midnite had said, *they were just dead convicts, after all, child molesters and the like; the guards sell them to me from the prison morgues on the QT. And you know, some of my employees are not human—and yet, ha ha, oddly enough, they can only eat human.*

On other shelves had been two frozen Yorkshire terriers, a frozen poodle, one anaconda, a dead Eskimo in furred parka (*Long story behind that one,* Midnite had said), the glassy-eyed head of a zebra, what looked like an earthworm as big as a python, an entire barracuda, a six-foot-long squid, a small bear replete with fur, a number of beetles and disgustingly large spiders in plastic sandwich bags, six roosters in full feather, the hearts of various unknown beasts, six kinds of brains, several cocoons (including one that seemed to contain a human shape), a trilobite, and a coelacanth. Also hundreds of chickens, hams, sausages, and turkeys, some frozen pizzas, Jamaican spiced beef, and seven gallons of Breyers ice cream.

"Is that really going to get hot enough to melt that metal?" Chaz asked, chewing a knuckle.

"Oh yes, we have to have some tremendous heat here," Midnite said. "Especially when you're cooking entire bodies down . . ."

Chaz winced, wishing he hadn't asked.

"Anything else blessed and portable enough?" Constantine asked, shaking the pot with a protective glove. "Even sacramental or totemic."

Midnite hesitated, then made a long low growling sound that seemed to express his annoyance with himself for giving in to Constantine so much, as he slid a gold ring off his finger; it bore the image of an ankh.

He held the ring up so it glinted in the fluorescent lights. "Do you have any idea what this cost?"

"Yeah—I sold it to you. Don't worry, it's fake."

Midnite threw him a sharp glare.

"What?" Constantine said, mugging like a borscht belt comedian. "Kidding here."

Chaz cleared his throat, wishing Constantine wouldn't be so easy with his sense of humor. Midnite was notoriously mercurial. If he started throwing around lightning bolts or something, Chaz could get caught in the cross fire.

Midnite dropped the gold ring into the pan. He grimaced as he watched it start to melt.

"It's not just the fellow with the spear who concerns me," Midnite said. "A thing like this takes centuries of planning."

Constantine knew what Midnite meant: Mammon would have taken every possibility into account. But then, he thought he had taken Constantine into account by sending assassins to kill him. Maybe by sending the cancer, too. And yet Constantine was still around.

Constantine beckoned to Chaz for the casting mold. Chaz picked it up, got a good grip on the metal container's handle. He was afraid that Constantine— who'd been drinking Midnite's cooking brandy while he waited for the pan to heat up—might drip molten metal on his hand.

Constantine was practiced, however, and with a steady hand poured liquid silver and gold metal into the mold casings: bullets. The room smelled of minerals, as if the air were reminiscing about caverns of lava.

Without their original shapes, some of the relics' virtues would be compromised. But Constantine figured they were still impregnated with divine emanations, if a little diluted.

"You might reconsider . . ." Midnite suggested.

Unspoken was the corollary: If Constantine *didn't* take action, where would there be to run, later, after Earth and Hell had become one? There didn't seem any real point in reconsidering. Hopeless as this likely was.

"You could come with me," Constantine suggested nonchalantly. "Two fools die as easily as one."

Midnite smiled, showing white, very white teeth. That remark had passed between them before.

"Not likely," he said. "No matter who rules on Earth, there will be sorrow. Fear. Loss. And I do run a bar."

Constantine suspected that whatever protection Midnite supposed he would have after Hell took over was illusory, and that the illusion was a product of Midnite's powerful ego.

The truth was that Midnite's power was also his vulnerability. He specialized in a kind of magic that was about self-belief and force of personality translated into magical energy. And the more vain you were, the more powerful you were, in that kind of magical arena. Ego became energy, somehow, with him. It was that way even with nonmagicians, among the great men of history: One of Napoleon's strengths had been his almost pathological self-belief. But it had also blinded him enough to make him invade Russia just before winter, a fatal step. With men like Napoleon, and Midnite, the power of self-confidence also meant that they had to stay in a state of fortresslike confidence in themselves to the point that they were blind to what might really threaten them—in Midnite's case, he might imagine himself important enough to be treated as an equal by the son of Satan.

Mammon wasn't likely to think so.

But Constantine couldn't say any of that to Midnite. The voodoo master wasn't constituted to accept advice—if he did, he might falter. That was the paradox of his power.

Constantine finished pouring the molds and put the pan down, then picked up the castings and dipped them into a big waiting pot of cold water.

There was a hiss, an emission of steam. The steam seemed to carry the faint fragrance of saintly virtue.

"How exactly," Midnite asked, "do you intend to get close enough to use those?"

Constantine cocked his head to one side, considering the question. He'd been putting that one off. But Midnite had a point.

When the answer came, it came from an unexpected source. Chaz cleared his throat, looked between the two magicians, and spoke up.

"They're not going to leave her unguarded . . . ," Chaz hesitated.

Constantine looked at him, frowning. Could it be that Chaz was going to be good for something besides ground transportation?

"Now as we know," Chaz went on, "half-breeds are most vulnerable when their outer skin is breached by holy water. And certain objects. Most notably, either of the two crosses of Isteria have been used by the unordained to bless and sanctify all commonly occurring waters. Even rain."

He hesitated. They were staring at him. Was he making a fool of himself? He plunged onward. Too late to keep his peace now.

"If one such item," he went on, "were available, it might give the good guys an advantage."

Midnite stared at him.

Chaz shrugged—spread his hands. "No use sitting on the bench if you're not ready to play."

Chaz looked at Midnite more seriously. "So—you wouldn't happen to have one of those magic crosses lying around here, would you? Something we could take with us."

"What do you know? A regular Babe Ruth," Midnite said, with just a suggestion of rolling his eyes.

" 'Us'?" Constantine said.

Chaz nodded. "No offense, John. But I don't think sending you to save the world on your own is the best idea."

Constantine shot Chaz a dark look.

Midnite chuckled.

"Take him along," he said. "Kill him after."

Chaz grinned. It was kind of a sickly grin. But he thought it best to act as if he were sure Midnite was only kidding.

SIXTEEN

~

Angela was spinning in orbit.

That's how it seemed. She was held in some kind of astral reserve, in a between-place till Mammon should decide the moment had come. There were no-man's-lands between the dimensions, twilight zones of nondefinition between the earthly world and the astral world, and between the various levels of the astral world. She was bound to one of these, as Mammon kept her, in a sense, on a shelf until he should need her. Out of the reach of John Constantine.

She saw Ravenscar Hospital below her, aware that the one who'd sent a powerful elemental to bring her here, Mammon, intended Ravenscar as her next destination—and she was orbiting it the way a satellite orbits the Earth, but faster, whipping around it invisibly in the air, in the world but not in it. She felt, though, like she was on a fast circular carnival ride.

She thought of many things, in a mild, nonjudgmental sort of way—she was in a detached state, in more ways than one. Her body was in a kind of time-space loop, her body and the finer body within it: her soul. And here she found herself contemplating the world as if it were just a process with no more significance than the blossoming and dying away of a hillock of wild plants.

All flesh is grass, says the Bible. So it seemed to her from here . . . this astral detachment seemed to suggest that nothing human beings did mattered; they were so temporary, so ephemeral. She could look psychically from her orbit, past the hospital and into the stream of time, and see people coming and going, rising and falling, a current of humanity in the stream of time. What seemed to be of agonizing importance to people in their mortal lives was in the long run about as important as an inconvenient twig to a snail.

She remembered agonizing over the men she'd killed. The why of it, the how. She knew now that her psychic talent had been struggling to emerge and that that was how it'd found an outlet. She'd sensed their murderous intent and she'd acted instinctively to stop them—and she knew now she'd been right to do it. In a way, she'd given the killers a kind of mercy. For they were trapped too.

Thinking about that seemed to open another realm of perception to her: She seemed to become aware of others contemplating the world from outside it, as she was. They were entities of various kinds, malign and benign. She knew the malign ones, somehow, all too well: The human beings she'd shot were just extensions of them, in a way. But the others were strange to her . . .

Who were they? The word *bodhisattva* came to her, from her reading. People who'd left the material world but still exerted a positive influence on it. She could feel them out there, also in a kind of orbit, trying to help. They were contemplating the suffering in the world and looking for ways to ease that suffering.

Her psychic sensitivity followed their lead, and she found herself aware of a churning, stormy sea of suffering in the mortal world: children being preyed on by men who regarded them as things conceived for their pleasure; women being knocked around by drunks; drunks being preyed on, in turn, by muggers, and pickpockets and whores who took their money; starving children by the millions, wondering why they'd come into the world only to raven endlessly for food and perish; paralytics who prayed for death to release them from their nightmare trap; lunatics in tiny cells, who'd done nothing to bring their lunacy on themselves; children beaten by parents in America; children in the Third World sold by parents into slavery; people of all kinds sunken into deep depression; animals tortured in lab experiments; men bleeding slowly, slowly to death on battlefields for causes they could no longer remember; mothers feeling their children die in their arms; people dying in fires set by arsonists; old folks sinking into senility and despairing of hope, sorry for a thousand mistakes; underfed people working in fields until they collapsed; people in sweatshops working as their hands bled, their eyes burned. . . .

Suffering. It was like a great discordant symphony ringing out from the world; like a klaxoning of a million million cracked bells.

She knew then that it did matter, despite how temporary people were: What happened in the world really did matter. What the devils and the psychopaths and the greedy did mattered. Suffering gave meaning to it; suffering alone. Because diminishing that suffering, modulating it, turning it into something a little better—yes, even making things just a little better—was worth doing.

And she realized that she'd nearly succumbed to the darkness; that Mammon had been whispering to her unconscious:

Look, and see: Nothing matters! Don't resist me. Don't struggle. Nothing matters in the great scheme of things. All flesh is grass, it all withers and dies; fighting it only prolongs your own misery. . . . Surrender, Angela!

But she would not be persuaded. She would not surrender.

When the time came, she would fight. With the subtle aid of the bodhisattvas, she would fight. Her chance would come.

Because she knew, then, what she was, what her

role in the world was. Her calling. An oracle? Yes. But more fundamentally . . .

. . . Angela Dodson was a warrior.

~

Midnite and Chaz and Constantine were standing outside the El Carmen, taking in the humid night.

The world wakes up for day in a certain way; there's another way it wakes up for night. The Los Angeles night was beginning to wake up. Cars honked, sirens wailed, music banged from radios, and all of it was given a kind of backbeat rhythm by the steady change of traffic lights, the pulse of cars going by.

People were gathering for the club; others were walking by with their kids, on their way to a video arcade, laughing about the money they'd waste. Couples walked by on dates, each with an agenda they didn't even know they had. Just following impulses, desires, lusts, or wistful longings . . .

Constantine shook his head. He had his own impulse—to shout, *You idiots! The world is at war with the powers of darkness! The doorway to Hell is opening! You're fiddling while Rome burns, you clueless chuckleheads! Rally with me and fight those who would make beef cattle of your souls!*

And how would he sound if he said that aloud? He'd sound like those lunatics who shout on street corners, making people shake their heads sadly.

How often were those lunatics talking about something real?

"Never ceases to amaze me," Constantine said,

looking around. Shaking his head in appreciation—
and sadness.

Chaz looked at him; Midnite didn't need to.

"Normal life," Constantine went on.

Especially now, he thought. *When a course that is
utterly insane is the sane course to take.*

Midnite handed Chaz something wrapped in a
cloth—not a sacred cloth, but one he'd gotten at Bed
Bath & Beyond with the rest of his hand towels.

"You get back," Midnite said, looking at Chaz
gravely, "you see me about membership. Maybe."

Chaz nodded—suppressing the desire to grin and
do a little buck-and-wing. Membership in Midnite's!

Papa Midnite waved his hands over Chaz, spell-
casting. Not too obviously; it could almost have been
some gangster-rap hand jive. His eyes were fixed on
Chaz, his lips moved, but he said nothing audibly.

"What are you doing?" Chaz asked. He just
couldn't think of any cooler way to put it.

"Praying," Midnite growled. His version of praying, anyway; praying to those voodoo *loas* who had
their Christian equivalents among the angels.

Midnite started the same prayer over Constantine,
but Constantine waved him away.

"Don't waste your time," Constantine said. He had
made up his mind that today would be, after all, a
good day to die. "Good a day as any," he said, as smirk-
ingly as he could manage, "to go to Hell, straight to
Hell; do not use your 'Get Out of Hell' card." He felt
the intricately interlocked and unbendable girders of
his doom all around him: an unyielding edifice of

karma. He figured he was like Samson—if he brought it down, it fell on his head. Midnite couldn't help him any more than he already had.

Chaz stuck out his hand to Midnite. Who just looked at it. Chaz dropped the hand, got into the taxi; Constantine got in behind him, waving good-bye.

Midnite watched them drive away into the smoggy L.A. night, weaving through traffic with increasing speed.

And Papa Midnite thought: *I shouldn't take sides. I shouldn't care who wins. What difference does it make to me? Even demons need a place to party. But still . . . somehow . . .*

. . . . he found himself hoping that Constantine found a way to put a new padlock on the door to Hell.

~

The time has come, Angela Dodson. . . .

The voice was like a whisperer in the dark. Like the touch of a spider lighting on the back of your neck.

We have waited for the most auspicious moment. The planetary influences are at their least problematic; the stars are quite neutral. The doorway is unguarded. The fools have left it so this millennium—or is it two. . . ?

Come, now, back to your world, and make it mine, Angela Dodson. Come! Come and marry the iron spear of Jesus!

Angela found that she was falling. . . .

Falling through a hole in space. Tumbling through the roof and walls of Ravenscar Hospital as if they were only fog. Entering the human world fully in the physical sense, only a split second before she fell splashing into water . . . a pool of chlorinated water four feet deep in the basement of the hospital. She floundered in the water, disoriented, feeling the grip of gravity like the hand of a giant dragging her under to drown. She fought her panic, and got her feet beneath her, standing up, dripping, realizing she still had her gun.

She looked around, spitting blue water and gasping, drawing her gun. She was in the large hydrotherapy tank, built right into the hospital's HT center's tile floor . . . exactly where Isabel had died.

A man was hunched in the water at the other end of the pool, fully dressed. A dark, gaunt man with a pockmarked face, black hair. He stood up, streaming water, and started toward her with an odd smile on his face.

Would her gun still fire? But it had only been immersed a moment. And she knew this man was an extension, in effect, of Mammon; that he was here to act as Mammon's hands in this world, until the door should open. She sensed all this in an instant, and in the same instant she raised her gun and fired.

And fired again. Again . . .

The man walked toward her, sloshing through the water, a stained spike of metal in his right hand. Unconcerned; his smile broadening a little more with each failed shot. She put both hands on the gun and fired twice more.

The bullets struck the wall behind the man, chipping away bits of tile—but didn't seem to touch him at all, though it was nearly point-blank range by this time.

He just kept coming . . . and knocked the gun from her hand. And grabbed her by the throat.

He said something in Spanish. He held the iron spike over her head and kept his grip firm on her, neither squeezing nor releasing. She found herself staring at the object in his hand.

Could it really be the point of the spear that had pierced the side of Jesus of Nazareth, the Christ, on Golgotha, the Place of Skulls? Had it traveled for two thousand years, to be here—like a spear thrown through time itself to pierce all that was good in the world? Could this homely little spike of ancient metal really be the Spear of Destiny?

She felt the power in it then, and she knew. This strange dark man held the key that would open the door. . . .

~

The sound that was coming out of the hospital turned Chaz's bones into icicles. A sound like seagulls on fire. But they were human sounds, really. Screaming. And the screaming would stop. And then it would start again. Screaming. And then it would stop. And then . . .

"What the fuck *is* that, John?"

Constantine, getting out of the cab, shook his

head. "I don't know, man. You sure you want to find out?"

Chaz thought about it. But from what he'd heard, there wasn't going to be much world to run to, not for long, anyway. "Yeah. May as well."

"You don't have to prove anything to me," Constantine said, looking at him. Smiling.

"Yes I do, John. Yes I sure as hell do." He hefted his shotgun—it wasn't a "Holy Shotgun" like Constantine's, but it was loaded with his divinely blessed ammunition.

Constantine shrugged. "You're just proving it to yourself. I already know you're a good man, Chaz." He looked at the hospital. The screaming had a pattern to it that was hard to work out exactly. "Let's go, then."

As they walked through the broken steel gate—clashing again and again, in some insane automatic mode, against the van—the very air began to darken. It was as if they were entering a bank of fog, but the fog was made up of granules of pure opacity, instead of water droplets; it was a fog of the essence of darkness, thickening around Ravenscar. There were streetlights behind them and electric exterior lights on the building—but the light didn't seem to penetrate, except dimly. It was like shining a flashlight into a cloud of coal dust.

"It's hard to see," Chaz said, peering around.

"There's always more than one kind of dark," Constantine said, carrying his Holy Shotgun up to the back door. The double metal doors had been broken in, as if by a heavy battering ram wielded by eight men—but in fact it'd been one man and an iron spike.

The darkness reached its maximal thickness—there was some light, some sense of material things around, but not much.

Six kinds of darkness, Chaz thought, thinking of a song.

They stepped through the door; inside the darkness was alleviated a bit. It was as if it were a warning belt around Ravenscar, to keep mortals away from the ground zero of Mammon's workings.

But Chaz's fear didn't alleviate. He seemed to taste metal in his mouth; he felt a clutching in his gut and something like the sense of inevitability a man in the middle of a street must feel as he turns to see a truck barreling down on him from a few feet away: It was too late to get out of the way. Chaz knew, somehow, that his destiny was coming to a kind of convergence here, at least in this life.

Constantine paused, listening to the staccato pattern of screams coming from the lobby—then turned to look Chaz over. A softness, a flicker of kindness, that Chaz had never seen before appeared in Constantine's face. And Chaz was afraid of it. It was too much like the look of a minister about to give last rites.

"Look, kid—," Constantine began.

"Don't, okay?" Chaz broke in. Sensing that Constantine was about to say something uncharacteristically sentimental. "I just don't think I could deal with the touchy-feely Constantine."

Constantine smiled crookedly. Then he racked a round into the chamber of his shotgun.

"Better?"

Chaz nodded. Pulling his own gun from its harness. "Better."

They stepped past the antechamber, through the swinging interior doors, into the lobby.

The strobing, damaged fluorescents overhead provided lighting for a nightmare. The ladies working at the desk, the passing nurses, the doctors, a middle-aged mother and father there about their mad son: All were standing frozen . . .

No, not quite frozen. They moved now and then. It was as if time stopped for them, then started and ran a second and a half's worth, then stopped again. And started yet again. They moved, sensing they were trapped . . . and they screamed . . . and the screams cut off, frozen again. And it would all start up again a couple of moments later.

"Holding spell," Constantine muttered.

"Why are they screaming?" Constantine asked.

"Dirty little casting," Constantine said. "Runs on fear."

Chaz stared, mesmerized, at the couple in front of the desk, the receptionists on the other side, all of them trapped in a loop of terror that could only be expressed in fits of screaming: step, one-two, scream and freeze; step, one-two, scream and wave your arms; step one-two, scream and freeze; step, one-two, scream and freeze; step, one-two, scream and wave your arms. . . .

Chaz felt a profound relief when Constantine led the way past those caught in the loop—it didn't affect Chaz and Constantine, as they'd not been there when the spell was cast—and through another set of doors.

Now where, Constantine wondered, *is Angela—and the Spear of Destiny?*

SEVENTEEN

Angela wasn't sure how the man had so completely overpowered her. It shouldn't have been possible. She knew two kinds of martial arts; she was a trained police detective. He wasn't a particularly strong-looking man.

But his hand on her throat had seemed to drain the strength from her.

His power over her must be flowing from the Spear of Destiny. Suppose she could get it away from him somehow . . .

But how? Right now she felt so weak, like a two-year-old faced with wrestling a gun from a commando.

As she was wondering this—and struggling, kicking at the water, trying to knee him in the groin, with no effect—he suddenly put his face close to hers, grinning.

She thought he was going to force his tongue down her throat. The thought had passed from his mind to hers.

Just for one horrible moment what was ironically called her "gift" opened a window into his mind, and Angela saw through the window into his memory. His name was Francisco, she saw. She felt a mix of pity and revulsion as she saw Francisco's childhood: abandoned on the streets, starving, having to steal food to survive; a man telling him he would have a new home . . . the momentary joy of it . . . only to be taken to a bathhouse and "rented" to sexual predators.

Francisco's running away, afterward, and joining a gang. Watching as his only friend was shot dead by a couple of fat, laughing policemen purely for sport. Watching his only friend bleed to death in a heap of trash as rats sniffed at his wounds. Learning to take and take and take. Running from the police. Learning to drive a taxi in another town. Driven away by the corrupt police there, too—ending as a scavenger in a dump.

And she saw herself in his mind. How he envisaged tearing her clothing away, thrusting himself into her, how he fantasized that she would respond with tender acquiescence, the happy slave ready to give and give again, as he took her repeatedly on a great pile of international currency on a garish red silk bed in a mansion like a child's fantasy castle. . . .

She sobbed, repelled, jerking her mind away from the psychic contact, and Francisco, putting the spearhead in a pocket, chose that moment to slap her, hard, the force of the blow spinning her around so he could use a length of snapped electrical wire to tie her wrists behind her with vicious tightness.

God, she prayed, *are you really going to let this happen? It's not just me, God—it's the world. . . .*

~

The sign read: CLOSED FOR RENOVATION.

They pushed the doors open, knocking the sign aside, and went through into a semiabandoned wing of Ravenscar Hospital. Constantine glanced at Chaz, wondering if he was going to be an asset when he so obviously was about to jump out of his skin.

As if playing with Chaz's nerves, a rat ran by around the corner ahead, and Chaz nearly shot at it.

"Easy," Constantine said.

But he remembered the demon made of vermin who'd nearly killed him on a street corner. Could there be more of that kind, just around the corner? Would the rat be followed by scorpions and maybe bird-eating spiders big as your hand?

But they saw nothing else move as they continued down the corridor, deeper into the darkness.

Chaz was chewing his lip. Sweat was beading on his temples. "Talk or don't talk?" he asked.

Constantine gave him a look that answered the question.

"Right," Constantine said. "Don't talk."

A repellent sound came murmuring to them. At first it was like the guts of a pig rumbling after just eating its young, perhaps one of them still alive in there, swallowed whole. Then it was like a psycho killer mumbling in his sleep, talking of someone he'd never met—of you, exactly you—and what he'd do to you once he got you alone in a dank basement, chained beyond hope of escaping. Then it sounded like a guttural language. But it was all the same noise.

"What is *that?*" Chaz asked.

"Hell-speak," Constantine said.

They both shuddered, listening to the language of Hell. Sounding like the babbling of a madman, yet freighted with meaning as fully as any language.

Constantine had never been in this part of the hospital, but he knew he was going the right way. He had extended his psychic feelers—and felt the feverish rage of Hell crackling in the air, in this direction, as a firefighter feels heat on his face from a flame hidden in the wall. There—that way. The sign on the door read: MAINTENANCE.

Constantine figured they were right on the edge of the spiritual black hole sucking at the heart of the hospital; a few strides more and they'd be well inside it. He looked at Chaz, wondering how he was going to deal with this. Constantine himself wasn't sure he could handle it—and he'd been to Hell itself, more than once; but his Holy Shotgun was slippery in his hands with his own sweat.

"I'm okay," Chaz said as Constantine glanced at him.

"I didn't ask," Constantine said.

He nodded toward the door to the maintenance tunnels. Looked at Chaz inquiringly.

Chaz knew what that meant. They'd agreed on what his mission would be—it was, after all, his idea. But there was more to their splitting up here than that—Constantine could have gone alone, after all.

They had to split up to increase what leverage they had by coming at the enemy from two directions. Maybe one of them could catch the demons unawares while the other one drew their fire . . .

The other one—whichever—might be like a goat staked out as a lure for the wolves.

Do what you have to do, Constantine told himself. *There are bigger issues at stake here than a "goat"— than any single human being. And maybe you'll get there in time to stop the wolves from feeding . . . maybe.*

But Constantine waited. He was waiting for Chaz to make up his mind about going off on his own. It was a decision he couldn't make for him. He couldn't order him to do it.

There was a long, lonely, fate-charged moment. Constantine almost hoped he'd say no.

Chaz swallowed hard—and nodded. He pushed through the door marked MAINTENANCE.

Constantine almost went after him. But Chaz had insisted on coming, carrying his own weight. He'd have to take the risks that went with going from apprentice to magician.

~

The light was so feeble here. Chaz seemed to hear it whimper.

He was walking down a low-ceilinged corridor lined in water-beaded pipes, holes tawdrily plugged with rags, some oozing reeking sewage. Pipes ran overhead, pipes ran to the right and left, exuding a humid closeness that threatened to choke him; that wanted to choke him. The air wanted to kill him, he thought, the air—

He caught himself hyperventilating, and thought:

Get a grip, you dumb asshole. You're psyching yourself out! Take charge of yourself or you're going to panic and drown in demon-spit!

He knew that it was possible that something *was* attacking him, psychically: psychological attack was the most fundamental weapon in the demons' arsenal. They took pride, as old Screwtape had pointed out, in allowing the humans to destroy themselves. A suggestion here, a little numbness there, an encouragement to sleepwalk through life, and human beings could be counted on to stumble into all the holes in the road of existence.

But demonic attack or just panic, it didn't matter: Fighting it was about being present enough to command himself, as Constantine and all the mystical books had taught him.

Chaz took a deep breath, and repeated a mantra he knew would bring on a certain degree of alpha state. His heart rate slowed; his breathing eased. He hefted his gun and took a few strides farther . . .

And there it was: a place where the corridor opened into a utility room dominated by a big tank, on the side of which was a sticker showing a flame.

He reached into his coat, found the relic that Midnite had given him. He unwrapped the cloth, revealing the bright silver Christian cross. He looked the tank over, found the cap on the tank, unscrewed it, and held the cross over it.

And he began to pray, to use the ancient words he knew by heart. Reaching out with his psychic field, as Constantine had taught him, summoning, conducting, directing. . . .

❧

Constantine felt the air seem to thicken with malignancy as he approached the turn in the corridor. He sensed that around that corner things would come to a head. That turn in the hallway was the cornering of his own destiny . . .

He was aware—he could *feel* it—that his whole life had been building toward this moment. He thought about Angela, and Chaz, and he figured they were going to go the way of the others who'd gotten close to him.

He remembered Gary Lester. He had been in a band, singing, with Gary—a new wave band called Mucous Membrane that used to play on the same bill with Obsession, Jerry Cornelius, and Bauhaus. Gary had only wanted to play bass, but getting involved with Constantine in any way had a tendency to be a wrong turn, for all too many people—and Constantine'd had to sacrifice Gary to the demon Mnemoth, so that he and Midnite could stop Mnemoth from eating New York City alive. Sure, getting involved with Mnemoth in the first place had been Gary's own doing. But it was Constantine who'd gotten Gary interested in the supernatural. Trusting, drug-addicted Gary Lester. Poor son of a bitch. Constantine sometimes still saw his ghost, trailing after him. . . .

There was no forgetting Astra Logue, either—the young girl had been an innocent bystander, caught in the cross fire when he'd botched the summoning of a dark spirit; pitiful little Astra had been sucked screaming down to Hell in the demon's psychic slipstream.

He'd done two years in this very institution, in another wing of Ravenscar, after that, trying to get over his sense of responsibility. Trying to let magic alone once and for all. But magic wouldn't let John Constantine alone; he was already notorious in the astral world. He was a marked man. Perhaps a cursed man.

After all, he'd murdered his own twin brother in the womb, or so his father had claimed. The Golden Boy had been strangled by Constantine's umbilicus: born dead. His own dead twin was one of the reasons he was shaken up by this close encounter with Angela and Isabel.

He was lucky that the first love of his life—the Irish girl, Kit Ryan—hadn't been murdered by the far-right extremists he'd pissed off back in 1993. They'd come close. She'd felt betrayed when he'd resorted to magic again, after he'd promised to leave it alone, and she'd left him for good. Best thing for her too, he'd decided. He wondered if she was still alive. . . .

Maybe the First of the Fallen—Satan, whom Constantine had frustrated so many times—had taken revenge on him by going after Kit. She could be addicted to heroin, selling herself for another fix somewhere, for all he knew; she could be dead in an alley somewhere, with rats chewing on her face, right now . . .

No, he told himself. *Don't think that way. You're playing Satan's game when you assume the worst. That's what he wants you to do. These thoughts could well be a psychological attack from one of his mind-demons. She's all right—somewhere, somehow, Kit is all right. She has to be.*

Still, the memories intruded, shoving into his mind like foul-smelling drunks pushing their way into an already crowded elevator. There was Rick the Vic—a British vicar who'd emigrated to the States and befriended Constantine, and probably wished he hadn't. Rick hadn't been clear about his own theology—killed himself to avoid facing Satan full-on, after getting entangled with Constantine, and found himself facing Satan in Hell.

And Nigel Archer—mildly psychic, a political idealist. Constantine had used him to summon the blade-demon Calibraxis, then embroiled him in an attempt to destroy Satan himself. Constantine had come out of the conjuring with his own life, for what it was worth, but not "Nige"—the First of the Fallen had torn the unfortunate Archer limb from limb. . . .

And Constantine's Scottish friend Header had died too—shot while caught with Constantine trying to steal a key grimoire: an ancient book of magic spells. It'd taken Header a painfully long time to die from his wounds. . . .

Then there was Father Hennessy, and Beeman. They'd still be alive if they hadn't gotten mixed up with Constantine.

All his friends, his true love, his own infant brother . . . all of them were blighted, cursed by association with him. Somehow the karma for all that had propelled him here, to this corridor and this corner.

And now he was about to sacrifice Chaz and Angela.

Well, he would have his punishment. No matter how this went for the world—chances were today was "the end of the world" for John Constantine.

He felt the atmosphere charged with fury . . . smelled the decay sweating from the wall . . . heard the nauseating babble of Hell-speak.

He walked around the corner in the corridor, and through two quite nondescript double doors, murmuring, as he went: "One. Last. Show."

EIGHTEEN

~

It was a waiting room packed with half-breeds. It was appropriate, Constantine decided, that he should come to a waiting room in that moment, when all the waiting for retribution should be over, because the whole human world was a waiting room. You waited to grow up, you waited to grow older, you waited to deteriorate, you waited to die. It was all temporary in this mortal world. Only the next world—whichever next world you drew—had anything truly lastingly real about it. Only then could the waiting be over once and for all.

This earthly waiting room was crowded with the unearthly. At first they looked like ordinary people, as seen strolling the streets or sitting placidly in restaurants: lawyers, brokers, soccer moms, truck drivers, PE teachers—several PE teachers. Each in their uniform, their department store clothing, their hairdo from Supercuts or Mister Gig. After a moment he shifted the filter on his psychic lens, and their real form flashed out: He saw their horns, their tails, their fangs, their taloned hands, and eyes the color of the La Brea tar pit.

And the sickening babble of Hell-speak broke off; they all went dead quiet as he came in. They were all turning to look at him, at once. They all had the same thought:

Constantine!

"Hi," Constantine said, his voice as cool and firm as that of the leader of a self-help seminar. "My name's John."

They all just stared at him. Incredulous that he should face them all at once—and that he should face them with so little apparent fear.

"Come on," Constantine continued. He lifted his hands like a symphony conductor. "All together now: 'Hi, John!' "

There was no response. They just stared balefully. Waiting for some signal to tear him to pieces. Each one hoping he'd get to be the one who got to disembowel John Constantine. Thinking that maybe the boss, the First of the Fallen, had reserved that pleasure for himself.

"This isn't a meeting?" Constantine said. "Damn! Okay, well, how about we all head home?"

He heard fragments of their psychic exchanges as they glanced at one another . . .

Who will kill him? And who feeds first?

We have received no instructions, fool! We were told to wait!

But he will be angry if we lose an opportunity to send him this human cur! I myself will . . .

But someone pushed from the back of the crowd to the front. Constantine felt a sick sinking feeling of betrayal as she came toward him. They hadn't been close, exactly, but still . . . it hurt him to see Ellie with this crew.

"Should have known you were in the game. Cancer." He shrugged his self-deprecation. "Makes you sloppy."

"Oh, John," Ellie said. She said it sweetly, really. Smiling apologetically. Her tail twitching. "You know how much I love it on this side. The human world. This was just an opportunity to make it permanent. . . ."

He guessed she hadn't been working with them all along—or she'd have killed him in that motel room. She was a recent recruit, back in the good graces of the boss. Who was definitely not Bruce Springsteen.

He figured that any moment one of them would take the lead—and shout to the others that they needn't wait, that it was time to kill John Constantine . . . right now.

~

Angela and Francisco waited in the pool. She no longer struggled. They were seated on the steps, wet and shuddering, both of them; he had his left hand around her throat, tight enough to hold her, not so tight she couldn't breathe. His right hand was clasping that metal spike.

She had no idea what he was waiting for here; she had an intuition that he didn't know for sure either.

He stared into space, seeming to listen, wondering what had become of the gargling shrieks, the sickening babble coming echoingly from beyond the doors behind them. Now, an eerie silence reigned. Sometimes it seemed to her that Francisco was listening to something else, someone she couldn't hear—he would cock his head, as if harkening. Even nodding to himself in response.

Now and then he muttered to someone that wasn't there. It might have been the mutterings of insanity, but lately insanity had jostled so-called reality out of the way and taken first place in line. An invisible being had carried her here, after all. She no longer had a reason to doubt the existence of such beings. So she was inclined to think he was muttering to someone she couldn't see. She might be able to see it, if she extended her psychic power, but she didn't want to. What good would it do? The first thing she needed to do was find a way to break away from this man.

Her chance came, then. He was staring at the spearhead, muttering to himself in Spanish. He seemed afraid of it. The hand holding it shook. Suddenly he thrust it into a coat pocket, as if to get it out of sight, and then drew his hand back out, empty.

She felt a change in his power then. No longer touching the spearhead with his bare hand, he now had only the strength of an ordinary man . . .

She had been stunned when the invisible thing had gripped her, smashed through walls to bring her here; she'd exhausted herself struggling with Francisco. She waited, now, gathering her strength. If she could keep him from bringing the spear out . . . maybe grab it herself. . . .

~

Constantine, still talking to Ellie, was aware that one of the half-breeds on his left had started to edge round, trying to flank him. The creature was aware that the Holy Shotgun was no ordinary weapon.

Constantine kept his eyes on Ellie, but he tracked the other half-breed with his peripheral second-sight. "You think Satan's son will be any different?" he asked. Constantine shook his head. "He'll just turn this place into his own Hell—and then where will you go to party?" He smiled thinly. *"Heaven?"*

She frowned. He was rather cruelly emphasizing that Ellie, at least, would never know Heaven.

"No need to get rough," she said.

Constantine snorted. "Never bothered you before."

All the time aware of that demon—a lawyer, predictably—edging its way closer to his flank.

Ellie smiled at his little joke about roughness. "I am so going to miss our little trysts. Hotter than Hell."

"Me too, kid."

The demon on his left was bending its knees, about to spring . . .

Constantine could feel it trying to keep its thoughts hidden so he couldn't read its mind, but he caught some fragments anyway.

One spring, tear out his throat . . . but don't kill him too quick. . . . The boss will get him soon enough. I can feed on his suffering as he bleeds to death, if I do it just right. I can almost taste the blood. . . . One step more, and then . . .

Constantine pulled out his cigarette lighter with his left hand. "You are in violation of the Balance," he said, addressing them all in a loud, officious, annoyingly reasonable voice. "Leave immediately or I will deport you."

"Oh, John," Ellie said, "this is so embarrassing. Where's your pride?" She gave him a look of saddened pity.

He knew it looked ridiculous, telling a roomful of demons he was going to deport them with a cigarette lighter. But there was precious little pleasure remaining to him in his doomed life, and he enjoyed the moment anyway. Constantine had always felt that the whole universe was inherently absurd—he'd felt an obscure pleasure, a kind of personal revenge, in helping to point it up by creating moments that showed the architects of the cosmos their own exquisite absurdity.

"All of you!" he went on, waving the cigarette lighter. "Beat it! Shove off! Take the first *down* escalator!"

The half-breed that had been about to jump him paused a moment in uncertainty, wondering what

Constantine was up to. Constantine took that opportunity to step up onto a lobby chair, raising the lighter higher, thrusting it at the ceiling.

Ellie shook her head sadly at him.

"Baby doll," he said to Ellie. "Go to Hell."

Ellie looked up at the ceiling—suspecting, then—just as the flame in his lighter triggered the fire-extinguishing sprinklers.

The water sprayed down on the roomful of demons—demons in business suits and doctors' coats and delivery uniforms, all looking cynically amused as they were doused.

The water had no effect at all, except to ruin the cut of their outfits. He heard one of them mutter disgustedly about just having gotten the suit from the dry cleaner.

"This was your plan?" Ellie said, sighing.

The water's downspray slowed, almost stopped—for a moment. Then came a new spurt in the lines, and suddenly it was as if a discordant music heard only by the demons was playing, sending them into a mad dance. They leapt about screaming, contorting, gyrating, as their skin began to fry, to sizzle away from immersion in . . .

"Holy water!" Ellie shrieked.

Constantine felt an unspeakable relief: Chaz had done his job. Constantine had been far from sure he would succeed. Chaz had used the blessed cross Midnite had given them to turn the water in the overhead fire sprinklers into holy water.

The demons danced to a violin tarantella of sheer

agony—it was a metaphysical agony as well as physical, their very souls tormented by the touch of the divine energy impregnating the holy water. Their human outer skins were melting away and Constantine could see the demons revealed beneath, for a moment—snarling bestial gaunt toothy faces that made him think of a moray eel—before those forms, too, began to collapse like Day of the Dead sugar candy in the rain.

But they weren't dead yet, they were still mobile, and some had the presence of mind to rush Constantine. They could still kill him before they went frying down to Hell. They could take him down with them.

The half-breed who'd been trying to flank him made his move now, even as his skin bubbled away: He leapt—and was struck full in the face by a blast from Constantine's Holy Shotgun, the bullets he'd made from sacred relics forming a core surrounded by shotgun pellets, disintegrating the demon's head. Constantine sidestepped the flying body—headless, but carried by its momentum—even as he heard the wail of the demon's soul spiraling back down to Hell.

And all the time the sprinkler water continued to spray down, jetting on Constantine and demons alike, making him sopping wet, the water streaming on his face and blurring his vision a little, hissing in his ear: pandemonium in a lobby turned into a locker room shower, the furniture puddling with runoff, the chair slippery under him. Losing his traction, Constantine jumped down to the floor, pumping the shotgun as he went.

He turned, just as another demon rushed him, its face almost gone thanks to the searing holy water, its weirdly sloping skull showing through, one eye melted and the other glaring lidlessly. Constantine shot that eye away, along with the top of its head, and it went shrieking to the pit.

He saw Ellie, then, writhing on the floor. He recognized her from her clothing, the remnants of her hair, but the rest was just a living cadaver, weeping without eyes, and he looked away.

A third demon grabbed at Constantine, wrapped a hand that was mostly skeletal bone around his throat, and snapped reeking fangs at his face—but Constantine jammed the Holy Shotgun against its gut and squeezed the trigger.

Nothing happened—he hadn't pumped the shotgun.

The talons tightened around his throat, and the demon cackled in triumph—but Constantine was pumping the shotgun now, squeezing the trigger, and the point-blank shotgun blast blew the demon in half, its lower half walking a step or two alone before falling. Its upper half clung to his neck a moment, like a grotesque pendant, gabbling in disappointment, before its joints fell apart in the holy water.

Others were coming at him—but they were reduced to crawling on all fours; some, legless, just pulling themselves along on their elbows . . .

One of them had gotten around behind him while he was distracted with the fight, and now it leapt onto his back, nails digging into him, shrieking in his ear, "I'm not going back!"

He knew the voice, however ragged it had become: It was Ellie.

Constantine grabbed her head, shoved her face directly into the spouting of a sprinkler right overhead. She flailed . . . and stopped moving, disintegrating into mucky ash. Her wet clothes slithered off him to the floor—empty.

"See you there, kid," Constantine said, sadly.

And then the water stopped spraying. The tank had run dry . . . and the demons were still coming. Some of them had died, but others, better covered with clothing, remained somewhat intact. Once it struck the ground the water was no longer holy, so the puddles couldn't help him.

And the demons were still coming.

He backed up, circled them, heading toward a farther door—

Saw a sign on the door: HYDROTHERAPY. That's where the Spanish guy with the Spear of Destiny had gone, wasn't it?

Constantine sprinted that way, got to the door, went through, started down the hallway—and heard a thudding, a phlegmy gasping, a clattering of bone on bone, behind him. He turned to see the surviving demons shambling after him, coming through the door. Some of them were mumbling castings, so that they were lifted up supernaturally, began to float down the hallway toward him, still falling apart as they came—a lower jaw falling off one of them to clump bouncing onto the floor, another's leg falling from where the demon floated near the ceiling, the limb breaking messily apart as it hit the floor, flesh and veins unraveling to bare bone.

Constantine stayed where he was, not wanting to lure them to Angela. He raised the shotgun to his shoulder, aimed at the nearest demon, cantering along on three limbs. . . . He fired, and blew it apart, but others were coming, demon after demon, rotting but still lethal, levitating and crawling down the hall, some of them muttering his name, over and over:

"Constantine . . . John Constantine . . ."

He fired the shotgun, again and again. One of them was crawling along the ceiling upside down, flipping to drop at him, he fired right into its gaping mouth and the round traveled through the back of its throat and down its spinal column, sending the vertebrae flying like dominos, and the demon flew apart into shrieking ashes. Another leapt at him from the floor like a jumping spider, and he had to knock it backward with the butt of the gun before he had time to pump the shotgun and send a round into the back of its neck. It spasmed, a broken thing, before quivering itself apart. And still the demons came on. . . .

~

Angela heard a low thudding, realized it was gunshots—sounded like a shotgun—from another part of the building, not far away.

The scavenger heard it too, and looked away from her in the direction of the shots, distraction loosening his grip on her neck.

That was her chance. She struck up at his wrist with the heel of her right hand in a tae kwon do move, knocking his hand loose from her, while striking at his jaw with her left fist, the blow coming straight from the shoulder as she'd been taught.

But he dodged and she caught him only glancingly, so that he staggered back but kept his feet, digging at his pocket for the iron spike.

She tried to climb out of the pool, hoping to get to her gun: He'd thrown it into a corner. But he grabbed her around the waist in snarling fury, pulled her back, and—off balance—they both fell backward into the water, thrashing.

Angela felt water invade her lungs, chlorine stinging her sinuses as Francisco rolled on top of her, straddled her, and forced her down. She heard him say something, the sound mostly muted by the water—and she didn't think he was speaking to her. She sensed that he'd been given the go-ahead: The time had come to kill her. He pressed his open hand down on her face, forcing her almost to the floor of the pool.

He had the other hand on the spearhead now, and she could feel the strength pour into him. She knew she was done for: She was drowning. Her lungs felt like they were about to explode. She thrashed helplessly, trying to get leverage, to find a way out, but it was no use; it felt as if every evil in the world had lumped together into a single weight just to hold her down. She saw her executioner's face up there, warped by the watery surface, and for a moment its shifting seemed to reveal an angry child, acting out over its abandonment.

After that the darkness began to close in on her. She couldn't see him anymore. She saw only shafts of light through shadow; blue darkening to indigo.

God, help me. I was trying to do your work on Earth. Can't you send someone to help me?

It was a heartfelt prayer. But the only response was darkness, a deeper darkness yet. . . .

But then came light—only it wasn't the light of redemption, it was the light of transition, of white-hot fire coming at her, to engulf her.

She screamed . . . and fell spinning, endlessly falling, sucked down and down. And then beyond up and down . . .

And found herself sitting alone, on the bone-dry floor of the pool. Only this wasn't exactly the same pool, the same therapy room. This was Hell's version of that room, she realized, looking around. The air was suffused with Hell's ubiquitous noise, overwhelming even the chorus of screams: the wet multitudinous gnashing of millions of jaws chewing at human flesh. She stood up and saw that the tubs in the room were full—with blood. The walls were cracked; she could see flame through the cracks, making them waver; the air was foul with ash and despair.

She knew she was not here as one of the condemned but as a visitor, with a connection to Earth that the condemned didn't have; she was the kind of specialized traveler to Hell she'd been once before—only this time she had been brought against her will. By whom?

Francisco was gone. But someone else was nearby, someone who was looking right at her. Someone behind her. He was coming at her from behind, focusing his terrible attention on her.

"*Angela . . . ,*" came the rasping voice. He repeated her name, almost lovingly, the syllables oozing with slime. "*An . . . gel . . . a . . .*" Somehow when he spoke her name he turned it into an obscenity. But then, any human word that Mammon spoke became an obscenity.

She made herself turn and look at him.

She was a strong woman. There weren't any stronger women. And she'd seen some terrible things, in her short life as a cop, that hadn't made her scream. She'd screamed only once before, seeing Hell. She didn't scream easily.

But right now, seeing Mammon, Angela Dodson screamed long and loud.

~

There were three demons still coming at Constantine, slavering for blood, flesh, and soul—when his shotgun jammed.

One of them, in a priest's collar, crouched like a cat

about to leap at a mouse, grinned at him . . . teeth falling out of the grin, the right side of its face sloughing off with the effort at facial expression.

"Now you're mine, my boy . . . ," it said, its voice thickly distorted by its rotting tongue.

Constantine recognized that voice. It was the priest who'd stood by when the other one had tried to exorcise him, in his boyhood. The demon masquerading as a man of God.

Constantine shouted and tried furiously to clear his weapon—he wanted with all his heart to blow the demon priest to Hell . . .

But it leapt at his throat, as the others came at him from the right and left, yowling with murderous delight.

Constantine couldn't get the gun unjammed in time. He was fucked.

But someone fired a gun from behind the demon and it exploded into wet ashes in midair. Constantine stepped back, striking out with his shotgun butt at the one on his right, stoving its skull in, as the other exploded from another shotgun blast.

Both demons fell away—one spasming, clawing at the air, as Constantine bashed its head to a pulp, the other flying into shrieking fragments.

Gasping for air, heart thudding, Constantine turned to see Chaz, his own smoking shotgun in hand, grinning from the doorway.

It was eerily quiet for a moment as they looked at one another—except for the sound of the shadows whispering. . . .

Then Constantine nodded his thanks, and got the bent shell cleared from his shotgun. It would fire now. He hoped.

"John . . ." Chaz said. "You okay?"

Constantine looked at him deadpan. "Why do you ask?"

NINETEEN

∽

Constantine and Chaz burst into the hydrotherapy room, crossed to the pool, and hesitated, taking in the scavenger—standing in the therapeutic pool, his hands trailing in the water—and Angela: floating . . . unmoving, inert, her hair swirling across the surface like seaweed.

She was floating facedown. Drowned, Constantine realized. Murdered.

Constantine pointed the shotgun at the scavenger, desperate for an excuse to fire. "Move! Get away from her, now!"

The scavenger looked at him—just a confused, frightened man without the spearhead. Constantine sensed the power had gone out of the man, as he no longer had the Spear of Destiny.

So who did?

The scavenger backed away from Angela's body . . . got out of the pool, continuing to move backward . . .

Constantine thought he ought to knock this guy out, see if he could do anything for Angela. Wondering if it was too late for CPR, or if maybe a real doctor could be found.

Then he heard a thrashing in the water, turned to see Angela stand up in the pool—she was looking right into his eyes.

But hers were black, solid black without whites.

"Shit," Constantine said, as she snarled at him.

She was possessed. By something powerful . . . and he suspected he knew who it was.

Mammon himself.

Constantine dropped the shotgun and jumped feet-first into the pool, charging her, shoving her hard with his forearm across her chest, trying to knock her off balance. If he gave her half a chance, she'd claw his eyes out, or bite right through his jugular vein with a single snap.

She staggered back, hissing, and he pressed her against the inner wall of the pool, with his free hand dragging out his key chain. He pressed an exorcism charm—the St. Anthony—to the side of her head, wondering if he could really pull off an exorcism on the fly. Her flesh sizzled and she flailed and roared in pain.

"In nomine Patris et Fili et Spiritus Sancti extinguatur in te ominus virtus diaboli!" Constantine cried, putting all his personal force in the words. *"In*

nomine Patris et Fili et Spiritus Sancti extinguatur in te ominus . . ."

Mammon reacted by trying to come through into the human world, instead of allowing himself to be propelled back into Hell. All along he had envisioned Angela as the doorway into the human world, the spearhead as the key to that door.

Now her body undulated as his shape tried to come through: grotesque, gnarled, and textured like a housefly, but with the face of an obscenely evil youth. The image pulsated in and out of visibility in her arms, her chest—and her face.

It made Constantine feel sick to see Mammon's visage forcing itself over the face of the woman he'd been falling in love with . . .

"In nomine Patris et Fili—!" Constantine shouted, ever more insistently. *"Et Spiritus Sancti—"*

But it was so hard to hold her—to hold her and concentrate—he was losing control—

Suddenly Chaz was there, rushing into the room, jumping into the pool. Chaz helped him drag her thrashing to the concrete floor near the pool, the two of them pushing her thrashing body down onto her back. Chaz slapped his own hand to Angela's forehead, intoning: *"Per impositionem manum nostrarum et per invoctionem . . ."*

John held her down, chanting with Chaz, *"Gloriosae et sanctae dei genetricis virginis Mariae. In nomine Patris et Fili et Spiritus Sancti . . ."*

Feeling a strange connection with Chaz, then. Something ancient, a communing going back before there were Latin invocations—to the earliest time men called, together, for the help of Someone Higher.

Angela—or Mammon—must have felt driven back, toward Hell. In desperation she turned her head and bit into Constantine's palm. Constantine recoiled, gasping with pain. She shoved him ferociously and he fell back against the tile of the steps into the pool, struck the back of his head, felt his scalp split.

Dizzy, struggling to stay conscious, he heard Chaz yell a warning at Francisco—then his shotgun blast. Francisco had tried to jump him . . .

Angela leapt out of the pool, past Constantine. He heard Chaz shout wordlessly—

His head cleared, except for the pain. He got up, wincing, and turned to see Chaz struggling with Angela, holding her from behind. Francisco's body lay crumpled to one side—shot through the heart.

"Finish it!" Chaz shouted as Angela thrashed in his grip.

Constantine staggered to her, feeling dizzy from the blow on the head. He forced himself to focus his mind and his psychic energy, and put his hand to her forehead. He incanted:

"El separatur a plasmate tuo"—he struggled to keep a coughing fit down, and went on—*"ut num quam laedatur amorsu antiqui serpentes! In nomine Patris et Fili et Spiritus Sancti—"*

Once more Chaz intoning, with him: *"extinguatur in te ominus virtus diaboli per . . ."*

And then Angela gave a great shudder, a gasp—

and went limp. The darkness in her eyes began to fade. But Constantine sensed that Mammon was still there—just retrenching, building his strength for another assault.

Angela blinked and looked at Constantine—spoke hoarsely. "Oh God, no, get it out of me, John—get it out!" And then her eyes darkened again—she began to spasm.

Constantine nodded to Chaz and together, in a fast whisper, they chanted—voices soft but inwardly roaring with all their spirit:

"In nomine Patris et Fili et Spiritus Sancti extinguatur in te ominus virtus diaboli per . . . !"

Angela quivered . . . and slumped, sighing. The shape that sometimes rollicked the skin under her face receded—and was gone.

Constantine sensed that Mammon was still connected with Angela, hovering between her and Hell. But he was weakened. It would take more to release him . . . it would take the spear. They had bought some valuable time.

He looked at Chaz and nodded. "Not bad, kid."

Chaz grinned. Paraphrasing Constantine, another time: " 'This is Kramer. Chaz Kramer, asshole—' "

But then his face tightened as he was lifted off his feet, by something unseen.

Then Chaz shouted in pain as he was pulled by the neck up into the air—pulled by the invisible.

Angela fell from his grasp, slipped to the floor, unconscious.

Constantine watched helplessly as Chaz was yanked up and up—and then slammed into the ceiling.

The invisible force twisted Chaz in midair, the way a farmer's wife spins a chicken to break its neck. It paused a split second . . .

And then it threw him with bone-crunching force to the floor.

Constantine walked numbly over to Chaz, who looked up at him, the light going from his eyes much the way the darkness had gone from Angela's. He was trying to speak. But the words died on his lips.

Careful what you wish for, young man, Constantine thought. *You wanted to know the supernatural world—to really know it. Now you know it as even I cannot. . . .*

Constantine felt a bubbling rage rise up in him, a sense of grief and loss that surprised him. He hadn't realized till that moment how attached he'd been to Chaz. His last real friend.

The grief and anger came out of him in one long scream—a scream that escalated into a roar. He turned, looking for his enemy, but saw no one. The killer was still invisible. There was only one trace: a shadow on the wall, cast by no one at all. A vaguely man-shaped shadow with perhaps the suggestion of wings.

Constantine rolled up his sleeves, exposing his conjuring tattoos, and slammed them together, roaring out:

"Into the light I command thee!" All his will invested in an effort to force his enemy into visibility. *"Into the light I command thee!"*

He could feel something resisting the spell. . . .

He marshaled all the force of his being, the very energy of his soul, and focused it into the words:

"INTO THE LIGHT I COMMAND THEE!"

The air seemed to thicken, and there was a shape like bottle glass outlining a man, floating above him. . . .

"Your ego is astounding," the voice echoed to him. A resonant voice, with something androgynous about it.

Constantine looked at the shape in the air, as definition seeped into it: a set of wings, two icy, ironic eyes.

"Gabriel?" Constantine said. He was shaken at the thought. The implications of it. But come to think of it . . . "Figures."

And he realized he'd been wrong to think it was an elemental sent by Mammon who'd snatched Angela away in the BZR building and carried her off to Ravenscar. It had been Gabriel.

Gabriel settled onto the ground in front of Constantine, alighting as gently as a butterfly, fully materialized now. In his hand was the Spear of Destiny.

"And the wicked shall inherit the Earth," Constantine said.

"You presume to judge me, John?"

Constantine snorted. "Betrayal . . . murder . . . genocide? Call me provincial." He was shaking with fury, trying to control it, to think of a way to get the upper hand. But to win over Gabriel? To beat an angel?

Especially an angel in league with the only begotten son of the First of the Fallen.

"I am seeking to inspire humankind to be all that was intended," Gabriel said gravely.

"By handing the Earth over to the son of the Devil?" Constantine said. "Help me here."

Gabriel's wings folded behind him as he walked around behind Constantine—walking by the body of the man he'd just casually murdered.

"*Why?*" Gabriel said, seeming to enjoy the ring of rhetoric in the question. "Why are you given this precious gift, each of you offered redemption from the Creator?" There it was—a surprisingly human tinge of resentment and envy in his voice. "Murderers, rapists, molesters alike, you have only to believe and God takes you unto his bosom. In all the worlds, in all the universe, no other creature can make such a boast. None is loved so, is forgiven so, save man. And what do you do with this gift?" He smiled thinly, not much taller than Constantine but seeming to look down at him from a great height as he went on, "You wallow in lazy slaughter. You take His grace, His undying acceptance, and you defile it, commit upon each other atrocity after atrocity of both body and soul, confident that at the end of your days a simple skyward Forgive-me-Lord will grant you acceptance unto His Kingdom . . .

"A seat by His side. No more. If sweet, sweet

God loves you so, then I will make you worthy of His love."

He smiled sweetly, and went on, "For you see, you are so like animals. Pleasure and reward have no lasting effect. But pain . . . pain is the language you best understand. Pain inspires you. I have watched you over the years. Only as your cities burn do you rush to save each other. Only when the threat of blood runs crimson through your streets and your very families are threatened do you turn your faces to God. Only in the face of horror do you find your nobler selves. And you can be so noble. So I will bring you pain. I will bring you horror. So that those of you who will survive this reign of Hell on Earth will be worthy of God's love."

"Gabriel," Constantine said wonderingly. "You're insane." He said it without any hope of persuasion. He said it simply in amazement. That an immortal could become so twisted with envy and malice that he could go mad.

And he said it in the hopes of distracting Gabriel for a moment—so he could grab the Spear of Destiny from the angel's hand.

But he never had the chance. "The road to salvation," Gabriel said, "begins tonight. Right now."

He beat his wings, once, hard—and Constantine was lifted up by the supernatural gust, blown through the air backward, carried over the pool, through the double doors, back down the hall, as if he were light as a thistledown.

Spinning through the air to find himself flung into the lobby waiting room, where—not at all like a thistledown—he crashed into the mesh-screened doors. He dropped into a stunned heap beside the mucky remains of the dead demons still steaming on the floor.

~

In the hydrotherapy room, Gabriel went to one knee beside Angela, enveloping her in his arms, his wings, cradling her to him . . .

And he began to open the way for Mammon.

~

Constantine lay wretched, broken in spirit more than body, on a clutter of broken shards of mirror glass. He forced himself to get a push-up position . . . trying to find the will to get to his feet . . . wondering how badly he was hurt . . . tasting blood in his mouth. . . .

He just didn't have the will to get up. The cancer, exhaustion, the blow from Gabriel, Chaz's death, and his own despair had drained his will away.

Only this extremity could bring him to do what he did now. Something he hadn't done in a long time.

He prayed.

"I know I'm not one of your favorites—I'm not even welcome in your house—but I could use a little attention. . . ."

He waited, breathing hard. Listening within himself.

Nothing. Well—what had he expected? A heavenly drumroll? A choir singing, a paternal voice booming from on high?

He let himself crumple onto the floor, cheek flat against the tile. Enjoying the coolness. His eyes were drawn to the shards of mirror glass glistening around him. He saw his reflection in one, skewed oddly, staring back. That's when the idea came to him. . . .

~

In the hydrotherapy room, Angela, cradled in Gabriel's arms, began to stir. She was alive—she hadn't been quite physically dead from drowning, and Gabriel had restored her just enough for what had to be done. Her feet dangled in the water.

She opened her eyes. Not seeing anything clearly . . .

Except a beautiful, benevolent face, smiling down at her. How could she resist that face? He was . . . angelic.

She waited . . .

And she felt a certain energy opening the way. Gabriel watched her eyes. Saw the darkness begin to gather there.

A doubt flickered through Gabriel then—something he was not accustomed to. He had long been "out of touch" with God's direct will, retaining his supernatural powers but not his angelic status. He had assumed that he was doing what was best for God's cosmos. He felt he knew the humans better than God did—God was lost in contemplating His creation, detached in His remoteness. Gabriel was doing what

God would want done, if He only understood. Surely He would see, when all was accomplished.

Gabriel began to wonder. Was this really what God wanted? Had he allowed himself to be infected by earthly emotion, earthly resentments, and anger?

He was supposed to be immune. He had been on the Earth only for some tens of thousands of years, really. Witnessing the growth and festering of civilization. Amazed at Sodom, amazed at the Roman circus, amazed at slavery, amazed at massacres carried out in India and China and America. Amazed at the Holocaust; amazed that in the twenty-first century slavery still existed in some parts of the world and there were people who sold their children to houses of prostitution. Even an angel could get cynical, after all that inhumanity on the part of humanity. Even an angel could become sickened, twisted—maybe especially an angel who'd all along secretly resented the importance God had placed on these ephemeral humans . . .

Okay. So maybe he had been infected by proximity to this race of madmen. Maybe the deal with Mammon was a mistake. Maybe he was doing the wrong thing. Maybe . . .

But it was too late now, of course. He had made the pact, and it could not be undone.

Nothing left but to see it through. He opened the way for Mammon into the girl—preparing to open the way from the girl into the world.

The darkness began to fill Angela's eyes, like ink slowly coloring a crystal bowl of pure water. Darker and darker.

~

Constantine was sitting up with his back against a corner of the corridor's wall, hard at work with a razorsharp piece of broken glass.

He was sawing at his wrist with the shard of shattered mirror. Blood was running, it would soon begin to spurt—whoa, there it was, a scarlet geyser, his lifeblood really pumping now, as if eager to get away from him.

He closed his eyes and made one last, decisive, swift slice . . .

And then he did the same to the other wrist. Soon both were gushing blood. He felt his blood pressure dropping; a dipping in the pit of his stomach, a sagging in his arms, a sleepiness growing on him.

Death wasn't so bad. Oblivion wasn't something you could complain about—you weren't around to complain. It was suffering, or dying, that was a drag. And it was what happened to your soul if you fucked up too much in this world. Or if you made that one certified blue-label USDA choice mistake.

Like suicide. And here he was, slashing his wrists again . . .

Constantine settled back against the wall, for once wishing the inevitable would hurry up.

"Hurry," he murmured.

~

Gabriel raised the Spear of Destiny over Angela's chest.

Mammon was trying to force his way out of her.

Her skin writhed with his hungry, childish, inhuman face, pushing from beneath, like a face pressing through a sheet of rubber—trying to break out, into the human world. He'd gone from Hell into a human; he would go from the human into the human world. Demons always did that—but never before so fully, so completely as now.

The blood on the spear—the blood of Christ—was the missing ingredient; would make the final connection. Gabriel would drive the spear into her skin, like a kind of cesarean section, letting Mammon emerge, born fully grown into the world.

He held the spear point at ready . . . a few moments more, to be sure that Mammon's spiritual force was fully gathered for the leap. . . .

The lightbulbs flickered overhead as the current ramped up and down. The moment approached like the arrival of a spear thrown at a target.

~

Constantine heard a distant metallic droning, like the reverberation of a gong struck a thousand years before.

He saw two feet descending toward him, coming down in a pose like Christ on the cross. "What took you so long?" Constantine asked.

"Hello, John," said a familiar voice.

The voice of Lucifer, the Light. Also known as Iblis, as Old Scratch, as Shaytan. As Satan.

"Your dying," Satan went on, his voice deep and echoing, "is the one show I wouldn't miss."

"So I've heard. . . . You mind?" Constantine asked, thinking about a last smoke. Why the hell not?

"Be my guest."

Satan even smiled. He flapped his leathery wings once, adopting a debonair pose. The classic Satan. He, after all, could come here. His son couldn't. The demons couldn't, except as half-breeds. But while the Devil didn't own the human world, he counted it as his turf.

Constantine reached into his jacket, lit a cigarette. He was aware that time was of the essence, but he also knew that time was in some ways malleable for Lucifer. They both knew he was asking for time for a smoke. So Lucifer had stopped the movement of Constantine's death, just enough so he could smoke a last cigarette—and so Satan could savor what he was about to do for all eternity, to someone who'd been a thorn in his side for a generation. Time was slowed to nearly a stop in the rest of the hospital too—something Constantine was counting on.

"Coffin nail," Constantine said, clamping the cigarette in his lips—they were so numb he couldn't feel it there without pressing hard.

"Fitting," said Satan, with a smile that chilled the room like a glacial wind. "I've got all manner of red delights in store for you, son."

Constantine blew smoke at the Devil. "Aren't you a peach."

Satan looked at Constantine's slit wrists. Puzzled by the apparent suicide. "I didn't think you'd make the same mistake twice."

Constantine smiled at him. Took a drag. Blew a smoke ring. He was weak as a starved kitten—it was hard just to hold his hand up to smoke.

"You *didn't*, did you?" Satan said. Make the same mistake twice, he meant. Realizing Constantine was up to something . . .

"So," Constantine said. "How's the family?"

"And why would that matter to you?" Satan asked, suspiciously.

"Word is that kid of yours is a chip off the old block."

"One does what one can."

". . . He's in the other room."

"Well, boys will be boys," Satan rumbled, yawning.

"With Gabriel."

"No accounting for taste, really." Satan was losing patience. His eyes flared between green and red. "Your point?"

"He has the Spear of Destiny," Constantine said Hoping, hoping like Heaven and Hell that the Devil didn't know that Mammon had the spear. Gambling that the Devil didn't know exactly what Mammon was planning.

The Devil was not omniscient. But if Satan *did* know that the rogue angel and Mammon had the spear, then this last-gasp effort had been a waste. Because if he already knew—he approved. Nothing went on in Hell without his approval, unless it was done behind his back.

"Like the old days, John?" Satan growled. "This another one of your cons?"

Eureka! The old boy hadn't known!

"Go look for yourself," Constantine said.

Satan glared suspicion at him—the glare was like a thousand-watt tanning lamp turned right on Constantine's face.

"You've waited twenty years for me," Constantine pointed out. "What's another twenty seconds?"

Satan thought about it. . . .

TWENTY

Detective Xavier closed his eyes and pinched the bridge of his nose. Then he looked again at the back entrance to this wing of the hospital, past the patrol cars pulled up, lights flashing.

The situation was still the same. He wasn't seeing things. There were two patrolmen frozen like statues, partway through the broken-open doors. Hard to discern in the murky air, the two cops looked like stills printed out from the tape of a surveillance camera, arms swinging impossibly at their sides—their arms never dropping at the end of the swings, though each carried a big flashlight. Nobody could hold their arms up completely motionless like that for this long. But that's what they were doing.

He looked at the night sky; a few stars gleamed blue-white through a break of cloud.

This had something to do with that guy Constantine who'd been hanging around Detective Dodson. Just an educated guess—but he'd been doing some checking on Constantine . . .

A young, Asian-American officer, Patrolman Yee, trotted up from reconnoitering the entrance. Xavier found himself watching the big silver flashlight swinging at Yee's side, half expecting it to freeze there in front of him.

"I found the nurse, the Filipino lady who reported all this," Yee said. The young cop licked his lips, not sure how to tell it. "She, uh . . . she says she heard gunshots, screams from this wing, says it was, you know, closed down for repair, no one supposed to be there. She thought maybe it was a patient run off from the lunatic part of the hospital smashing things up. So she went to have a look."

"Nervy lady," Xavier remarked.

"Yeah. Figured she'd seen it all anyway, I guess. But she hadn't seen this—people in there caught up in some kind of . . . like a time loop or something."

A year ago, Xavier would have said that the nurse had been smoking pot while watching *Star Trek* reruns on her break, or something. But with the things that had been happening lately around town—and those two cops frozen in the doorway—he was inclined to believe the story.

"So—time loop. Fine. Whatever. And?"

"And . . . she found some dead . . . creatures. All half melted. Like . . . 'devils,' she said. What was left

of them. And that was, I guess, the end of her nervi-
ness. Hightailed it out of there."

"And those two in the doorway?"

"Yeah, that's Officers Morrisey and Garcia, answered the call from the nurse. I shouted at them—
no response. I started to get closer and I got a strange
feeling. Like . . . things were slowing down. I took a
step back and the feeling went away. So, well . . ."

"So you decided not to go any farther. Sensible,
Officer Yee. You'll make sergeant yet." Xavier was not
at all sure what to do. He was sure only that he didn't
want to push things too far till he knew what the hell
was going on.

"Detective . . ." Yee turned and looked at the hospital. The two frozen cops hadn't moved. "It's like
something's got a . . . some kind of wall of . . . I don't
know how to say it . . . like time is frozen there and
you get a sense that it's like a kind of warning. Like the
incident tape we use. Like . . ."

"Like don't go in there."

"Yeah. But *somebody's* in there. I heard . . .
sounds. I don't know how to describe it. But, uh . . .
you know the other day, that little girl . . ."

"I think I get the idea. Constantine's behind this
somehow."

Thing was, this guy Constantine was more quali-
fied than LAPD to deal with this. This was the excep-
tion of all exceptions. "Yee—I decided to chill a bit
here. Don't call this in, either. Let's wait."

But privately, he thought: *Someday, by God, I'm*

going to get Constantine alone somewhere, in a bar or a back alley, and I'm gonna get the goddamn truth out of him. With a bottle of Jim Beam or a nightstick. Somehow I'm gonna make that son of a bitch sing.

~

Time was stopped for Gabriel and Angela. Satan had frozen it. The Spear of Destiny was poised over her chest—a split second from tearing into her. A frozen tableau.

Then Satan walked into the room.

He walked around the static Gabriel, slid his horny hand under Angela's head, ran his fingers tenderly over her mouth . . .

Nice.

Then he swept her up in his arms, away from Gabriel, nodding to Time to let it know . . .

. . . that it was Time to start again.

Sound and motion returned to the room as Time began to flow in the room once more. Gabriel's spear hammered down into the tile—where Angela had been a moment before.

Gabriel gazed up at Satan in wonder. Stunned.

"Lucifer!"

Satan chuckled grimly. He held Angela tight to him.

Gabriel looked down at the water under Angela. He saw Mammon's image reflected there instead of Angela's.

"This world," Satan said, "is mine. In time. You best of all should understand ambition . . ."

"Son of perdition," Gabriel said. "Little horn . . . most unclean."

Satan chuckled. "I do miss the old names."

Gabriel took a step toward Satan. "I smite thee in His honor!"

Gabriel swung a fist, and Satan simply caught his hand. Like a linebacker gently stopping the fist of a five-year-old boy.

Gabriel was confused. He looked skyward, to Heaven. ". . . Father?"

Satan smiled wolfishly. "Looks like Someone doesn't have your back anymore."

A new expression flashed in the angel's face. A stranger to him: Fear.

Then water exploded upward from the pool, engulfing them—Gabriel's wings bursting into paradoxical flame at the contact. Mammon shrieked from within Angela. . . .

"*No!*" Gabriel screamed.

Satan vanished, carrying something dark and wriggling in his arms. Taking Mammon with him. Where Satan had been, Angela lay moaning on the tile.

Satan went back to Hell. A very short trip. Just to drop something off, you understand. The building quaked at his going . . . and his return.

~

Constantine felt the building shake, rocking to its foundation. And though time was suddenly flowing normally again—and that meant so was the blood from his arms—he smiled. He figured the jolt meant Satan had kicked some ass.

He looked up as Satan reappeared in front of him. A glare of impatient expectancy from the First of the Fallen.

Constantine gave him the look that said: *You owe me.*

Satan knew it was true. He was at a metaphysical disadvantage if he let Constantine restore balance in his kingdom for him. He had to take authority back by paying off the debt. It was just another law of spiritual physics.

"So . . . what do you want?" Satan demanded, his voice taut with impatience. "An extension?"

The weakness of blood loss was making Constantine feel like his face was made of soft lead; his lips were too heavy to move. He managed to say, "Isabel. . . ."

Even in Hell, it's all about context. Satan knew who he was talking about. "What about her?"

"Let her . . . go home. . . ."

Satan wasn't easy to surprise. But Constantine had genuinely surprised him. "You would give up your life so she could go to Heaven?"

Constantine managed a nod.

And Satan was pleased. Constantine wasn't asking for his own life. That meant that Satan could have Constantine to play with, and right away. Satan disliked delaying gratification. And he would get far more personal satisfaction from torturing Constantine than in playing with Isabel, whom he scarcely knew.

"Fine," Satan said.

There was a pause. Things were done, invisibly, in the space of that pause.

~

In the hydrotherapy room, Angela was awake, lying on the floor, weak but breathing—and at the same time she was in a kind of dream state, a condition of psychic receptivity that brought about visions. True visions.

So it was that she found herself with her sister again, the two of them once more little girls on a swing set in the park. The swings were moving together, and Angela and Isabel, two little girls, were holding hands as they swung . . . looking at one another, waiting for the right moment to let go. The two of them, holding hands, would jump as they had so many times from the swing, to land together laughing in the soft dirt. . . .

Now! Up they went, out of the swing, holding hands for a moment in midair.

Angela was coming down, about to land on her feet—but Isabel kept going upward, kept flying up, slowly, into the air, like a helium balloon released to ease into the sky. She kept the grip with her sister's fingers for just a moment. Beaming at her . . .

And then Angela let go—knowing she was doing something for her sister by letting go. And Isabel drifted upward, spiraling slowly into the sky, into a blue that was unimaginably deep, astonishingly perfect.

~

Things were accomplished, in that pause, after Satan said, *Fine*.

A spirit was released from Hell—and found itself in Heaven, where there was celebration at her arrival, and many things came clear to her at last. . . .

"Welcome, Isabel," said her grandmother. "Welcome, my darling. I'd like you to meet some friends of mine—and I don't think you ever met your grandfather. . . . Oh—and here's a friend of a friend. His name is Chaz. . . ."

~

". . . it's done," Satan finished. He looked at Constantine—and it was a look that contained a continuum of torment. "Time to go."

Constantine nodded. All he could manage. Lifted one hand, just a little, toward Satan—to show his readiness.

Satan reached down and took his hand, pulled him toward him, toward the doors. On the other side of the doors was something other than more hospital. It was now a doorway to Hades.

Satan drew Constantine after him . . .

. . . but the corridor seemed to stretch out on the way to the door. They couldn't seem to get there. They moved, and yet the door remained the same distance away. They weren't really going anywhere at all.

Constantine's other hand lifted up—something was pulling him in another direction. Away from Hell. Constantine's other hand was held by someone else.

His hand was in God's.

Satan dropped Constantine's hand—recoiling in ineffable, infinite, space-spanning anger.

"The sacrifice!" Satan roared. Realizing that Constantine's willingness to sacrifice himself for Isabel had been noticed: had saved him. Constantine was dying, nearly dead—but he wasn't going to Hell. He was going to Heaven. Satan was to be cheated.

Satan shook his fist at the light shining from above. *"No! This one belongs to me!"*

Constantine's rising hand—drifting up toward Heaven—now drifted down toward Satan for a moment, middle finger extended.

But it wasn't Constantine doing it—God was giving Satan the finger.

Satan combusted with rage, lifting his fists and igniting into a figure of fire. He pointed a flaming finger at Constantine. "You will live, John Constantine! You will live so you will have the chance to prove that your soul truly belongs in Hell. Damn you—you *will* live!"

Satan plunged his blazing etheric hand into Constantine's body, deep into his breast, lifting him up off the floor with the thrust.

Constantine screamed in agony as Satan scooped the cancer from his lungs, ripping out a mass of diseased tissue with a nasty yank, trying to make it as painful as possible. He released Constantine . . .

. . . and Constantine dropped to the floor in a heap.

On his hands and knees, Constantine felt strength pour into him. He took a deep breath . . . filling healthy lungs for the first time in years.

He looked at his wrists. They had sealed up—he was healed top to bottom. Satan had given him a new lease on life—but he'd done it only so that he could one day try to get an eviction.

Constantine heard Satan's voice in his mind as the dark angel went through the door, back to brood at home—and to beat his son.

I'll have your ass sooner or later, Constantine. What's a few more years to me? You're a fuckup. And you're mine.

And then Satan was gone—as much as he ever is.

Constantine looked around. Didn't see any heavenly glows. Didn't feel that divine touch that'd been so exquisite, moments ago. God was gone too.

But then again—He *never* is.

~

Constantine walked into the hydrotherapy room, looking for Angela . . . and seeing her against one wall, sitting up, hugging her knees. But smiling at him. Alive.

He knelt beside her. Saw the spear lying near her. The Spear of Destiny itself.

"Thank you," Angela said.

"No problem," Constantine replied, as casually as he could manage.

She couldn't help but smile at that. He couldn't help but smile back.

He heard a moan, turned to see Gabriel, hunched up, shaking near the opposite wall. Stumps of torn cartilage protruded from his back. A pattern of sinew and bone, burned into the floor near him, was all that remained of his wings.

There was red blood, very human blood, dripping from the stumps of the angel's wings. Constantine grinned in satisfaction, as he retrieved his Holy Shotgun from the floor.

"Human . . . !" Constantine chuckled.

Gabriel grimaced at that verdict. But didn't deny it. He had been punished by being turned into a mortal. Without God's protection—withdrawn when he made the pact with Mammon—he'd been subject to Satan's superior magical powers . . . and Satan had punished him by turning him into one of those he despised. A human being.

"You don't deserve to be human," Constantine remarked, hefting his shotgun thoughtfully, approaching the erstwhile angel.

Gabriel cleared his throat. "Then . . . pass judgment on me now."

Constantine set the muzzle of the gun against Gabriel's forehead. He was going to enjoy this. . . .

"Do it," Gabriel urged. "Seek revenge! End my life."

Constantine's finger tightened on the trigger. He

needed to put only a micromillimeter more squeeze on that trigger . . .

"Pull the trigger!" Gabriel begged. "Be the Hand of God!"

Constantine's finger relaxed. He understood, then, what Gabriel was trying to pull. *I shoot him—and I'll be condemned again.*

Still . . . Constantine wanted to pull the trigger more than he'd wanted his first sex with a real live girl—and that was a lot. He wanted it as much as he wanted to live.

But he lowered the gun. Knowing that Satan was behind this—had whispered the suggestion to Gabriel. The First of the Fallen was trying to trap Constantine, already. To trick him into condemning himself to Hell once more.

Constantine looked at Gabriel for a moment . . . shifting his gun to his other hand . . .

And then hit the former angel hard in the face with a right. Gabriel was knocked back against the wall, slamming hard into the concrete. He slumped, stunned.

"That's called pain," Constantine said. "Get used to it."

Gabriel surprised Constantine by smiling. "You could have shot me, John. But you chose the higher path instead."

Constantine turned and went to Angela.

"My plan's already working," Gabriel said. "Look how well you're doing."

She gazed up at him, lips parted . . .

Constantine bent toward her and picked up the Spear of Destiny, lying at her feet. Straightened up, smiling at her. He could tell—he could feel it—she knew about Isabel being set free from Hell.

Gabriel was looking upward. As if right through the ceiling. Speaking to God. "No recompense for such love. And who will keep your dominion now."

But he did have a problem—nothing he couldn't handle. The time barrier had dropped from the building. Xavier was coming in with Officer Yee and at least five other cops.

They were going to want an explanation. He was tempted to tell them the truth.

Let them put that *in their report.*

He put his arm around Angela and led her out of the room.

Behind them, Gabriel shuddered, sensing the opening of a doorway . . .

And the room filled with light. A silhouetted figure appeared, in a shimmering doorway. Heaven illuminated behind him with higher-dimensional clarity. Heaven's newest half-angel: It was Chaz, adjusting his cap, casually. Smiling sardonically at Gabriel. "S'up, Gabie."

Chaz rubbed his hands together. He had a lot of work to do in his new gig, and he was looking forward to it. "P.S., man," Chaz said to Gabriel, walking past him. "You have one shitload of explaining to do."

~

Another L.A. night on the rooftop of another building—Constantine's building. Standing near the edge of the roof, Constantine gazed at the electric tapestry of city lights. Leaning on the roof's rim near him was the Holy Shotgun.

He wasn't surprised when Angela came up the fire escape: He'd asked her to meet him here.

She looked around at the damp, tarry roof littered with old paint cans. "Nice spot," she said.

Constantine smiled at her. "Got something for you."

She raised an eyebrow as she joined him. "I'm guessing you're not a flowers kind of guy."

Constantine reached into his coat pocket. Handed her an object wrapped in cloth. She opened it, but she already knew what it was by the feel, the weight, the tingle. The vibratory association with both suffering and the transcendence of suffering: the Spear of Destiny.

"Why the hell are you giving me this?"

Constantine's smile became rueful. "Rules."

He couldn't keep it—it was something he could never bring himself to try to conjure with. And he knew that a genuinely holy relic should be disposed of—or "put away"—according to the rules of the tradition it sprang from. Angela was closer to that tradition than he was.

"Hide it," he advised, with a heartfelt solemnity. "Somewhere no one will ever be able to find it."

"And I'm supposed to know where that is . . . exactly how?"

"Hey. The son of the Devil didn't want *me* for my psychic ability." His was minor-league compared with hers.

"Always a catch," she said.

He looked at her. Thinking that he wanted to go the next step with her, if she wanted that too. But there were things he had to do first. And maybe she wouldn't be interested anyway—could be he was just putting off the inevitable rejection. A relationship with him would be a constant reminder of things she'd want to put behind her. Literally: her time in Hell, among other things. Still . . . she wasn't looking at him like she wanted to put John Constantine behind her.

"So?" Angela prompted.

"I've got some cleaning up to do."

She looked at the Holy Shotgun. She nodded. "See you around?"

He smiled. Feeling real relief. Seemed to him that was an invitation. "Yeah. I'd like that."

She wrapped the relic up again, put it in her purse. She walked away, and he watched her go down the fire escape: a woman carrying the spearhead that pierced Jesus Christ in a purse she'd bought at Neiman Marcus.

Constantine turned and looked at the city. Wondering what he'd say to that city, if its inhabitants could hear him, right now . . . Maybe:

I'm everything that never happened to you. I've seen young boys strong enough to snap your neck in one hand. And women sell their babies for the promise of a throne of fire. I've seen Hell blaze through these streets. I don't have the usual map of L.A. in my head, not the one everyone else has. L.A.'s got a different geography for me. Spilling blood and the last breath before dying mark it all out, in dark wet borders. And no one giving a damn about it. No one at all.

Constantine took a pack of cigarettes from his coat. Looked at them. And crumpled them up, tossed them over the edge. Then he took something else from his coat pocket: two special shotgun shells. Their casings embossed with arcane symbols.

God has a plan for all of us. I had to die. Twice. Just to figure that out.

He loaded the shotgun shells into the gun's chamber. Racked the shotgun.

Like the Book says, He works His work in mysterious ways.

He peered down over the roof. The lure he'd arranged earlier was working. The thing was coming . . .

Wait—he lost sight of it for a moment.

"John—"

He glanced at Angela at the door. She pointed. "On your left!"

He stepped back, aimed the shotgun as she went through the door.

Some people like it . . .

The winged demon swooped down at him—the

one that had gotten away at the mission downtown . . .

Over his head now, angling down, coming right for him . . . He saw its teeth plainly in the streetlight shine, gleaming as it opened its jaws, preparing to tear into him . . .

. . . *Some people don't.*

The demon came right at him. He had just time to aim the shotgun. . . .

And he blew the demon into leathery fragments. Two rounds, just to be sure. Then he blew the smoke away, and went to the fire escape. There was still more for him to do out there, this night . . . but he couldn't get Angela out of his mind.

The way she'd said it . . . *See you around?*

Just a tone of voice, but definitely: an invitation.

And going down the fire escape, thinking about Angela and God and Heaven, John Constantine had a strange sensation, a strange feeling deep inside him. What was it exactly? It was something he hadn't felt in a long, long time, and it took him a while to recognize the feeling.

It was hope.

About the Author

JOHN SHIRLEY is the author of numerous novels, including *Crawlers*, *Demons*, and *Wetbones*, and story collections, including *Really Really Really Really Weird Stories* and the Bram Stoker Award–winning collection *Black Butterflies*. He also writes scripts for television and film, and was coscreenwriter for *The Crow*. His authorized fan-created website is www.darkecho.com/JohnShirley.

Not sure what to read next?

Visit Pocket Books online at
www.SimonSays.com

Reading suggestions for
you and your reading group

New release news

Author appearances

Online chats with your favorite writers

Special offers

And much, much more!